Peace

The Other Side of Anger

Helping Teens with Anger Management

by

Dave Wolffe

Peaceful Minds Press
Rye Brook, New York

Peace: The Other Side of Anger
Helping Teens With Anger Management

Peaceful Minds Press
Rye Brook, NY
http://www.peacefforts.org

Copyright © 2011 by Dave Wolffe

Book design by Robin Simonds, Beagle Bay, Inc.

ISBN: 978-0-615-40090-7
LCCN: 2010936175

First Edition

Printed in the USA
15 14 13 12 11   1 2 3 4 5 6 7 8 9 10

Dedication

In Loving Memory of my parents, Morris and Yvette Wolffe, Frieda Forman, who gave me life, my brother Fred, my Cousin Jeff, my Aunt Clara and all those family and friends who have so greatly contributed to my life.

Table of Contents

An exploration of the causes of teen anger and adolescent perceptions of different situations they encounter daily. Tools introduced
are the "Top Ten Causes of Anger in Teens," Anger Managers and
the Anger Scale. Using a case study, these techniques are demonstrated in effectively teaching a teen how to manage their anger.

Many adolescents experience anger for reasons not clear until some
investigation occurs. This chapter explores the effects of physical
and emotional mistreatment. A three-step process for helping
young people feel comfortable enough to express these concealed
reasons for anger are described, along with the kinds of situations
that can occur with its use.

Frustration is a common cause of anger in teens. The causes and
effects are examined. Ways of empowering adolescents to handle
these sources of frustration are also explored.

that have been presented up to this point. Examples and possible responses are examined.

Chapter Ten

In this chapter we'll gauge the effectiveness of the Anger Management training. Tools used are the Anger Management Power Program's Feedback and Follow-Up Surveys and how to elicit responses to the questions and ideas presented in these two documents.

Chapter Eleven

This chapter provides you with the results of the A.M.P. Program Feedback and Follow-Up Surveys and the conclusions that were reached by participants. Also discussed are the peer facilitated workshop and focus groups.

Chapter Twelve

Parents, educators, social workers and youth workers are offered ideas specific to their concerns and their relationships with teenagers.

Information Boosters

Foreword

A couple of years ago I received an e-mail from a gentleman named Dave Wolffe who was interested in some of the things I had written related to anger management. Dave and I struck up a "cyber-friendship" and began corresponding about our work. At some point, he mentioned that he was working on a book and wondered if I would be willing to take a look at it. I said, "Of course" and assumed I'd never actually receive the manuscript because people often fail to realize the amount of time and energy it takes to actually write a book. It's easy to talk about—hard to do! Well, Dave Wolffe is a man of his word and the proof lies in the fact that you are, at this very moment, reading his book.

In *Peace: The Other Side of Anger*, Dave Wolffe provides a very engaging book that is replete with common sense approaches to helping adolescents manage their anger. Dave's experience as a clinician shines through as he includes many practical tips from years of being "in the trenches" with students. These are not just a collection of ideas he has read in a book. These are practices that Dave has fine-tuned to be used with adolescents. The book is also filled with interactive sections to help the reader connect to the concepts being explained.

My favorite part of the book was the detailed description of sixty-four (64) techniques to help adolescents manage their anger. Several scenarios that require the reader to apply the ideas follow the explanation of the techniques. Mr. Wolffe understands that people have to practice what they've learned if they hope to ingrain the ideas into their beliefs and behaviors. As a clinician, Dave knows that simply reading the ideas will not get the job done.

This book is far more than just a collection of techniques to be used with angry adolescents. There is a depth and complexity in this work that is often lacking in similar books. Dave gets to the heart of the matter by spending a considerable amount of time discussing relational and developmental issues that are often at the core of anger management problems. Mr. Wolffe recognizes that parents and counselors, social workers and youth workers have to understand teenagers to help them. There are no shortcuts.

After reading this book, I am confident that you will have a deeper understanding of the issues that confront adolescents on a daily basis. *Peace: The Other Side of Anger* is a well-constructed manual on anger management and adolescent development. Read it and enjoy!

Jerry Wilde, Ph.D.
Author of *Hot Stuff to Help Kids Chill Out: The Anger Management Book*

Acknowledgments

First and foremost, I'd like to extend my gratitude to the teenagers, college students, parents and professionals who participated in the Anger Management Power (A.M.P.) Program. Without their responses and suggestions this program would not have evolved to the point it has, and become the inspiration for this book.

I'd also like to thank my wife, Janet, for her thoughts and suggestions for making this book more understandable and reader-friendly.

A great amount of appreciation goes to Jacqueline Church Simonds, of Beagle Bay Inc. Without her encouragement and expertise in editing and putting all the pieces of this book together, *Peace: The Other Side of Anger* wouldn't have become a reality.

My gratitude also goes to Dr. Jerry Wilde, my "Cyber-buddy," whose unselfish advice and support allowed me to take the ideas for this book from a blueprint in my mind to a finished publication.

My appreciation also goes to three people who took their valuable time, careful efforts and expertise to help me develop this book. Thank you Michael Blumenfield, M.D., Psychiatrist, Dr. Susan Blumenfield, and Richard A. Giaquinto, Ph.D., Chairperson of the Teacher Education Department of St. Francis College in Brooklyn for your input.

Finally, thanks goes to the members of my family, and the friends, colleagues and students whose thoughts and support have so greatly influenced the writing of *Peace: The Other Side of Anger* and helped me make it the book that it is.

Peace

The Other Side of Anger

Introduction

Columbine, Virginia Tech, and other acts of violence caused by young people dramatically bring to light the kind of extreme reactive behavior that is fueled by anger. But these are rare events. Other displays of this emotion are not as severe. They appear in different degrees, in different settings, in many kinds of relationships. How to understand anger in a teen, and learn ways to empower them to express this feeling without hurting others or themselves, are the goals of *Peace: The Other Side of Anger*.

Anger is a feeling, just like love, hate, boredom, excitement and pride. It is important to know how an adolescent views this emotion, as well as stress to them that there is nothing wrong with feeling angry! It is how they act when they experience this feeling that needs to be addressed.

We'll be discussing ways to help a teen understand their reactions and how to minimize their negative responses throughout this book. We'll also be addressing such questions as:

> What makes some kids so angry?
>
> Why do teens explode for no apparent reason?
>
> How can someone tell when these kids are getting angry?
>
> How can we help them calm down before they lose it?
>
> What are different ways to help adolescents better manage anger?
>
> What kinds of situations are common to many young people?

What are ways to see that what is done with teens is working?

Throughout this book, typical adolescent behavior will be pointed out.
The shrugging of shoulders, the "are you crazy?" look, the often uttered
"I don't know," are examples of how young people often respond to adult
questions. Their overall attitudes toward grown-ups is that they don't want
us to know what's going on with them—it's their private world, we don't
have any idea of what their world is like, and what adults have to say is
dumb. This is a common roadblock to our work with teens. But they are
listening, even if they don't seem to be.

A teen growing up in today's world certainly faces many different challenges than we had during this stage of life. You might not immediately
understand their challenges, since you can only evaluate things from your
own experiences. For others, the behavior you recognize in an adolescent
may be consistent with your experiences working with them. What you
read can give you a different perspective on dealing with adolescents and
their anger.

Why I Wrote This Book

Who am I to write about anger in teens? The answer may be helpful
for you in evaluating the information found in *Peace: The Other Side of
Anger*. I have been an educator with the New York City Department of
Education for over thirty years, as a teacher in grades 1-9, and worked as
a high school guidance counselor during the last thirteen years of my em-
ployment. One of my responsibilities in this capacity was to train teens to
become peer mediators. This function allowed me to view adolescents who
were involved in conflict and see how they tried to resolve these conflicts
with the help of their specially trained peers. In addition to this responsibility, deans and the principal would often refer youngsters with an anger
problem to me. As a result of this kind of referral, I worked with a group of
teens and developed a program to use with them, and later on, with other

adolescents. This was the foundation from which the Anger Management Power (A.M.P.) Program, on which this book is based, was developed. More details about this program are presented shortly. Once I retired from the NYC Department of Education. I began to work more intensively with this program. In the last eight years, the A.M.P. Program has been presented to over one thousand high school students, as well as to over six hundred parents, professionals and college students. As time went on, changes to the original format of this program were made, along with the activities and tools that were used. Many of these modifications were based on adolescent suggestions. Their peers have also presented this program to teens—a powerful way to get the information to young people. Much of the information found in this book is based on these experiences; along with that provided by many readings, conferences, and work I have done with teens and other children.

It is important to note, the material found in this book is educational in nature. It is not therapeutic, or a substitute for any form of intervention that may be necessary for individuals with severe emotional and/or social problems. It is a training process to follow, with ideas and activities that can be useful to readers in empowering young people to handle their anger in positive ways.

The Anger Management Power Program

The material found in this book is based on the ideas and activities taken from the Anger Management Power (A.M.P.) Program, a developmental process created for use with teenagers. This program came about as a result of work with high school students who had difficulty managing their anger. The A.M.P Program furnishes the participants with a means of understanding anger and provides them with ways to maintain control over their reactions to anger-provoking situations. It also gives the participants the opportunity to help others take control of their own anger. These objectives are met through the presentation of a variety of materials and interactive experiences including group work and role-playing activities. The training originally took the form of a four-session workshop with youngsters in different subject classes.

Through a skills-based approach, the program enables the participants:

To recognize anger in themselves and in other people

To express their anger without harming themselves or other people

To learn how to de-escalate anger—their own and others

As a result of the activities and information presented during the Anger Management Power Program, the participants are able to identify:

What Anger Management involves

The causes and effects of anger

Some of the different positive ways of managing their own anger, and dealing with the anger of other people who are part of their lives

After about a month, a follow-up survey is distributed to the participants to see if the training was useful in their lives. Those who have used some of the skills are given an opportunity to receive additional training in the form of a focus group and/or may be considered for becoming facilitators. Some of the high school students who received the initial training in one of their subject classes became facilitators and taught these skills during single period peer workshops.

I'll be showing how the lessons I learned from the A.M.P. Program participants can be applied to your work with a teen as you continue to read through the pages of this book.

Chapter One

The Anger You See

Our starting point for understanding anger in teens and how to help them deal with it is to look at the reasons they experience this feeling. The whys of anger take into account many influences and appear in different forms. There are causes that are obvious, and then there are those that are more difficult to detect, the ones that make you wonder, "What's going on with this kid?" All of these reasons influence how an adolescent is going to react to the different people and situations that provoke this feeling.

In this chapter, we will examine the most apparent causes of anger in young people. To better understand how to deal with the reasons for this feeling, you need to view them through a teen's eyes. When you don't take their perceptions of situations into account, wrong conclusions are often drawn. Thanks to over 1000 youngsters who participated in the Anger Management Power (A.M.P.) Program described in the Introduction, much valuable information on teen viewpoints has been provided.

The Top Ten Causes of Anger in Teens

Below are the anger triggers described by A.M.P. Program participants. After the list, we'll explore each of the reasons for these feelings.

1. Being Lied To
2. Being Yelled At
3. Being Blamed For Something They Didn't Do
4. Being Put Down For Something
5. Being Told To Do Something Over And Over Again
6. Another Person's Nasty Attitude
7. Being Betrayed by My Boy/Girlfriend or an Adult
8. Having My Private Conversations Repeated
9. Being Ignored
10. Being Made Fun of in Front of My Friends

Now let's examine these in detail.

1: Being Lied To. Whatever the relationship is between an adult and a teen, it faces serious damage when the grown-up tries to deceive an adolescent. Some of the lines a teen is given are:

"I wanted to protect my child"
"I have to keep my kid from doing something harmful or
    dumb"

These describe some of the reasons an adult may "stretch the truth," or out-and-out try to trick a youngster. A teen wants to be leveled with. If they aren't—for whatever the reason—their general reaction is not to trust the grown-up. "Why listen to that adult? They lied to me before so why believe what they say now?" becomes the thought process. When something happens in the future, the offending adult shouldn't expect the young person to listen to their advice, no matter how helpful it can be. Once a teen's trust in a grown-up is shaken, the damage to a relationship is often irreparable

Honesty with a child, no matter how young, pays off in great dividends. As a youngster's life becomes more pressure-filled, their need for guidance from a trustworthy adult becomes greater. Level with a child early in the relationship and the influence on how they think and act is bound to be greater.

In the short run, it is sometimes seems easier to skirt the truth. However, over a longer period of time, this is more damaging to your relationship with the young person, and, more importantly, to their ability to effectively cope with life's challenges.

2: Being Yelled At. This is not to say that when a teen does something wrong, they shouldn't be held responsible for their actions. It is both the manner and location of the scolding that upsets the young person. If they are berated in front of their peers, they may "lose face" or suffer a lowering of self-esteem. Because of this feeling, their response may be more severe than if they had been confronted alone. The most common response from A.M.P. participants to being shouted at is: "It made me feel like a little kid."

In most cases, it's best to ask a teen that is misbehaving to move to a private place to talk when you discover them doing something you wish to correct. This does two things: it gives you a chance to speak privately, and it may allow both of you to calm down before you discuss the situation. Very little is accomplished or learned from shouting at someone.

3: Being Blamed for Something They Didn't Do. Without a doubt, there are many good reasons to think that a young person is responsible for doing certain things. These infractions may include: doors being left unlocked, siblings crying or screaming, disturbances that occur in classrooms or in other places where a teen hangs out, damage to property, or the use of cars, computers, clothes, without the owner's permission. This list can certainly be extended. Adolescents do these things frequently.

But suspicions are not conclusive evidence. It is important not to jump to conclusions. To paraphrase a quote, an ounce of prevention is worth a pound of aggravation, for both a teen and an adult.

When allegations are made, a young person is the subject of adult prejudice. This, in turn, creates the impression in a teen's mind that adults are not being fair. When this happens, adolescents can feel as if they are being verbally attacked or given the "Third Degree," and will frequently respond to this accusation by shouting or shutting down, compounding the situation.

Care should be taken before accusing an adolescent of doing something. The best way of dealing with improper behavior is to either base your conclusion on direct observation of a young person's behavior, or an admission of responsibility by them. Unless you can be sure that the teen is responsible for a particular situation, it is wise not to make assumptions about their guilt. When the time comes that you see some inappropriate behavior taking place and speak to a teen about it, their reaction will be less severe.

4: Being Put Down for Something They Did (poor grades, sports, chores, other responsibilities). An adult wants an adolescent to achieve their best. However, some grown-ups use comparisons or put-downs instead of encouragement to meet these goals. Remarks such as:

> "Why can't you do as well as Bobby in algebra?"
> "This stuff is easy. Anyone with half a brain could do well with it!"
> "That was such an easy play, a five-year-old could have made it."
> "You're just lazy!"

illustrate some of the reasons behind this source of anger. Very often, a young person will realize how badly they screwed up and get down on themselves for these mistakes. Harsh remarks just rub salt into the wound, or make a teen feel even worse. Adolescents describe their reactions to these kinds of criticisms by remarking:

> "I know I [expletive]-up. Why does the coach have to make me feel even worse than I do?"

"Here's another time Mom treats me like [expletive]"
"So I'm not Mr./Miss perfect? So what!"
"Why can't Mr. Harrison just stay off my case?"

This manner of criticism produces negative reactions and so should not be used. Focus instead should be on discovering ways for them to improve in whatever area needs improvement. This can be achieved without put-downs or unfavorable comparisons.

Young people tend to blame others for their shortcomings. If this occurs, have them concentrate on what they could have done differently. The idea that a person controls what they do and don't do introduces the concept of personal responsibility. Listen to what they think of the situation and their feelings. Hearing a teen's views of this situation helps meet the need for recognition, that is to say, how they see things is worthwhile enough for an adult to hear. Taking this approach sets the stage for both parties to work together to discover the road to improvement.

5: Being Told to Do Something Over and Over Again (chores, homework). It is not unusual for a teen to need to be reminded to do something—usually those are things that they find difficult, bothersome, or that take time away from other more important activities. These priorities include, telephone calls to friends, using computers or watching TV. There is no doubt that there are many other diversions. The most common response to a reminder is, "I'll do it later," uttered more than once. Based on my previous experiences with young people, when the task is finally done, it is accomplished in a rush, and isn't done well, or it becomes one of those forgotten, things that a teen thinks won't be remembered. All these reasons for reminders with an adolescent are logical and establish just cause for being used.

Teens see these reminders as another way to put them down or question their abilities. They think:

"Does Dad think I'm stupid?"

"Does the teacher think that I'm deaf or don't listen?"

Acknowledging the possibility of this kind of adolescent thinking first, and then sharing your thoughts, is a way to avoid more stressful situations between you and a young person.

6: Another Person's Nasty Attitude (shown in their tone of voice or by sarcasm). How an adult approaches a teen will determine the direction of their relationship. Coming at an adolescent in a loud tone of voice or making a comment expressed with sarcasm describe negative approaches that are going to be met by negative reactions.

This is not to say that you can't be upset with a young person. It is how things are expressed that causes an escalation of hostility by a teen. "Constructive criticism"—telling an adolescent about the troublesome behavior without worsening the situation—is an essential skill to work with a young person successfully.

Try the "I Statement," an Anger Manager to be discussed later in more depth. With this method the adult's feeling about the upsetting behavior, the specific actions that led to it, and the reason why they felt this way are described. "I felt angry when you cursed at me because it was a disrespectful thing to do," is an example of this approach. You are modeling this approach for a teen, and by doing so, making it part of the learning process. This technique was something adolescent A.M.P. participants felt was useful. The next step would be to have the young person try using this method by responding to the adult's constructive criticism. "I felt happy when you didn't yell at me because you showed me respect" describes such a statement.

7: Being Betrayed by My Boy/Girlfriend or an Adult. With this cause of anger, parallel situations involving adults and teens will be described. Let's look at the problem of the perception of adult betrayal first. In this case, two reasons for an adolescent's anger are possible. The first involves "being lied to" directly. The next source arises from a youngster's observations of some form of deceptive behavior. This can involve an adult making excuses for not going somewhere or doing something with particular individuals, or saying things that a teen knows are absolutely not true. This category of deceit may also include exaggerated details about a situation or about the individuals themselves. The bottom line is, an adolescent's trust in the adult suffers major damage when they observe this kind of behavior by a grown-up. By acting this way, a young person feels an adult is a cheat. Without trust, the likelihood of any kind of strong relationship diminishes. The young person who sees this kind of behavior reacts to it in the same way they would as if they had been deceived by their boyfriends or girlfriends.

In a close relationship, either party may say or do something different than what their partner was told. This may be about being somewhere or with someone that the other person wanted to go with, or someone who they had a close relationship with. Once this deception is discovered, the girlfriend or boyfriend loses trust in the other. Their reaction may result in screaming or hitting the other person. Without trust, the relationship is severely damaged or ruined, and often revenge for this deceit becomes the reaction. This response often takes the forms of lies about what the other individual did or said, or turning peers against the offending person and treating them like an outsider.

8: *Having My Private Conversations Repeated.* Very often, an adolescent will tell a grown-up something in confidence. It may not appear important to the adult. However, it is significant to a teen. This information can be about a relationship, or something that may be said about another person, or an incident about to happen to someone else. However, once a betrayal of a confidence has taken place, adolescent anger quickly surfaces. The most obvious reason for this happening is that a trust has been broken. In addition, revealing of confidential information may cause embarrassment. In this situation an adolescent may feel they may lose face by looking foolish, or by appearing "soft" or weak to peers who find out the details of their secrets.

If the reason for revealing this information is expressed by an adult as, "I didn't think that it was that important," the idea of prejudgment, enters the picture. A youngster's identity is constantly evolving; judgments by an adult, as to what is important or not, takes something away from their feeling of self-worth. "That person is trying to tell me what is important to me," expresses their reaction. No one likes to be told by another person what they are thinking or feeling.

Confidentiality Exclusion: This confidentiality excludes finding out about things that may be potentially harmful to a teen or other people. Such subjects require mandated reporting. Knowledge of weapons, drug and physical abuse and threats fall into this category. In my role as guidance counselor, before I had any conversations with an adolescent, I would let them know about the kinds of things that needed to be reported. This kind of honesty, when shown at the start of conversations, or of relationships with a young person, ensures that you are a person who can be trusted and are someone a teen is able to speak to.

9: Being Ignored. When a teen is ignored, what they have to say or want to do has little meaning. An adolescent has a strong need for recognition. It involves giving value to their achievements, thoughts and opinions. This desire is frustrated when what a youngster has to say is ignored. When it is, a teen may become angry. An adolescent's self-worth seems to be questioned. "That person doesn't think what I have to say is important," conveys this idea.

Another, more complex dynamic comes into play. "If that person doesn't want to listen to what I have to say, why should I listen to what he / she tells me?" This kind of thinking reflects a mutual respect—or lack thereof—between an adult and an adolescent. It is a two-way street. The adult must have the willingness to understand a young person's ideas when they are expressed, without making any judgments.

What Shouldn't Be Ignored: We are not talking about inappropriate behavior. Cursing, tantrums, hurting others and destroying property are not acceptable actions. This kind of conduct necessitates an adult choosing whether or not to directly confront a teen's behavior or ignore it. The message being conveyed to an adolescent about their behavior is, "Act like this and you'll get nowhere or nothing."

> You don't have to agree with what is said. Listening to and respecting what is said is the important thing. The advantage this approach has to your relationship and influence on a teen outweighs the time and effort spent on using it.

10: Someone Making Fun of Me in Front of My Friends. The value of peers to an adolescent is immeasurable. The need to belong is one of the strongest forces in their lives. Being respected by friends is also very important. When a youngster is put down in front peers, reactions become nothing short of an outward explosion or severely hurtful action. A teen will act in whatever way they think is necessary to save face and restore their status with peers. They may forcefully challenge an adult by using a loud voice, cursing or hurling insults. At the other end of the spectrum they may become severely depressed and withdrawn.

Some adults may feel that embarrassing an adolescent in front of their peers will force them to correct inappropriate behavior. The effect of making fun of a young person in front of friends or associates (people in a peer group but not part of the teen's inner circles) is more likely to be a call to arms. Public confrontations with an adolescent yield the most severe reactions. For some teens this kind of treatment works. What you have to decide is whether or not the course of action you have chosen is worth it in terms of the effect on an adolescent and on your relationship with him/her.

Reasons to Explore These Causes of Anger

Looking at these causes of anger has given us the following information:

Adolescent perceptions of these causes
Effects of these reasons on teen behavior
Possible ways to limit severe reactions by young people to these causes
Ways to avoid these sources of anger in teens

This list can be expanded to include many other anger activators that adolescents feel apply to them. It is a jumping-off point for discussions with a young person.

The Anger Scale: A Measure of Levels of Anger

To help understand more about the causes of anger in teens, the next thing we need is to have an adolescent identify the intensity different causes of this feeling create. "How can seeing how angry certain situations make you feel be helpful in managing this feeling?" is a question young people who participated in the A.M.P. Program were asked. One of the conclusions these teens reached was that by being aware of situations that make them really angry, they learn to avoid them. Another result of the use of this tool was that they were able to see that when a situation occurs that causes them to reach top of the Anger Scale, they can make preparations to get away from the event, or find a way to calm down before they lose their temper completely. Another way to explain the second benefit of knowing when something really gets a teen upset is to compare this idea to a situation where people know that a car accident is going to occur. When this experience begins to occur, they find their car skidding on ice and headed toward another car. In this incident the person involved would brace himself or herself to minimize the severity of injury. In both the case of an anger activator, and that of a car accident, the consequences of the situation can be limited.

Dave Wolffe

The Anger Scale

The use of a visual aid puts an idea into a more concrete form. When a young person is able to see things, they become more real, and are more likely to be understood and discussed. Let's look at this visual tool.

You are in control of Anger						*Anger is in Control of You*			
1	2	3	4	5	6	7	8	9	10

Looking at the scale, you see two opposite points numbered 1 to 10 respectively, and what each represents. A teen may describe these places differently. For example the "1" position on the scale may be described by an adolescent as the point where someone is "chilled out," "calm," or "cool." The "10" on this index may be described as the place where a person is, "crazed,""nuts, "psycho," or has "lost it." When you work with a young person, putting things in terms that they are familiar with makes ideas more relevant and acceptable. Having a teen describe the meaning of these points, as well as those numbered 2-5, and then 6-9 may provide them with the feeling of "personal ownership" and furnish a good reason to use this tool.

For our purposes, 2-5 are points that show that a person is still pretty calm and is able to express anger about a particular situation without causing harm to themselves or others. However, once a person passes a "5" on the scale, things can start to escalate, as their reaction becomes more severe. "At what point do you have to be to handle your anger without getting into hassles?" is a helpful question to ask a teen. The response to it creates a goal to achieve with an adolescent, and establishes a foundation for using this tool again.

How to Use the Anger Scale with Individuals or Groups of Teens

Let's use "Being Ignored," one of the top ten causes of anger cited by young people, to illustrate how to use the Anger Scale "Where on the scale

17

would you be if you were ignored?" and, "Why?" are two questions to ask to get things going. If you are dealing with an individual teen, have them indicate the number on the scale that best describes the level this cause of anger creates.

If you are working with a group of young people, you can use two possible approaches. The first involves having the group of participants choose the points on the scale that describe how angry they get when they are ignored. The second way, suggested by a teenage participant in the A.M.P. Program, is to have people physically place themselves where they feel they would be if they were ignored. This method involves having three people come up to the front of the room. Each one is given a number. These are the numbers "1", "5" and "10," respectively representing three points on the Anger Scale. The other group members are then asked to stand at the point on the Human Anger Scale that represents how angry being ignored makes them feel. (The number of adolescents chosen to participate depends on the size of the group you are working with.) Since this idea was suggested, it has been successfully used with many program participants.

Whichever method you choose, the next step is to have individual young people explain why they felt the degree of anger they experienced over being ignored. Not only are you having them view this cause of anger from their own perspective, but you are also allowing them to see that for others, being ignored may have a different meaning.

A "Teachable Moment" with the Idea of Accepting Differences

At this point, you have a "teachable moment" and can explore the idea of accepting differences—another Anger Manager. Start with the question, "How can this idea be useful?" If you get a shrug of the shoulders, or an "I don't know" response, (typical adolescent reactions) suggest that accepting differences can be a means of preventing anger from surfacing, or at least be a way to keep another person from going too far up the Anger Scale.

Another approach is to ask, "Did anyone ever try to get you to change your mind about something that you really felt strongly about, like the friends you have, or music you like to listen to?" If a young person shows some sign of recognition, ask, "What happened?" The teen response may go something like, "The harder my mom tried to change my mind, the angrier I got." If this is the case, you've made your point.

You can take it one step further and ask, "How do you think your mom was feeling?" Then try to have the adolescent look at the situation from the other person's viewpoint as a way to de-escalate anger in others. Describe the term empathy and what it means. This is another Anger Manager. If a youngster gives you the "I don't know" shoulder shrug, use a teen-relevant, situation. For young men, this could be something taken from sports. One example is to have them imagine what it would be like when a New York Yankee baseball fan tries to convince a New York Mets fan that the Yankees are a better team. This is the example used successfully with A.M.P. Program participants. For young women it may involve having them point out different ways they and their friends look at "What's cool" in styles of clothing, or in boys to date. What you want a teen to be aware of is that certain beliefs—things that are important to people—are areas that arguing about leads only to frustration and anger. Along with this realization, have them try to recognize that different ways of thinking about things are okay and then move on from there.

Implications of Accepting Differences for Adults

Challenging certain beliefs an adolescent may have, for example their thoughts and feelings about certain peer groups, whether they value certain styles of clothing, or wear their clothing in certain ways (butts showing, etc), or enjoy a particular kind of music (rap, hard rock, heavy metal) or who think that certain kinds of groups are cool or necessary to be a part of (teams, or gangs), is a mistake. The point is not to argue about what you think is right or wrong about certain groups or preferences, but to find out why it is so special to them.

The suggestion is not that these groups are positive. What needs to be understood is the young person's thinking, even though you may not agree with it. Keep in mind that accepting their ideas and trying to understand the reasoning behind them keeps the doors to two-way communication open.

The Role of the Needs for Recognition and Belonging in a Teen's Life

Two very strong needs for teens come into play with this notion of accepting differences. The first involves the need for recognition—in this case, valuing an adolescent's opinions. It cannot be emphasized enough that by listening to what a young person is saying, and by letting it be known that you understand the thinking, rather than jumping in with opinions and making judgments, the door to having a dialogue, rather than an argument, is open. As a guidance counselor, this is what many teens told me that they wanted and needed from adults. It is the kind of behavior that an adolescent will respond to most favorably. By listening to what a young person has to say, the chances that they will be willing to hear your thoughts will also be greater.

The "Staring Incident" and the Issue of Respect

Although being "dissed" (disrespected) was not listed specifically as one of the Top Ten Causes of Anger In Teens, some of the reasons for a teen's anger fall into this category. "Being stared at" is one major source of disrespect described by many adolescents. A fight between two young people often occurs as a result of this behavior. This is a form of conflict that often takes place in the hallway of a school, or in any public area where teens congregate.

Individuals "looking hard" (staring), are often accused of looking down at the other person, (dissing them), or looking to start trouble. An adoles-

">Dave Wolffe

cent receiving this look, "the Victim," may notice this action taking place themselves, or have it pointed out by peers. "That guy/girl is staring at you. Don't take that from him/her," are remarks that signal a call for swift action by the "offended" youngster. If this act isn't dealt with quickly, peers may regard the "offended" individual as weak, or a person who takes [expletive] from others, making them vulnerable to other such acts. The need to respond to being stared at becomes urgent. Another reason to react to a person's stare may stem from some previously unresolved difficulty that took place between these two teens. This episode becomes an excuse to refuel that fire. Either of these reasons can cause an adolescent to react to another's "hard" looks.

> Accepting a teen's viewpoint doesn't mean agreeing with it, only that you understand it.

An adult may view an intense look from different perspectives. They may think that the person is daydreaming, looking in the direction of some loud sound, or noticing some other person. In other words, they may view things more rationally. However, for a teen, when this situation occurs, it often doesn't call for calm thought. Instead, it becomes a signal to do something, and do it quickly.

After learning the reason for an adolescent's reaction to being stared at, the next step is to accept their evaluation of it. Keep in mind that in helping a young person manage anger appropriately, it is their perception of an incident, and the feeling it arouses that counts, not yours.

Now that you have shown that you understand how an adolescent views the situation, have not made any judgments, or given any unwarranted advice, the door for a youngster to hear other reasons for staring is opened. Steps are taken toward moving away from reacting based on emotion and toward responding reasonably. Your aim here is to help a young person reach a point at or below "5" on the Anger Scale, where positive

21

However, many times a teen responds in a way that is purely about saving face, something common to this age group. It means they are covering up an entirely opposite view. Regardless of an adolescent's answer, proceed to discuss other possible reasons for an incident.

Anger Management ideas may have a chance to flourish. It is time to test the waters where changes in behavior can be found.

Let's explore the effects of a teen's reactions to staring. This part of the process begins by asking a teen "Was the fight worth it?" (Looking at the consequences of behavior is an Anger Manager that will also be examined in more depth later on.) Here's a place where many adults find themselves being frustrated. After paving the way for this discussion, an adolescent may respond to this question with an emphatic, "Yes!" Don't be too dejected. With a young person this is always a possibility.

Some adults may feel that a teen doesn't care what happens after an incident has taken place. This may be true. However, whether or not you agree with this view, the idea is to expose an adolescent to different ideas. The value of fighting over the "hard" look can be taken one step further by asking, "What can happen after you fight with someone?" Many young people were asked this question. Their responses included being,

Suspended

Grounded

Hassled by a parent, school or agency staff member or
    police

Deprived of certain privileges

The victim of payback (This response meant being hurt
    by the other person's family or friends, or by the other
    individual coming back some time later to take care
    of unfinished business) will see that the adolescent is
    punished for their action.

After these consequences are explored, finding out if these results were what a teen really wanted brings them further down the road to reason. At this point, nothing is being suggested. Instead, an adolescent is given the opportunity to express what they see as the effects of fighting over the issue of "staring," and have a chance to evaluate their value. This process may influence how a young person handles a similar situation in the future. Having a teen look at the consequences of their behavior can be a productive Anger Management tool. As a matter of fact, many A.M.P. Program participants chose this method as a way they would use to handle different situations.

After having an adolescent look at some of the results of their reactions to this incident, finding ways to resolve this situation becomes the next topic of discussion. One method, totally out of a youngster's control, involves the use of punishment, something certainly discussed as a consequence of fighting. Another form of dispute resolution involves some authority figure mandating that the two teens involved in the situation talk it out.

A third way of handling this incident involves both teens volunteering to discuss the incident by themselves without adult intervention. One form this kind of discussion can take place is through peer mediation, a process facilitated in many schools and other youth organizations.

The realities of using this method are that:

> The two disputants (people who fought) are involved in mediation because they have been told to do so. This is done just to ward off any other consequences the fight may have brought on them as mentioned above.
>
> It often represents a forced truce and doesn't really involve any effort to discuss and resolve the issues that brought on the conflict. As young people often have said before sitting down to discuss the issue in mediation, "It (the fight) is squashed (over)."
>
> With this method of resolution, a band-aid is put on the wound and doesn't deal with the cause of the problem.

It often doesn't take into account ways for a young person to prevent this kind of situation from happening in the future. This is not to say that this, as well as the other forms of conflict resolution, isn't productive. They all can be, and, at the very least, they help to end particular situations.

Keep in mind that a teen likes to feel in control of their lives. Having someone else decide how an incident is going to be handled demonstrates an inability to take care of business. "Do you really want someone else to decide how to fix this situation or do you want to have control of its outcome?" is something to explore when an adolescent is involved in conflict. It is a thought that may encourage a young person to find an alternative to handling an incident with violence or any other destructive means. Finding other, more positive ways of fixing a problem can also prevent more problems from happening in the future is something else that can influence a teen's willingness to try positive Anger Management methods.

Chapter Summary

Some of the more obvious causes of anger described by participants in The Anger Management Power (A.M.P.) Program have been explored in this chapter. Along with these reasons for an adolescent experiencing anger, were their perceptions of different situations they encountered, and different Anger Managers that can be used in dealing with these incidents. The Anger Scale, as an Anger Management tool was also explored. Finally, a situation involving "being dissed" was discussed, along with different methods for handling this kind of incident with a teen.

How can the information found in this chapter be helpful to use with adolescents? is a question to think about. Reading about the causes of anger that had the most impact on the participants in the A.M.P. Program creates an awareness of what situations to look for with a young person. Knowing how a teen views these anger activators and reacts to them can help you understand and relate to them with a more open mind. This responsiveness can result in a teen's being more willing to hear what you have to say. The tools that were provided introduce some methods that can help an adolescent understand their anger and offer ways to assist them in expressing, avoiding and better managing this feeling

Chapter Two

The Hidden Causes of Anger

The reasons for anger are many and varied. Those that were more obvious were explored in the previous chapter. This chapter and the two that follow will examine the causes young people find hard to disclose because they are too painful, frightening or embarrassing to relate. They are things that require gaining a teen's trust. Without some kind of intervention taking place, an adolescent will remain angry and continue to react negatively to situations that occur.

Before getting to the "How To's" of convincing a young person to disclose these hidden experiences, looking at the kinds of incidents that take place is helpful.

Symptoms of Physical Mistreatment

Physical abuse represents the first category of hidden events. This type of injury may have resulted from a teen being a victim of sexual or physical abuse, or being bullied by peers. As a consequence of this kind of treatment, an adolescent may show hostile behavior toward others, or withdraw from any kind of relationships. You may notice that they flinch or move back from anyone who physically approaches them. They often resist any kind of physical contact, whether it is a handshake or an attempt to put an arm around a shoulder. A youngster will also clearly and often loudly tell others that touching is not acceptable to them. More information on how to use these observations, and get to the sources of a teen's mistreatment, will be presented in depth later on in this chapter.

Emotional Mistreatment

Other, less talked about causes of anger in adolescents arise from emotional sources. They are also more difficult to describe and underlie the irritation that is openly expressed. They often take longer to get over than injuries inflicted physically. Emotional pain often leads to depression, which, in its most severe form, can result in self-mutilation or even suicide.

The anger that is observed represents the tip of the emotional iceberg. Beneath its surface may lie many feelings. These take a lot more effort to discover than the anger that can be directly observed. Without getting to these feelings, a young person will only be able to see relationships and the world around them through "angry eyes."

Sources of Emotional Pain

Knowing the source of this kind of damage is the starting point for helping a teen reveal, discuss, and find ways to lessen its impact on their lives.

Fear: This is one feeling that lies beneath the surface of an adolescent's anger. It is an emotion that will not readily be expressed. This feeling may come from different sources. A young person may be afraid of physical harm, losing a relationship with a family member, friend, or girlfriend/boyfriend, or someone's love, respect or attention. A teen often fears admitting this feeling to others because they believe it will make them look weak or "soft," and become a target for others to take advantage of, "to be played." Maintaining a strong image is the reason for much of an adolescent's behavior. Keeping fear hidden enables a youngster to save face, remain strong in the eyes of his or her peers, and secure a measure of safety and acceptance. It is a key to survival. These beliefs need to be addressed to help bring this and other feelings to the surface. Once the fear is uncovered, a teen can be helped to find ways to cope more effectively with people or situations that create it, and have the opportunity to experience a more peaceful life.

Criticisms: Different kinds of repeated criticism represent another source of emotional pain. A comment made about an adolescent's physical appearance is one contributor to this kind of hurt. Being told over and over again that they are, fat, skinny, a slob, or look like they just got out of bed, illustrates this type of remark. How a young person looks is very important. Remarks made about a teen's appearance are attacks on self-esteem. If this is how they feel, two very important parts of his/her life will be affected: the ability to have a girlfriend or boyfriend, or be a person others want to hang out with. As a result, an adolescent might withdraw from any contact with peers, perhaps develop an eating disorder to make themselves more attractive, or they may act out against other young people or themselves by self-mutilation or even by committing suicide.

Another source of emotional damage comes from constant references to a teen's behavior. They may be described as, stupid, bad or rotten. In this case, an adolescent may start to believe they fit this profile and act accordingly to maintain the mistaken image. The thinking behind this is, "This is what my dad thinks of me, so why not be this way?"

A young person who doesn't achieve good grades in school may be described as thick, stupid, lazy, or irresponsible. These inferences add to the list of emotional bullets that are directed toward them. With this kind of image, a teen who already sees school as a challenge may adopt a "Why try?" attitude.

Differences in an adolescent's preferences in dress, friends, music or sexual orientation serve as another source of criticism. Their friends are described as weird, geeks, or as people who are a group of losers. A young person can have a variety of thoughts about these kinds of judgments. One thinking process goes, "I'll listen to whatever, or be with whoever I feel like, I'm old enough to make my own choices." Another way a teen may look at this kind of criticism, particularly from peers, is "Screw them." This idea may be followed by criticism or threats to individuals in different groups that can result in some form of physical or verbal confrontation.

These kinds of comments may come from a variety of critics, parents, siblings, peers, other family members, educators, or anyone else who is part of a young person's life. Those who make these remarks may say they do so to motivate a teen to act in more positive ways. For others, these remarks are made out of frustration. Whatever the reason is for such criticism, it can greatly contribute to a teen's anger.

An adolescent may react to these attacks in different ways. They may ignore references made to these subjects and choose not to talk about them. A young person may become defensive about these topics and lash out at the "attacking" individual. This kind of treatment by another person also lowers an adolescent's self-esteem. When this happens, a teen may think, "Why talk about something that's going to make me feel worse than I already do? My dad doesn't want to understand or help me." All these criticisms can result in pushing an adolescent away.

A Method for Reaching Hidden Causes

Before any other reasons for teen anger are described, there are three steps that can be taken to help an adolescent reveal these anger activators, and be willing to discuss them. This is a process analogous to peeling off the layers of an onion. It requires time, a lot of effort, and much-needed patience. There are two benefits to using this method. The first is that it can pave the way for a young person's emotional growth. By looking at the causes of their behavior, a teen is able to look at painful or bothersome situations and learn how to confront, rather than avoid them. The second reason for using this process is that by taking these steps an adolescent may show a willingness to accept your involvement in their life.

A young person needs to be given reasons to feel comfortable to talk with you. The first involves trust. This is demonstrated by your ability to keep what is told to you private and not use this information in any way that can damage them. What this means is that you will not use what was told to you in any way that would embarrass or make an a teen feel more vulnerable to the comments or actions of other people. The next thing that he or she wants and needs, is to be able to see that their thoughts and feelings are heard and understood—and more importantly—that they are not being judged.

With this foundation being laid, the first step toward getting to the source of a teen's behavior can be taken. It involves letting them know that you are aware that something is bothering them, and that you are concerned about it. Care must be taken, so that an adolescent feels comfortable enough to describe the source of unhappiness, rather than keep it to him or herself. Your patience, ability to listen without saying anything, or make any judgments creates the kind of atmosphere that allows a youngster to reveal this information.

A recent incident that you have been made aware is one way to discover the underlying causes of a teen's anger. Their reaction to this event represents the starting point for this process. There are two categories of behavior that can be helpful. The first notes the more obvious behavioral demonstrations of anger. These include yelling or expressions of defiance, characterized by remarks such as, "What are you going to do about it?" or "I felt like [expletive]!" or may include such actions as slamming doors or getting into fights.

The second type of response to a situation isn't as clear or as easy to detect. It can be characterized by sad facial expressions, denial that something is wrong, lack of eye contact, secrecy, or a desire not to be around other people.

The general demeanor of an adolescent needs to be considered. If you have observed a behavior over time that requires attention, be sure it is not just a reaction to a single incident, although a particular event may have triggered the hidden source of anger. It can also be the kind of situation that a young person repeatedly finds him or herself involved in. These behaviors go beyond the moodiness and need for secrecy and privacy that normally accompany adolescence.

The next step is to look at a method that can help you discover the underlying emotional causes of a teen's anger.

The Three-Step Information Gathering Process

You may have become aware of an adolescent's involvement in a situation in different ways. Directly witnessing, or being near enough to have heard the commotion and responded to it, represent two ways of finding out about an incident. Another means of getting this information comes from a young person's peers, a colleague, a neighbor, or a friend. Regardless of the source of this knowledge, a teen's actions become something that you need to handle as a parent, counselor, social worker or youth worker. After finding out that an incident has taken place, the next step is to discover the real source of an adolescent's anger.

Step One: Gathering Information About the Recent Incident: An approach to take after a youngster has publicly acted out—one of the hardest for many adults to follow—is to stay silent and wait for a response. A teen may react to this tactic by giving an observer a long hard look (the one with daggers), respond with a curt, "So what?" or say nothing at all. The recognition that something happened, and that you are aware of it, is the message that needs to be conveyed.

Another way to approach this situation is to ask direct questions. "What's going on?" or "What happened? and then be ready to follow these up right away with some comments or questions. Typical teen responses to these questions include:

"Nothing."
To which you can reply: "People usually don't get upset over nothing."
"You wouldn't understand."
Ask: "Why don't you think I'd understand?"

For the "Because I feel like it," and "None of your [exple-
tive] business!" response, leave the subject alone for
the time being. A nerve has been touched and an adolescent needs to have a chance to calm down.
"I don't want to talk about it!"

Sometimes the word "now" is added. If so, it is an invitation to discuss
this subject later. The timing of a future conversation may come as a result
of another "clue" a youngster may furnish.

Your knowledge of the incident may be considered a reason to be attacked. If this is the case, not immediately responding to a teen's reaction
makes good sense. Waiting for an adolescent to tell you about the incident
often is rewarded. In many cases, a young person is aware they did wrong
or could have handled a situation differently, but need to let their thoughts
out without being interrupted. The value of using this approach with a
teen cannot be underestimated. Its benefits rest in having an adolescent
more open to discussion and willing to hear what you have to say. "I only
want the counselor to listen to what I have to say and not tell me what to
do or that I was wrong," is a comment that I heard as a guidance counselor,
stresses the importance of following this advice.

Taking this approach is something that takes practice and much
self-restraint. Using it does not mean you are agreeing with how a
young person has handled a situation. It is a means of discovering
what is bothering a teen and can result in helping to resolve this
type of incident in more positive way.

Looking at two different ways of explaining an adolescent's conduct
can also be helpful. A comment like, "It's really not healthy for you to
walk around angry so much," is both a judgmental remark, as well as one
that makes an assumption about how a youngster feels. Instead, by using,

32

"When people slam doors, sometimes it is a way of telling other people that they are angry about something" is an objective, non-judgmental way to describe a teen's actions. It gives them the chance to tell you what is going on and prevents an adolescent from shutting down. It is also a way to head off a "Don't tell me how I feel" response and avoids escalating the anger and having it directed at you. Keeping your opinions out of the discussion shows that you are trying to understand their actions rather than criticize or judge them. The goal of this approach is to start to gather information about the incident that took place, not dead-end this possibility.

Once a teen accepts your interest as genuine and your approach as non-accusatory, they are ready for you to discover the source of their behavior. This is not an easy thing to do. Here again, time must be taken, a lot of effort must be expended, and much patience is required. At this point an adolescent may be ready to reveal the "whys" of their reactions to the situation. If this is the case, you can get right to it. If they aren't prepared to take that route, the next step is to finding the reasons for a youngster's resistance to talking about past incidents.

Step Two: Overcoming Resistance to Discussing Past Experiences: A teen may be reluctant to speak about troubling experiences for many reasons. One cause for this silence may be that they feel as if they are the only ones who have had these things happen. If this is so, they may also think that other people who hear their stories will think that they are strange, different, weird, abnormal, crazy, weak or make other negative judgments about them.

Another explanation for not talking about these experiences is that they are too painful to talk about. Recounting these situations means reopening a deep wound, or dealing with something that the youngster doesn't want to acknowledge ever happened.

A third reason for a teen's unwillingness to talk about the past may be that it will make them feel more vulnerable. By revealing something that they experienced an adolescent may appear weak and place their image or safety in jeopardy.

Whatever the reason is for their hesitancy in telling their story, it needs to be overcome. To get through this resistance, "Objectification" is useful. With this tactic, the focus is removed from the individual and generalizations are used instead. "Lots of times people go through experiences that they think no one else has gone through," illustrates this behavior. These kinds of broad statements can also be made to cover other possible concerns:

> "Other people have suffered abuse and recovered with help."
> "Other people have had feelings of shame and embarrassment over incidents that have taken place."
> "Don't worry that your behavior will be discussed with outsiders."

These kinds of remarks may permit a teen to be able to identify with experiences that have occurred in their lives. If they do, an adolescent will feel more comfortable about talking about these situations with you.

A young person may still not want to discuss these kinds of subjects when they are first brought up. They may refer to this discussion some time later. "You know when you told me that sometimes people get embarrassed by a situation" provides one way a teen shows their readiness to talk. Other ways an adolescent may indicate their "discussion readiness" are by a nod of the head, or saying something like, "Stuff like that really does happen." Whatever forms this willingness to talk takes, they have opened the door to more conversation. The question, "Did something like this happen to you or someone that you know?" can keep information flowing. When it does ask, "What happened?" After you do, just let them give their response without interrupting. For many teens, this "conversational green light" represents a time to open their emotional floodgates. It's a time when everything an adolescent has been holding in is allowed to come out and the emotional injury has a chance to start to heal.

You may also get an, "I don't want talk about it" or an "I don't want to deal with it now" response. At this point, a youngster has been taken as far as they want to go, and the subject has to be left alone. However, before it is, a teen must hear that whenever they are ready to discuss an experience, you will be prepared to listen. When they put up a red flag on discussing an incident, it is often a test of your willingness to meet them on their own terms. In other words, an adolescent wants to see if you will give them the time and space to decide when they are ready to discuss a situation. In this way, they are exercising some control.

Building Trust

An adolescent has different ways of seeing if you can be trusted. Letting them know from the start that the conversation you are having with them is confidential is a small part of establishing whether or not you are trustworthy. Words alone don't determine whether someone is honest. How you describe your willingness to respect a teen's need for privacy carries a lot of weight. This "trustworthy test" takes into account your body language and tone of voice. They communicate more about the sincerity of your message than the words alone do. An adolescent may also network with peers to check you out. This has much value to them. Much of what a youngster learns, in just about any subject in the peer culture, comes from other teens.

It is also wise to let an adolescent know that certain subjects that may be discussed require notifying the police or some other authority further helps to build trust. The rationale for giving them this warning is simply, if you are given information about something that can be harmful (knowledge of weapons, drugs, threats, abusive behavior) and you haven't let them know about this obligation, when an incident is reported and action is taken the trust you are trying to build disappears. A teen may respond to this disclosure with a doubtful or questioning look, or ask you for the reason you would report what was said. Whether or not they raise this point or not, it is beneficial to the relationship to describe the negative consequences of not reporting an incident. One point to make is that if someone is aware of something and doesn't report it, someone, (an adolescent or another individual) might get hurt or even die. The question, "How would you have liked to know about something that has happened to a person before, not have said anything and then this individual gets hurt again or even dies, and you may have been able to prevent this from happening?" drives home this idea. Another reason to give is that reporting certain incidents is your legal responsibility. If you don't report an incident and something happens, you could risk losing your job or be charged with a crime. How much influence these explanations may have is hard to say. At the very least, you have given a young person honest reasons for reporting an incident. A teen is more likely to respect and trust you when you are "up front" about what you say and do, then if you omit telling about actions you might have to take.

Discovering the Emotional Effects of Situations

The emotional impact that past incidents has had on an adolescent is also something that needs to be discovered. This information may take days, weeks or even months to discover. Imagining a "Patience Is Required" sign flashing in your head is helpful when trying to get to the whys of a youngster's hostile attitude.

Helping a teen peel off the layers of protection that surround these events requires not only hearing the words that are spoken, but also being aware of what is not said. There may be details that are left out or skimmed over. These descriptions may not only contain limited information but may be told quickly. When an adolescent is anxious about describing an experience, they often tell their story rapidly. Unfinished thoughts are also something else to pay attention to. They may start talking about something and then switch to another topic. "My dad was yelling at me and started to move toward me really fast "pause, and then continue with, "The next day we went to the movies," illustrates this tactic.

Another clue to watch out for is a description of experiences that other teens have gone through, or something they saw in a movie or on television. These kinds of descriptions allow a young person to tell you something without personalizing it, that is, give you information about a situation without saying it is about them. It's the "objectification" mentioned earlier. Looking at something as if it were happening to someone else has less of an emotional impact on an adolescent.

Listening Beyond the Words that Are Spoken

All these signs necessitate recognizing that there is often more to a youngster's descriptions of events than what you hear directly. Whether traumatic incidents are being described, or experiences relating to school, peers or everyday events, listening beyond the words that are spoken is important. You need to listen to the way a teen describes a past incident. The phrase, "Listen, not just to the words people say, but also to the music they play," makes this point. Do the descriptions pour out, or are they related slowly, with hesitancy? Are they uttered softly, or in a loud tone of voice? Do you hear deep breaths or gulping? What facial expressions or physical gestures, (eye-rubbing or foot-shaking), are noticeable? Is an adolescent looking at you or at other places in the room?

As you get the information about their experiences, specific details not only about the events themselves, but also a young person's reactions to them, are important to observe. Questions should be posed in a matter-of-fact way, as though you are asking them to describe a party. This is a non-invasive, approach to finding out about situations. Details about the kind of incident, the people involved, the frequency of an event, and the time and location of these incidents need to be explored. The following questions are helpful in getting this information,

> What was going on? (physical actions, put-downs or threats)
> Who was around when these things were happening and what did they do?
> Did this kind of thing happen more than one time?
> When did this happen (a particular time of the day?

Where did it take place (at home, outside, in a hallway)?
How did you feel when whatever occurred was going on?
When it was over and things calmed down how did you
   feel?
Who did you talk with after this happened?

Your goal is to make sure you fully understand what a teenager has gone through, both rationally and emotionally. Seeking to clarify what is being described communicates to them that they are really trying to be understood. An observation made as an unfinished "fill in the blank" statement is one way to check out what an adolescent is saying. "When you were telling me about this incident, you looked down at the floor," illustrates this tactic. After making this comment, silence is golden. If a young person doesn't respond to this communication gap within a minute or two, ask, "What was going through your mind? or "What were you feeling?" If you get a typical shoulder shrug, hands raised in the "I don't know" position, or a "nothing" reply, use "Objectification" and say something like, "People who have gone through this talk about how upset they were." At this point look for a gesture of agreement or denial. If you receive a negative response, ask, "What else do you think that they could be feeling?" If you still don't get a response, leave it. At some point they may decide to comment on this observation. Once again, patience is required. Using a phrase such as, "It seems" or prefacing a remark by using the words "I thought" gives a teen the chance to admit or deny having a particular feeling, while not making them feel as if you are telling them how they feel. By doing this you prevent an adolescent from getting angry with you and keep the conversation flowing.

Another way to help an adolescent express their feelings is by giving an interpretation of their behavior. A statement like, "It seems a little frightening," or "When you did this, I thought you may have been feeling angry," is useful. A young person may respond some time later, or not at all.

One last consideration should be taken into account. Sometimes, other people will make a request to be present during a conversation between you and a teen. It is better talk to an adolescent alone. The presence of another individual often inhibits a young person's discussion with you. A teen may be afraid that the other person may not like what they have to say and do something to them for telling these things to a stranger. They may fear saying something that can be hurtful. The may also be concerned about being embarrassed, or be made to feel dumb after describing a situation.

However, there are times that another person insists on being present during a conversation with a particular adolescent and they stay for it. This individual can be a parent, another family member, a staff member or an agency supervisor. There are two reasons why a person wants to be in the room while a conversation with a young person is taking place. One concern is expressed as, "I am worried that Darryl's reactions to what is being described may be too difficult for you to handle." The second possibility is that this person thinks that a teen may be trying to con (manipulate) you, to avoid punishment or other consequences for their behavior. Acknowledging and appreciating these concerns and letting the individual know that you will take this information into account when you work with an adolescent can help prevent these individuals from being present during your conversation with the youngster. At this point, thank this person, and talk with the teen by yourself. This response recognizes the other individual's misgivings and shows your confidence in handling them.

There may be other sources of apprehension that underlay those mentioned above. If these do exist, this individual will still insist on their presence while you talk with the adolescent. This is the case when there is something that may be potentially harmful or embarrassing to a family or agency. Their opposition can occur because of substance or physical abuse taking place in a family, or for the failure of an agency to report or effectively deal with a situation while a young person was under their supervision. These kinds of incidents do occur and should be considered.

For whatever reason, another individual may be present during your conversation with a teen. If they are, notice the non-verbal interaction that takes place between them. In particular, be aware if either one shakes their heads, vertically or horizontally, when particular subjects are being discussed. Glaring, gently pounding a fist against a hand, or holding up a finger by their mouth also fall into the "signals to notice" category. These gestures are often made subtly to escape detection. Making these observations often explain the reasons for an adolescent's hesitancy in describing all the details of past situations, and furnishes clues to the causes of their behavior.

Getting to the root of a young person's anger is a time and effort consuming process. Once this task is accomplished, you are that much closer to helping a teen to effectively manager anger. Once an adolescent is able to reveal details of past experiences, they have been able to reach below the surface of their emotional icebergs and you both are ready to take the next step in this process.

Step Three: Using the Knowledge: The last part of this process, perhaps the hardest, is to decide what to do with the information you have gathered about a youngster. To see how far to take your knowledge of the causes of their behavior requires you to consider different options.

One possibility is that a teen doesn't want you to go any further. By revealing the source of anger they have been able to open the door to the past, and are able to shake free of the pressure of having to keep these experiences a secret. This in itself is a big step, and may be the only one they will be able to take.

Your attitude about what was described may also determine how much further this process can go. If you jump in with advice on what an adolescent should do, or say something like "That's nothing to have been scared of or feel hurt about," the conversation has been dead-ended. However, if the young person's emotions have been accurately described, and you have shown a genuine understanding of the effect these experiences had on them, then the path to further discussion has been opened. Asking something like, "Now that you've been able to tell me what happened, what would you like to do about it?" can take you further down this road. The teen may say, "I don't know," or provide the familiar shoulder shrug response. If this is their response, try the following approach. "If you could get over this fear (pain or other feeling) and not let it get you as upset as it did, would that be something you'd like to try?" highlights this idea. Their tone of voice, smile, or a "What ideas do you have?" responses indicate a readiness to continue. If they reply, "Nothing," a frown, or show some other negative sign, the process has been taken as far as it can go, at least for the time being. At the very least, you have opened another path for a teen to take.

Another avenue to pursue to is to revisit the situations that were described. Using this approach, asking an adolescent how they think this incident could have been avoided or handled differently is helpful. If there is a pregnant pause, an "I don't know," or a shoulder shrug response, ask them to try to remember how someone they knew handled a similar situation. The energy that a young person expends expressing responses to these questions, their expressions, or a "Let me think about it" reply, gives you the green light to pursue this approach. If they frown, or say "Nothing," that is exactly what has to be done at this point.

Overview of the Information Gathering Process

Keep in mind the goal of this process not only involves getting information about an incident, but also focuses on helping a teen deal more effectively with anger. In addition, revealing the source of this feeling often helps to reduce its intensity. Once this happens, an adolescent has the opportunity to discuss the effects of past situations on them, and then they have the opportunity to find different ways of handling similar experiences.

Chapter Summary

The hidden causes of teen anger involve situations and people that evoke feelings of embarrassment, fear and hurt that are difficult to express. Some of the issues that were explored in depth were physical and emotional mistreatment, criticisms of appearance, friends, and their efforts in school. A three step process for helping an adolescent feel comfortable enough to express these concealed reasons for anger was described, along with the kinds of situations that can occur with its use.

Chapter Three

Teen Frustrations

In this chapter, the different kinds of frustration an adolescent faces will be addressed, how these effect a young person's behavior and what you can do to help a teen deal more effectively with this source of anger.

Frustration

A big contributor to an adolescent's anger is frustration. Its sources vary. One basis for this feeling occurs when a teen's beliefs are challenged. When their thinking about styles of dress, groups of peers, or the kinds of music they find enjoyable is questioned, the message they receive is, "Your opinions don't count." The stronger the beliefs a youngster has, the higher the level of frustration is when these views are challenged. It is important to understand the role these beliefs have in a teen's life, not judge them. By accepting that these things are important to an adolescent, without making any judgments, you give them value. By doing so, the need for recognition that a youngster so strongly desires is met. After finding out this information, having a teen describe the pros and cons of following these beliefs, keeps the discussion flowing, and eliminates or keeps the level of frustration to a minimum.

By following this pattern of behavior you have also added yourself to the list of adults that a young person will listen to and may accept different viewpoints from. If you challenge their beliefs, you enter the "You're wrong,

I'm right" zone. Once this happens, it is a "lose-lose" situation; an adolescent's frustration is escalated and negative reactions reign supreme. At this point, any chance of influencing a young person plummets like the stock market.

When you take the time to hear and understand what an adolescent has to say, you have a better chance that your thoughts will be heard.

Emotional Needs

The frustration of emotional needs in a teen represent a real sore spot for them. When the desires for recognition, belonging, freedom, security and safety aren't met, an adolescent often reacts strongly. Defining what the requirements for meeting these needs are, noting what happens when they aren't, and finally, discovering how to handle a youngster's reactions when they occur will help you understand more about this source of anger.

The Need for Recognition

The need for recognition involves giving value to a teen's opinions, achievements, and decisions. What is important to an adolescent is to have someone notice they are achieving some level of mastery in a particular area, starting to develop a skill or completing tasks they have been given. These observations can involve accomplishments in school, sports or in dealing with situations that arise. It is important to notice the efforts being made—not the results or adult expectations. Any and all attempts by a teen to improve in any area of their lives must be recognized. To illustrate this idea, let's look at academic achievement. As an example, an adolescent has improved their grade in Math from a 70 in the first marking period to a 75 for the second marking period. For many parents, although there is an improvement, this higher grade isn't high enough. They remark, "You should be able to get an 80 or 85!" There is nothing wrong for a parent to want a child to get this higher grade, however, the improvement that was made went unnoticed. This is something that can negatively influence a young person. The same attention should be paid to gains in ability and achievement in sports, or in any area of a teen's life. Adolescents react negatively to comments about what they should do. As a person on a tape I heard quipped, "People get tired of being 'should of' on."

Another source of recognition for a young person is being heard. Adults really listening, not just to a teen's words, but really understanding the message, helps fulfill this need. It gives a feeling of being understood and heightens their self-esteem. It also gives you the opportunity to understand more about a young person's perceptions: "All I want is for someone to listen to me" is a comment made by many teens. It is something I heard from many students as a high school guidance counselor. It is something that underscores the importance of helping to fulfill this need.

> Once again, listening to and accepting what an adolescent has to say doesn't mean you agree with them. It means, "I am paying attention to what you have to say and think it's important."

Frustrating the Need for Recognition

Frustrating the desire for recognition takes different forms. The criticisms mentioned earlier describe one cause for this feeling. The "How To" of reaching the kinds of concerns that are noted by disapproving remarks in a constructive way involves a different approach. Listening is a key factor. Very often a teen's anxiety over physical appearance, school, family, relationships, come out in conversation. These can surface directly, with such remarks as:

"I can't stand how dumb I am in Math."

"I hate to look at myself in the mirror."

They may also be masked in such comments as, "Sally's mom doesn't put her down about her weight. Instead, she waits until Sally asks her for ways to lose weight before she says anything"

"Brian's parents don't yell when he gets a bad mark."

By making these kinds of direct or indirect remarks, an adolescent furnishes a conversational lead and opens the door to a discussion.

Sometimes asking general questions such as,

"What's happening?"

"How are things going for you?"

"What's new with school?"

"How are things going with girls/ boys?"

can get to some of the concerns in a non-threatening, matter-of-fact way. Often these questions are answered with a shrug, or with short, evasive responses such as "Nothing" or "Okay." Knowing that youngsters often want privacy makes these remarks predictable. The key is to keep asking questions. At some point, perhaps in some indirect way at another point in time, you'll get some more details about a their life. Continued interest in them also shows concern. Keep in mind, an adolescent will pick the time and the place to speak with you. Be ready for it.

Another strategy for getting more information is asking more open-ended questions (those requiring more than a yes or no, okay, nothing, response). The information you are trying to obtain is based on previous knowledge about specific areas an adolescent brought up, either directly or indirectly. Using questions beginning with, "How" "When" "Where" may help you to tap into these parts of a teen's life.

Dave Wolffe

The Need to Belong

Closely related to the need for recognition is the need to belong. Being part of a particular peer group, be it the, jocks, cheerleaders, the In Group, in other words, those people regarded as cool, or being considered a Metal Head, Geek, or Gang Banger, individuals who are viewed as weird, or those who are on their Shouldn't Know or Don't Want To Know" list, has tremendous value . Being part of a group is as essential to a young person as having food, clothing and shelter. Belonging also extends to family and other intimate relationships. "I feel important because people (peers, particular groups, family) want me to hang out (go places, do things, invite me to) with them," illustrates the connection between the need for recognition and that for belonging.

Other times peers or adults ostracize a teen for their differences in dress, music, and lifestyle, and consider them outsiders. When an adolescent feels this kind of rejection, their need to be a part of a community, school, or peer group is frustrated. Anger and resentment sets in. These feelings can lead to a variety of reactions. Some of these can escalate to the point that leads to a Columbine, a Virginia Tech or some other horrible senseless, violent behavior against others. A youngster sometimes reacts to this source of frustration by turning their anger on themselves with a self-inflicted injury, or, in the most severe instance, they may resort to suicide.

Needing to belong and be recognized seem to be among the strongest desires for young people. Understanding how intensely a teen experiences this feeling, and the kinds of reactions they have to it, is helpful knowledge. It is at this point that you can have them identify where on the Anger Scale they find themselves when a particular situation frustrates this need. A variation of this idea is to have an adolescent list different situations in which this desire is frustrated, and put them on the Anger Scale. Once the degree of anger is noted, analyzing the incident becomes the focus of the discussion. How to prevent the reaction from going too far up the Anger Scale then becomes the focus of the conversation. Using a visual tool, as mentioned earlier, can offer a concrete, more understandable way to see the effect of an incident.

Another approach to use, is to explore the consequences of different reactions to situations where a teen is made to feel left out.

The Need for Freedom

Another source of frustration arises from the pressure to do something that a teen doesn't want to do. It can come from peer pressure to go certain places, or be with a particular group of friends. This stress can also come from parents who want to impose a curfew or have certain chores done. In these situations the need for freedom and independence is being threatened.

Limited freedom is a major source of frustration for teens. Put another way, adolescents have the desire to have control over their lives. When they feel they don't, this need is being challenged. A young person wants to be viewed as being capable of handling different responsibilities on his or her own. School, sports, chores and relationships represent these areas of accountability. A teen also wants to be viewed as being capable of making the right choices. The power they have in deciding to do certain things, be with particular people, enjoy going where and when they want, describe the kind of decisions that an adolescent wants to be able to make. If they are regarded as responsible, both their need for freedom and for recognition are being met.

Objections an adult has to allowing a youngster freedom are:

> Tony makes the wrong choices.
> Carla doesn't have any sense of responsibility.
> Joey needs me to be on top of him.

There is no doubt that teens may have a history of not doing things, not achieving or caring. This behavior certainly needs to be addressed. How it is handled, in a way that creates the least hassles, offers the greatest opportunity to gain influence with adolescents.

What happens when a youngster isn't able to have the need for freedom met? You can expect reactions to this source of frustration to come across loud and clear. Responses can take on many forms. Some typical teen remarks are:

> "You treat me like a little kid!"
> "You don't trust me!"
> "I can do what I have to when I feel like it!"
> "I am fifteen years old. I can do what I want without you
> being on my back."

Some of the adolescents who participated in the Anger Management Power Program described the following frequent behaviors to their freedom being challenged by:

> Yelling.
> Storming out of the room.
> Slamming doors.
> Cursing.

These participants also expressed the idea that when their freedom was restricted or taken away they did exactly what they were being told not to do. This kind of rebelliousness resulted in:

> Staying out late purposely.
> Getting involved with people who don't go to school.
> Participating in illegal activities.
> Hurting others.
> Doing something harmful to family members (stealing,
> hurting a sibling or being physical with a parent or
> other caregiver).

These actions carry the message, "I'll show them! I don't have to take their [expletive]!" A youngster usually knows that the things they are doing are wrong, but anger takes over their behavior. A major nerve has been hit. A teen's chance of maintaining control over their life has been taken away. What you are trying to accomplish is to have an adolescent deal more effectively with this cause of anger, not add to the frustrations that they experience. Suggestions on how o accomplish this objective will be presented throughout the remaining sections of this chapter.

This is not to say that an adolescent shouldn't have structure. In fact, having guidelines to follow, whether they admit it or not, is something they want and need. This period in a young person's life is a time when the need to be both free, and have the security of knowing they can go to a parent or other adult for help. Many times these mixed needs result in an internal conflict and becomes another source of confusion for a teen. This conflict that they face is something that should be understood and handled.

Educational Frustrations

School can be another source of frustration for adolescents. Articles of clothing that cannot be worn (hats, "butt-showing jeans," 'do-rags, etc.), items that cannot be used (cell phones, iPods), examinations, grades, and subjects that are described as "useless in real life," make up the menu for causes of this feeling in the educational setting. The comments that parents, caretakers and educators often make, heighten their reactions to school. The remarks, "How come your little brother can do this stuff and you can't," "You really don't want to learn." "You're wasting my time and your time in this class. Why don't you go for your GED (equivalency diploma)" illustrate this kind of criticism. Adding to this feeling of incompetency, the frustration of not being able to meet the needs for recognition, safety, security and freedom, both from school, as well as other sources, and you have a more complete picture of the impact the educational environment can have on a teen.

The remarks an adolescent can make about school range from:

"I just don't get this (subject)!"

"There's no way I am every going to graduate, so why should I try?"

"I'm quitting!"

"Screw school, the teachers and you!"

These kinds of reactions often come after an exam, a report card, or in anticipation of some other indicator of academic progress. Avoiding doing any assignments, cutting classes or dropping out of school entirely are actions that can accompany educational frustration.

To help an adolescent overcome the challenges that education brings, requires using different strategies. The first approach involves gathering information on how strong the frustration with school is, and what about it gets them upset. The questions, "How frustrated does school make you?" and "What about it makes you feel this?" focus on these details.

The Anger Scale is a good barometer of how strong a reaction a teen may have to this source of dissatisfaction. If they say it's a 3-6, you know their displeasure with school is annoying and bothersome but not overwhelming. If their assessment is a 7 or above, then there is a chance their reaction will become more severe. If they can't come up with a place on the Anger Scale, then have them compare the frustration school creates with other sources of this feeling. Another indicator of how intense a young person's reaction to school is demonstrated in their description of it. A teen's tone of voice (matter-of-fact, forceful, soft), and facial expressions (glaring eyes, puzzled look), provide clues to how severe this cause of anger is. Observing and listening to them provides a more effective way of trying to deal with their frustration with school than trying to explain the reasons why they shouldn't be so upset over it. Once you are able understand how angry they are, and why, you can make the assessment of whether or not they are just venting (letting off steam), or are about to act out more severely.

If it's just a matter of getting the frustration out, creating an atmosphere in which an adolescent is able to freely express their feelings is the road to take. Doing nothing but listening to them gives a youngster the opportunity to sound off about things or people that are annoying about school. This reaction may come out all at once, or in bits and pieces. After he or she has finished describing the source of frustration, they may sigh or take a deep breath. If this happens, it's a sign that what was bothering them is out and the "siege of frustration" is over. It is the peace that follows a storm. At this point, an adolescent is ready to describe why school is so frustrating and discuss what can be done to help him /her feel less upset about it. Another possibility is that a teen just wants to leave the subject alone. Whichever path is taken, follow and respect it.

If an adolescent appears extremely agitated, describing or reaching an 8-10 on the Anger Scale, they are heading toward a crisis point. If this is the case, steps need to be taken to bring down the intensity of this feeling. The first involves acknowledging the frustration being experienced without judging it. The remark, "Yeah, when something like this happens, a lot of people just want to forget about it or not deal with it all," illustrates this tactic. Once this comment is made, watch and wait for a reaction. If they smile, nod or show any other sign that you are on target, try to find out the reasons for these feelings toward school. "What's stopping you from doing better in school?" represents a good starting point for this discussion. A young person may remark, "I'm just dumb," or hold teachers, an educational system or any number of other people or things responsible for their problem with school. If they describe themselves as someone who lacks intelligence or ability, accept this feeling without agreeing with it, by saying something like "Some people feel that way when they have a hard time doing or understanding things." A way to treat this view is to bring up how people that are not as good in some things can still do better in them. The question, "What kinds of things can people do to improve themselves?" addresses this idea. If a teen can't think of a response, describing other things that they can relate to is another way to stimulate their thinking. Asking what athletes in different sports do to improve or get out of slumps, or musicians and singers do who want to get into a band or become recording stars, describe some of these areas of interest.

If a youngster plays the "blame card" the remark, "In addition to (whatever the blockage is), what else is getting in your way?" helps them focus on what they may not be doing to succeed in school. If there are some areas that they admit they can do something about, that is, take responsibility for, the path to a lower level of frustration can be opened.

Another approach is to introduce the idea of control. Asking if they like the idea of being in control of what they can do, starts you in this direction. An adolescent may respond to this apparently "dumb question" by commenting,

> "Who doesn't?"
> "You've got to be kidding!"
> "Are you serious?"
> or a resounding, "Yes!"

After this obvious conclusion is reached, saying, "What you can't control is how others behave toward you, (teachers, counselors, principals other school staff, or your parents, the objects of blame) or what the requirements are for your diploma," can help to lead down the road leaving blame behind and look for ways they can achieve more in school. Let this thought sink in for a minute or so. After you have, add, "You have the power to deal with school, if you want, and do something about all the things that are keeping you from passing (the subject, test, being promoted, graduating). It's your decision!" You have empowered the youngster to take charge of this part of their life. Whether they do or not, is another story. His/her reaction to this train of thought will determine whether this idea will work or not.

Another tactic is to have a teen think of a time when someone had a problem that seemed unsolvable at first, but was successfully handled. If they can remember, have them describe what was done to remedy the situation. If the problem wasn't resolved, look at what might have been done.

Previous experience can be helpful. It is another area that will be considered in a later chapter.

Looking at the big picture is another road to take. In this case, have the teen try to put their difficulty with school in perspective by pointing out problems that other people face. Describing individuals who have to deal with a physical difficulty, being crippled or blind, or having some kind of life-threatening disease, serves this purpose, Making the point that many individuals with these limitations just don't quit and don't stop doing what they need to do to get on with their lives, may help them see the light out of their "educational tunnel." If their eyes open wider, they nod, or make a remark something like, "Maybe my problem with school isn't all that bad," their frustration level with education has been diminished.

If you get an expression of doubt, or "Yeah, but I'm not smart," or, "So what!" response, add, "When anyone goes through a tough time, they often don't want to look at anyone else's problems, or feel what they are going through is much different." This remark shows empathy toward the youngster. By sharing this attempt to understand a teen's viewpoint, you may soften their reaction to your thought. In addition, having thoughts and feelings heard and understood is often all an adolescent wants or needs to get passed a situation.

> Trying different approaches, that is, using Trial Balloons, often pays off. Your gut reactions to situations that arise with a young person are often right on target. Go with them. It is something that I have found useful in working with teens. You never know what idea is going to make sense to an adolescent or when they will use it.

Frustration with Peers

The last, and perhaps the strongest source of frustration for a young person, comes from their relationships with peers. Much of a teen's life centers on friends. Identity and recognition are part of this picture. "If I have friends and belong to a group, I am a worthwhile person," expresses this idea. Belonging, being part of something, is another important need for an adolescent to meet. Having a network of friends can fulfill this desire, as well as those for security and safety.

There are many ways an adolescent can experience this source of frustration. Not wanting to do what friends want to do, go where peers want them to go, or not being a part of a particular group—Jocks, Cheerleaders, Metal Heads, Geeks or Gang Bangers—illustrate some of the reasons a young person can experience frustration with their peer group. What makes this area more upsetting is that the need to be independent (free) comes into conflict with their need to belong, to fit in, to be accepted by peers. When this happens, a great amount of internal tension is created. When a young person chooses independence, they not only face criticism, but also leave themselves open to ridicule, ostracism and sometimes verbal or even physical hostility. Comments like:

"What's the matter, you think you are better than us?"
"You're a snob."
"Forget you!"

are some of the remarks they face when they demonstrate their need for freedom from their peer group's influence.

When this behavior towards a teen takes place he/she often reacts strongly. In their most extreme form these actions may be violent. This kind of behavior may be directed toward others or at themselves. The young people who were responsible for the Columbine and Virginia Tech tragedies illustrate this response in its most extreme form. "[Expletive] them!" "I'll show them" coupled with hand-pounding, fist-clenching, banging objects, bullying and frequent fighting represent other kinds of reactions to being criticized, ostracized or experiencing other forms of alienation.

Sometimes these responses result in self-destructive behavior. Hitting something hard, or punching a window or other glass object illustrate this kind of reaction. Another way a youngster may hurt him or herself is engaging in risky behavior. They may find themselves frequently fighting, engaging in dangerous activities (walking across railroad or subway tracks, or busy streets) or taking chances with their health (smoking, taking illicit drugs, or participating in unprotected sex). Self-mutilation and attempted suicide are the most extreme examples of self destructive behavior.

Less obvious behavior also occurs. It can develop anywhere from one month on, and is often hidden from parents, other family members, teachers, boyfriends/girlfriends and close friends. A young person can physically distance themselves from others. A teen who does this often tells other people that they want to be alone or need their own space. Sometimes they push others away by yelling, sulking, or behaving in ways that keep other individuals from wanting to be around them. Some youngsters go on eating binges or starve themselves. This behavior can also be symptomatic of bulimia or anorexia, both serious conditions that are often hidden. For more information about these illnesses consult a mental health agency or search the Internet.

Sleeplessness is another form frustration with peers takes. Problems with friends can cause the degree of anxiety that often keeps them awake. During these sleepless times an adolescent thinks a lot about ways to handle this kind of trouble. If they are unable to resolve this difficulty, to them, it means an end of their life. This idea may seem overly dramatic to an adult. However, this kind of thinking expresses how great a problem, in this case the frustration with peers, is to a young person.

Sleeping too much, offers a way for a teen to escape dealing with this source of frustration. When an adolescent sleeps a lot and doesn't want to get up to go places and do things they usually look forward to, this represents another sign that there is a problem. It is true that red or droopy eyes may be caused by allergies, getting something in their eyes or waking up late. However, these symptoms and behaviors may also be attributable to drug abuse, or frequent crying, and be indicative of depression. All of these reactions require serious attention. These signs do not necessarily mean the worst fear you may have, only that you ought to be aware of them. When these signs last over two weeks, or whatever time they usually display this behavior, that's the time to act. Without help, the results to a young person, their family, and to others who are part of their lives can be catastrophic.

The behaviors that are being attributed to an adolescent's frustration with peers,, can also be reactions to other sources of anger, or their inability to express this feeling. They should be noted, discussed and dealt with directly.

Acknowledging a youngster's behavior is a good first step to take. What you see or hear needs to be objectively described.

> "I noticed that you have been hanging around by yourself
> lately."
> "I saw you punch the wall after you walked away from
> your friends," or
> "You look like you haven't gotten enough sleep"

illustrate this kind of recognition. If you've observed these kinds of actions over a period of time, let the teen know. "It seems to me that you've been unhappy for awhile" describes this kind of observation. Once you have made this kind of a remark watch and wait for a response.

An adolescent may say, "So what!" "Yeah," or stare, nod, or not react at all. When this happens they may be waiting for you to keep the ball rolling. If this is the case, saying, "You looked like you wanted to let me know more about what I said to you," can keep things going. Once again, pause, be patient and give the young person the chance to respond. If there still isn't any response, try something like, "What I said or saw seemed to be something that you want to talk about." Wait for some kind of reaction. Whatever form this response takes, ask, "What's going on?" and see what happens.

Keep after an answer, no matter how many attempts you make. This effort should be made periodically, not at one particular time, so you don't get the "Get off my case" response, and ruin the chances of discussing this problem with a teen. The purpose in pursuing this direction is to establish a connection between their behavior and the reasons for it. When the adolescent responds, the path to helping them limit the effects of their frustration is opened.

If an adolescent gives you a hands up gesture, a look of doubt or disgust, or just walks away, the conversation has gone as far as it can go, at least for the time being. Don't be too frustrated! A youngster will often return to a subject some time after it has been dropped. The topic of frustration with peers may resurface in different ways. It can come spontaneously as something they are ready to handle at a particular time or perhaps when something else happened with peers that they don't want to let continue. "Discussion readiness" may also come in the form of descriptions of situations other teens are going through, or as an observation they make of a television or movie character.

After discovering the reasons for their frustration with peers, and discussing them, the next step to take is to find ways to limit the results. Having a teen take certain steps helps to reduce the effect this feeling has. Rather than repeat the strategies already described to accomplish this goal, return to the section entitled, "How to Deal with A Teen's Frustration with Education" to get more ideas on how to handle this source of frustration with an adolescent. These ideas can also be used to limit other causes of anger.

The Need for Security and Safety

Some of the sources of anger in young people have been connected to the frustration of the needs for recognition, belonging and freedom. Not meeting their desires for security and safety represent two additional reasons for teen frustration. Some of their roots are not as easily revealed as others because they can cause them the most embarrassment, shame or fear.

Sources of Security

The need for security can be met in different ways. One means of achieving it takes place when youngsters feel part of a stable family environment. A strong marital relationship, a steady family income and healthy parents characterize this atmosphere. Having food, clothing and shelter consistently available represents another way this need is met. The knowledge that a teen's home and neighborhood is safe also contributes to this feeling of well-being.

This need can be threatened in many ways. A parent losing a job or taking one in a new location, having a close relative with a long-term or terminal illness or dying, or a fire that destroys a family's home can shake an adolescent's foundation of security. When these events occur, they can find themselves separated from parents and siblings and living with relatives who are unfamiliar, or in a foster care or a group home setting. The peace and comfort they once felt is replaced by anxiety. A young person can face the possibility of not knowing when and if they can live with their family again, or where they might be living. When these kinds of changes occur, a teen may also have to move to a new neighborhood, attend a different school, and worst of all, be unable to see friends they've made, as often, or even ever again.

With these circumstances occur in a teen's life, it is no wonder they are angry. This feeling comes out in many ways. They may appear defensive when asked about their family. A quick and loud," Nothing!" or they may ask, "Why do you want to know?" expressed in a distrustful manner may meet a simple question like, "What's going on in your life?" An adolescent with this difficulty is sometimes resistant to having close ties with other people. Their thinking can be, "Something else may happen and make me move again so why bother with other people?" A youngster experiencing this insecurity may also walk around with constant scowls, and find they get into frequent confrontations. They may also cut classes, or have a strong desire to stay away from wherever they are living, whether it's in their own home or somewhere temporary. This kind of behavior avoids having to face the sources of uncertainty.

Whether this feeling is based on reality, or is created by the fear that certain events may take place, its effect is great. It is safer for a teen to show anger, a feeling that covers up this insecurity, rather than to admit to being fearful. The thought process goes like this, "If I show I am worried, people will think I'm soft (weak) and think they can play (take advantage of) me." "Toughness" in appearance and action is the key to survival for many adolescents.

As with other causes of the anger that a young person experiences, objectively describing their actions represents a good starting point. The remark, "Seeing you staring into space when someone asks you about your family makes it seem like something is really bothering you" illustrates this idea. The more specific the details of their actions are, the clearer the path is to having them tell you what they are going through. Using a "pregnant pause" after making an observation gives a teen the opportunity to decide to say something or not. The absence of sound can really be uncomfortable, requiring them to break the "quiet barrier" quickly. Looking at it another way, for an adolescent it can be their opportunity to take control of the moment.

If there is no response, asking directly, "What happened?" may get you some information. If there is still no reaction, you have reached the end of this path for the time being. A youngster may provide information sometime later through a conversational lead. This information can come veiled in a situation an adolescent describes involving a peer, a character in a movie or television show or from something they read about on the Internet. After a youngster has dropped this hint, saying, "You spoke about what happened to your friend. Some people your age think this sort of thing is going to happen to them," may reopen the dialog. If after a minute or so they haven't responded, ask "Do you see this kind of thing happening to you?"

Once you have discovered the reasons for their insecurity, the next step involves helping a teen to find a way to experience some degree of comfort and well being. Uncovering the source of this feeling is one way that can help reduce the intensity of the insecurity for a teen. The role of previous experience can be another way to help an adolescent contend with this source of unhappiness. "Have you seen anyone else deal with (divorce, illness, or whatever situation they are presently faced with)?" is a way to get this information. If they have, continue moving in this direction by asking, "What happened? How did the other young people deal with it? What helped them? What didn't help them? Do you see any of these things helping you in your situation?" describes this information gathering process. If an adolescent cannot come up with any responses, have them try to think of how a character on a television show or a movie handled a similar situation. If they can, have them describe how the person managed their problem. This method encourages a youngster to deal with the situation while also keeping the spotlight off of them. It uses the "Objectivity" method.

The idea of dealing with change is another area to explore. Moving from one neighborhood to another, from elementary, to middle school to high school, or managing the loss of a close relative or friend, represent the kinds of adjustments that a teen may have already made in their life. Having them remember these types of changes can give them some degree of confidence in dealing with their present situations. "You were able to handle that situation, so I really think that you can find a way to take care of this now," reflects this belief.

The sources of stability that still remain in a young person's life offers another approach. If, for example, the situation involves a divorce, discussing the consistencies that remain in the teen's life is worth trying. Having them look at ways to see the person who may no longer be living in the same house is something to discuss with them. Asking if the individual who no longer lives in their house works or lives near enough to be seen easily and frequently illustrates this idea.

Finding out if decisions effecting an adolescent's education, health care and behavior will still involve both parents points out another consistency in their life. Having them think about family members who will still be living with them, and the roles these people play, is also worth pointing out. By discussing these possibilities a youngster is shown that even though there are major changes taking place in their family, there are still things that will remain the same.

Other relationships that are part of a teen's life represent another source of stability for them. These individuals may include friends, classmates, teachers, guidance counselors, other school personnel, priests, rabbis, social workers, agency interns or store owners. These are people they feel comfortable speaking to and spending time with and can continue to do so. Having these consistent relationships pointed out can help diminish the intensity of the feelings of insecurity, isolation, abandonment or rejection that can accompany the changes that are taking place in their life.

Another source of stability are the activities that still remain a part of their lives. Attending school, participating in or attending different sporting events, or going to parties, rock concerts and dances are things that remain the same in spite of a changing family environment.

A young person's reaction may be a resounding, "So what!" The unwillingness to accept the changes in their life, or the idea that there can't be anything positive once the family is being split up is common. A teen simply cannot accept these differences emotionally. The key to seeing stability in their life rests with their ability to get through their emotional upheaval and to calm down enough to be able to cope with these changes in a rational way. As with any kind of loss people experience, a young person must go through different emotional stages. These steps can involve a variety of feelings including anger, denial, fear, disappointment and pain. The final stage in this process allows them to reach the point of acceptance. When they realize what has happened in their life is a reality and is something that they cannot make go away, they are ready to deal with the situation differently. Helping an adolescent to reach this stage can mean giving them time to express these feelings to you. By hearing, understanding and not giving advice, a youngster's thoughts and feelings are valued. Once this "venting" has taken place, you can expect a calmness. It is at this point that some of

---

"Gut Reaction" Advisory: There are ideas that just pop into your head. Call them gut reactions, instincts, or mental thunderstorms. They are thoughts that have been stored in your memory bank. For whatever reason, they are knocking on your mind's door ready to be called to action. Don't be afraid to let them out and follow their lead, at any point, with any situation that may arise with an adolescent.

the sources of stability that were suggested to them can be considered. The goal in using these approaches is to help a young person understand that as disruptive as things may be in their life, there are people and parts of it that will remain consistent. Once this idea is accepted, they may also see that their world is not totally falling apart. By realizing this they may see that their need for security can be met, at least to some degree and they may also not feel as frustrated as they were before looking at these possibilities.

Meeting the Need for Safety

Safety is another strong need for a young person. Reaching this goal requires that they feel protected from both physical and emotional injury. Being shielded from physical pain can be accomplished in different ways. A teen who experienced physical abuse at home often avoids this treatment by coming home late, spending time in other people's houses (friends, other family members) or getting involved in extracurricular activities, positive or not. Another threat to their physical safety can come from violent peers. To avoid this source of harm they may cut classes or school entirely, make sure to do things outside of their neighborhood, or join a group, often a gang, for protection. The thinking for membership in this kind of an organization is, "They (other gang members) have my back." Self-preservation is a powerful motivator.

Ways a young person finds safety are often those that they see and hear from their peers. Joining a gang or giving payback to the offending party describes the methods learned from close friends or other peers, often

It is important to note that in no way am I saying that gang involvement and violence are positive ways for an adolescent to gain protection from physical harm. Hearing and understanding their reasons for thinking these actions are necessary for their safety is important. The more information you have on their thinking on these subjects, the better the chances of finding safer alternatives.

referred to as "associates." Using these kinds of methods involves a strong belief that the way to deal with violence against oneself should be with violence—an "eye for an eye" philosophy. Challenging this attitude only alienates a teen and shuts down any further conversation on this subject.

Finding a Positive Path to Physical Safety

Physical and sexual abuse against teens must be reported to the police, or some other governmental agency, as mandated by law. All the methods described below do not replace or substitute for this means of protecting them. Violent acts can occur within families, in dating situations or in other intimate relationships. They can also occur between members of the same or different peer groups. Wherever, and with whoever these incidents of mistreatment occur, agencies and groups are available to help victims of this kind of crime. There is a wealth of information available on referral sources from state and city mental health and other agencies and organizations and on the Internet relating to this topic. Without some form of intervention, the chances of repeated abuse and perhaps death are very strong possibilities.

Physical abuse is no doubt a very sensitive and emotionally painful subject for a young person to describe. Discovering the How? Where? When? and Why? of physically harmful situations is the first step to take. These should be open-ended questions that require more than a "yes" or "no" response. They are useful in gathering the most details about situations and help to keep conversations going. Getting this information from an adolescent requires time, patience and gaining their trust.

There is much that can be discovered. How the injury occurred is something to find out: Was the adolescent struck with hands, fists, or objects like irons or brooms? How often has this kind of incident happened? Does this behavior occur once in a while, every day or weekly? Find out whether or not the person hurting the youngster does so when he/she experiences stress (financial, job-related), or when they are drunk or high on some other drug. Look at what took place prior to the event and the steps the youngster or others took to stop, prevent or avoid this kind of treatment. Where this abuse takes place is another piece of the abuse puzzle that needs to found. Do these actions take place at home or somewhere else out of sight? Once you have answers to these questions, strategies can be developed for helping the teen to protect themselves from future injuries.

There are several different steps that can be taken to get information from a victim of abuse. The use of objective descriptions of an adolescent's behavior is helpful. "Lots of times, people your age who have been hit a lot need lots of space and don't like to be touched" is an example of this kind of remark. It is a statement that can be made and then left alone. Whether in response to this statement, or as part of a description of an incident, careful attention must be paid to the youngster's tone of voice, pauses that are made, and to other non-verbal cues. Does a teen's body look rigid or relaxed? Are their hands and arms folded or resting on their legs? Do you see tears welling up? Does he/she look sad, angry, scared, describing abusive situations? These are signs to be noted and questions to be answered to fully understand the effect of this type of treatment.

Once this information is obtained and observations are noted, there are several ways to help prevent this mistreatment from taking place again. Some of these have already been described in the "Safety" section. Another direction to take is to look at the past attempts they made or that have worked to prevent the abuser from hurting them. You can also have them describe what peers or characters in movies, television programs or in other forms of media did to successfully prevent themselves from being mistreated.

Culture and family patterns often play a role in knowing why abusive behavior takes place. These are things that are sometimes inadvertently mentioned by a young person. "This is how people in my family do it" or "In my culture hitting a kid is the way we get punished," describe how this kind of information is revealed. This is the kind of knowledge that counselors, social workers and youth workers should take into account when dealing with teens.

For some adolescents, using weapons or physically striking back at an abuser can be a way of handling the abusive behavior that is hurting them.

To an adolescent who describes this pattern of behavior, the consequences (another anger manager to be explored) can be pointed out. Asking, "What happens to your mom, brothers, sisters or other family members if you are sent to jail, or if the abuser isn't hurt and comes after you and does more damage to you or others in your family?" expands on this idea. Sometimes young people who are reluctant to see any other way of dealing with an abuser will say, "I don't really care." If this is their response, ask, "What else can be done to stop this from happening again where you won't get in trouble with the law or get hurt again?" You are not agreeing with the teen's vengeful thoughts, only hearing them, and giving them the opportunity to find other ways to manage this situation.

Prior to having an incident reported, victims, as well as family members, may fear retribution by the abuser and not want these situations disclosed. There are several ways to handle this objection. One thing that can be done is to let an abused person and their family know that there are places that abuser won't be able to find about where they can stay until the situation is handled. These locations may be in the homes of relatives or friends, or in temporary shelters.

Another thing to let a victim know is that people under investigation may not attempt any more acts of violence out for fear of facing jail time or financial penalties if they are found guilty of this crime. Even if abusers aren't punished as a result of a particular investigation, if accused again, they may have less of a chance of escaping punishment, causing them to think twice before physically harming anyone else. Impressing on the victim that not reporting this behavior may allow the abuser to hurt other people, or possibly cause someone's death is another important idea to get across.

Even with these apparently strong reasons to let others know about these destructive people, young victims may still not want you to file a report. Fears and concerns outweigh any reasons that can be given for turning in an abuser.

Some things need to be considered by a professional who works with a teen victim of physical abuse go beyond the legal responsibility to file a report. Failure to undertake this obligation results for different reasons. Feeling sorry for the victim and not wanting to be the cause of any more grief for them because you think that you can help them steer clear of any further mistreatment by helping them develop a plan to prevent the abuser from hurting them again, represent two of these ideas. However, if you have knowledge of mistreatment, and it isn't reported, there is the chance that this same adolescent could be physically injured again, or even die at the hands of the abuser. It's an outcome that no one wants to have on his or her conscience. It's sometimes a professional dilemma many people face. The expression, "It is always better to err on the side of caution," I believe can helps resolve this confusion. Your role as an advocate for a young person involves taking the action that will best serve them, having the least negative effects on their life. This is often a delicate balance, and requires you to be flexible enough to try several approaches.

Emotional Safety

Emotional safety has its partner in the need for recognition. Rather than feel the pain resulting from some of the criticisms that were described earlier in this chapter, a teen will seek out people who provide protection from this source of hurt. These individuals are those who will listen to an adolescent without making harsh judgments about them, their interests, opinions or friends. These "emotional safe havens" include, school counselors, teachers, coaches, custodial personnel, school safety agents, ministers, social workers, relatives, friends and their parents' or any individuals who touches them.

Another way that you can help youngsters handle this source of frustration involves a three step analytical approach. The format used in this method is the same as that found in an Anger Journal, another Anger Manager that will be explained in more detail later on. Using this approach requires a teen's readiness. It is a time when their emotional reactions to situations have run their course. Their angry energy, the power that causes reactions without reason, has been released. It is the point when an adolescent can express this feeling without hurting themselves or others. Many Anger Managers have been and others will be introduced to be used to help young people reach this goal. Once their anger has been diminished to this level, the following approach can be used.

The first step requires analyzing the situation that was the source of their frustration. They look at what was said about them to cause this emotional injury, and find out why it was upsetting, that is, to discover what "hot button" was pushed.

The next part of this process has them focusing on ways to diminish or eliminate the effects of a situation. It has them view an incident from different perspectives in order to develop better means of managing it. This stage enables them to answer the questions, "What else could the other person be trying to tell me?" and "How could I have handled this situation without getting so upset?"

The final stage of this process has teens looking for ways to protect themselves from experiencing this emotional damage in the future. If they care about their relationship with the critical person, they may decide to tell how and why that individual's remarks are so damaging. The "I Statement," another Anger Manager to be discussed later on, helps to accomplish this task. A youngster may also consider the reasons that some people criticize others. These critics may be individuals who themselves have received much criticism, or are people who don't feel very worthwhile. The reason they put down others is to make themselves feel bigger or better than those they criticize. Given these two possibilities teens may decide to ignore remarks made by particular individuals.

Chapter Summary

Many sources of frustration were revealed and discussed in this chapter. These included the needs for recognition, belonging, security, physical and emotional safety and freedom, along with those having to do with peers and education. Ways of empowering a teen to handle these sources of frustration were also explored

Chapter Four

Other Sources of Anger

In this chapter we'll focus on some very different sources of anger: unmet expectations, injustices, traumatic experiences, domestic violence and drug abuse by a family member. While there are methods to help teens deal with all of these situations, keep in mind making sure adolescents are safe, by reporting any abusive situation is the most important consideration in working with them.

Unmet Expectations

Unmet expectations are another major contributor to anger in young people. When the hope that something will happen, or someone will do something is smacked against a wall, the disappointment that follows can lead to varying degrees of anger. Whether or not this is a frequent occurrence can determine the intensity of an adolescent's reaction to being let down. Specific events also carry their own weight. Going to see a movie or a ball game, celebrating a special event, a birthday or graduation, working on a special project, or having a visit from a parent, describe some of these sources of dissatisfaction.

Managing Unmet Expectations

Once you find out what expectations weren't met, several approaches are possible. The first is to have the young person put different sources of disappointment on the Anger Scale. Once the intensity of different kinds of setbacks is defined, plans can be developed for handling those that create the strongest reactions.

Another way to deal with setbacks in the adolescent's life is to try to depersonalize the offending person's behavior. In other words, have the youngster think about whether or not this behavior occurs with other people as well. If it does, ask, "What does this tell you about that person?" The reply may describe this person in a derogatory way. This perception of the "disappointer's behavior" may help diminish its effect on the youngster.

Having a youngster look at the disappointing behavior as a "promise deficiency," describes another way of helping them handle this offense. This can be accomplished by having them compare this deficiency with physical limitations, such as being unable to walk or see, or educational challenges like not being able to read or do math well.

Self-talk and affirmations are two Anger Managers that can be used to empower a teen to handle this source of anger. "This is something that I can't control" and "I am not going to get upset" illustrate two examples of self-talk. "I am a patient person" and "I am an understanding person" are self-affirmations that can be used to handle changes in plans. These techniques will be discussed later on in more depth.

Another approach to use with an adolescent is having him/her try to remember when they handled disappointment well. Past experiences are useful tools. Once a youngster makes this connection, the thought, "I know ways being letdown can be handled well, so I have an idea of what to do now," may come to mind, and give the confidence needed to handle a recent disappointment.

No doubt these ideas may be hard for a teen to understand and accept. As with so many other suggestions that are made, you never know what might appeal to them, in certain situations, at particular times. It is important to develop a repertoire of ideas to use. The motto "Try, try, again" is something that bears repeating and keeping in mind.

Dave Wolffe

Injustice

A young person usually describes certain things that do not seem right as "unfair." Some of the causes of this feeling may be directly expressed and observable, while others may be harder to detect. Others can be both. Criticisms over appearance, lack of achievement, and choice of friends, as well as some of the "Top Ten Causes of Anger in Teens" describe some of these areas of discontent.

Discriminatory statements made about teens as a group or other stereotypes describe another basis for this feeling. Individuals who are part of a specific culture, have different sexual orientations, are a particular religion, or live in a certain neighborhood are often referred to as "You people" "Those people" or are described with racial, specific religious and other kinds of slurs. Where these remarks are made, whether in public (at school, a workplace, in a mall, at a movie theater, or on the street) or in private, and who makes them (people who are part of the same or different groups, parents, siblings, teachers, police, supervisors, coworkers) determine an adolescent's reactions. Sometimes these things aren't expressed directly to a youngster, but are overheard. A teen may react immediately, or as is often the case, can't or won't say or do anything at the time of the incident. When responses are not immediate, the anger they experience gets pushed down and rears its head at a later time.

You may see an adolescent walking around with a scowl, or cursing and yelling at anyone without any apparent reason. When asked about their mood, you may get,

"I don't know."
"I don't want to talk about it."
"Get off my case!"

responses, or none at all.

The frustration of a teen's emotional needs describes another area of grievance. This occurs when the desire for freedom and recognition are

71

challenged. Regulations dealing with dress codes, the use and possession of beepers and cell phones, smoking or drinking and the setting of curfews, and academic requirements (homework, papers, examinations, courses needed for graduation) describe the basis for this feeling.

When injustice can be described as unfairness, you have one way of getting to an adolescent's dissatisfaction. "Does something that's happening seem unfair to you?" initiates this approach. If you get a positive response, asking, "What's going on that makes you feel that way?" can keep the information flowing. Having them tell you directly, or being aware of a conversational lead that they give you, provide other ways of finding out more about this cause of anger. Questioning a teen's behavior by remarking, "You seem to really upset about something you heard from that coach a little while ago," or mentioning other situations that have surfaced in the past that might be going on now, can be helpful information-getters.

A great resource to tap into is a "peer network." This can be found in schools, neighborhoods or any other place an adolescent hangs out, or on the Internet. It is used to provide information about potentially harmful or upsetting events that are going to take place. These include impending fights, knowledge of weapons, rumors being spread, or anything else that could be potentially damaging to young people. These are things that peer information distributors feel just aren't right, are unfair, and want to see stopped. These things may be told directly to the person being targeted, or to a trusted adult.

Once these sources of unfairness are uncovered, the next step is to help them look at ways to handle them. Discussing the reasons people say what they do is a good starting point. The answer to the whys of the actions these people take furnish clues on how a teen might deal with the different types of injustices. Their responses may range from,

> "It makes the person feel bigger than me."
> "They think they are 'all that' (cool, knowledgeable, fashionable) when he or she puts me down (what I wear or how I dress, taste in music, friends)."

"That person just doesn't know anything about us (teens,
ethnic groups, religious groups)."

"He/she is just stupid"

or may make some other comment. Listen to these remarks and *don't judge them*.

The next step to take is to find out how an adolescent reacts to these kinds of unfair judgments. They may say, "I yell at them and tell them how stupid they are," or "I walk away from them really mad and don't want to talk to them." After they describe their behavior, the question, "What else can you do to keep the other person's talk from getting you so upset?" If you get a response to this question, the teen has been able to come up with his/her own way to resolve this source of anger. However, if this isn't the case, some other approaches are helpful. These need to be put in a youngster's own terms. For example, the question, "If the person says these things to get you angry and you get that way, who is in control?" uses the idea of power, something a teen very much wants to have in a situation.

Another area to discuss with an adolescent is the "Ignorance Factor." The remark, "Some people don't know anything about groups they put down" starts you in this direction. Asking a young person how he/she learns about teachers, programs, organizations, neighborhoods, or subjects like sex puts this thought in teen terms. Their response will more than likely be from friends, brothers or sisters or other family members. If this is the case, more than likely some of what they learned from these sources isn't accurate. This network of information is based on what these individuals have heard from others, and has not been from personal experience. A young person may see this point and understand what you are trying to tell them. If you get a positive response to this line of reasoning, ask, "If the people who said these things haven't really met (members of different groups) or been to the places they are putting down, what does that tell you?" Finish this idea with the question, "If they don't know what they're talking about, then why get upset about what they say?" This is another case of, "You don't know what's going to appeal to a teen unless you try it." These different approaches are trial balloons. They are different attempts to use what can appeal to an adolescent to better understand a situation, and pave the way for them to be less reactive to this kind of experience.

Traumatic Experiences

Traumatic experiences include divorce, death or having a home destroyed by a fire. These are the kinds of situations that result in major life changes for a young person.

Chronic Illness

This could be a disease that develops in the teen himself or herself, or in close family members. In both of these situations, there are the constant pressures to control the illness and also try not to let it severely limit the lives of the affected person or their family.

During my career as a guidance counselor, I had occasion to work with a young man who had Multiple Sclerosis. He was referred to me because of the anger that manifested itself in frequent outbursts in class. During a conversation we had, he admitted that over 90% of his anger was caused by the disease. A question that helped me better understand his anger and the frustration he faced on a daily basis was, "Why can't I be normal?" This desire, along with the pain he faced on a daily basis, and comments made about his appearance by insensitive peers, contributed to the anger he experienced.

The road to diminishing the anger this teen felt rests in his acceptance of the way his life is going to be, something difficult to accomplish. For him and others who have such a limiting disease, or to those who have someone in the family with something similar, going through the steps found in grieving the death of a loved one is to be encouraged. All of these stages need to be experienced, without lingering on any one step too long. This analogy can be pointed out by a mental health professional and used to help an adolescent go through the entire process, until they finally reach the last stage, acceptance. Once this is done, a youngster can move on with his or her life.

This approach takes time and specialized effort, often requiring a professional who has worked with people with a particular disease. The American Cancer Society, the American Heart Association and those that deal with specific illnesses provide these kinds of services. You can open the door for a teen going through this experience with comments relating to the stages mentioned above, and then guide them to someone who has the specialized knowledge and experience to help them move on with their life.

As with any kind of disruptive influence in a person's life, the idea of connecting with others who are experiencing the same illness and developed a positive outlook on their life can also be helpful. In the case of a physical illness, as with this young man, perhaps his doctor or an association specializing in a particular disease offers some sort of support group for helping him get past his anger.

Abnormal Behavior

This category includes depression, eating disorders, brain injury or substance abuse. These are conditions that were not previously noticed, or may have developed over a period of time. In some young people, these disorders are diagnosed and treated. When these problems aren't noticed, taking note of certain behavioral signs can be helpful. Among these indicators are:

- *Increased Nervousness and Anxiety:* A teen may seem fidgety, constantly looking around, may cough (not from a cold or allergy), blink their eyes often, or pace a lot. This behavior may be new, or something that you noticed has increased over a period of time, ranging anywhere from a few weeks to a few months.
- *Withdrawal from Previously Enjoyed Activities:* An adolescent may have liked going to the movies, being with friends and hanging out, or participating in sports or other activities. At this point they no longer

want to do any of these things. "I just want to be alone in my room" is a statement that often accompanies this behavior.

- *Changes in Eating and Sleeping Patterns:* Eating or sleeping too little or too much should be noted. Both of these behaviors can go together with a lack of energy or enthusiasm. This conduct goes beyond how a young person usually acts. If you notice these behaviors lasting more than a week or two, there is something really bothering them. These reactions go beyond those attributable to a cold.

- *Increased Irritability:* Aside from the usual moodiness and need for independence that often is very much a part of the teen years, comes an unusual display of temper. This behavior appears more quickly, intensely and frequently over things that hadn't bothered an adolescent before.

- *A Drop in School Performance:* This is not only reflected in a drop in grades, but also in a youngster's lack of effort and energy when it comes to anything related to their education. The way assignments are done, the desire to stay in bed, or being oblivious about when tests are given and assignments are due, illustrate this behavior. This isn't about their usual complaints and attitudes toward school. These reactions may have resulted from a particular incident involving a teacher or peer, threats or bullying by other students or some kind of trouble that is going to take place near or around the school.

- *Increased Acting-Out and Reckless Behavior:* These actions can include frequent fighting, cutting school, shoplifting, drug use or engaging in careless acts such as walking across train tracks and hanging on to moving buses or trucks. These actions are all flags that mean, "I need some help. Something is really wrong and I can't handle it myself." These reactions can be the result of divorce, a parent's illness, or bad treatment that a teen feels has taken place.

When these signs appear they must be addressed. "What's going on?", "I've noticed you shut yourself in your room more than you used to," moves the conversation in this direction. Whether or not a teen says anything, the fact that these signs are noticed is a good jumping off point for getting at the causes of their actions. School personnel, close friends or family members become excellent sources of information about a particular adolescent who is exhibiting these signs. Whatever the source of this knowledge is, a youngster's behavior needs to be addressed immediately.

Environmental Stress

Noise: This kind of anxiety can be created by different living conditions found within a teen's home, or neighborhood. Different sounds, ranging from parents arguing, younger children screaming, to screeching sirens, blaring horns, people yelling are contributing factors.

Living Under Crowded Conditions: Whether an adolescent lives in a house with many people or in an overpopulated neighborhood, they face unwanted circumstances. In a household with many people, the need for privacy and quiet is often frustrated. Whether they want to listen to music, work on a computer, read or do other things that require concentration, they cannot because of too many distractions. When a teen lives in a crowded neighborhood they often cannot do things as quickly as they want, or even at all. This could be waiting for a basketball court or a place to play ball. Space is just not available. Often the frustration they experience translates into violent reactions. The need for freedom, to do what they want, is greatly challenged.

Once environmental stresses are uncovered as the source of a teen's anxiety, the next step is to help them deal with these circumstances with less stress. In other words, find ways for them to fulfill the need for privacy and space outside of changing neighborhoods or their family. One way to accomplish this goal is to ask if there was ever something that really bothered them that they couldn't change. If there was, find out what it was and how they dealt with it. Perhaps, it was a teacher they didn't like and wanted to transfer to another class but weren't allowed to. In this case, they may tell you that they had to deal with the individual for the rest of the semester, and added, "I kept out of his way," or "didn't answer many questions he asked in class," as ways to avoid further problems with the teacher. You can use this experience to apply to the uncomfortable environmental situation affecting a youngster by asking, "What do you think you can do to get the privacy and space you aren't getting?" They may respond:

> "Talk to my parents."
> "Move out."
> "Make a time to do what I need when I know people in my family are doing other things (watching TV, doing their own homework or go to their room to play games)."
> "Wait until my brother (sister) is asleep."
> "Keep yelling at whoever is bothering me until they stop."

You can have a teen try out these ideas. If any of these methods work, they have found a way to reduce their own level of anger. If they haven't been successful, then making other suggestions can be helpful.

If a youngster hasn't dealt with this unchangeable condition before, or can't think of a way to handle it, find out if they think that they are going to move to another neighborhood, have their brother or sister go away, or suddenly have a lot of people moving somewhere else might be something that can happen, eliminates some of the unreal possibilities for fixing this problem. These solutions are those an adolescent can be aware of, but sometimes has to hear from others. You may get a funny "Are you crazy" look, or "Yeah, right," response to this inquiry. However, the point that conditions probably won't change comes through loud and clear. With these possibilities ruled out, find out other things a teen can do to be able to do what they want, when they choose, becomes the focus of attention. One of the most powerful motivations for an adolescent is knowing ways to have control of a situation. Asking other questions and offering suggestions will help them accomplish this goal. It's surprising how ingenious and creative teens can be when they are given the opportunity. They don't even realize this about themselves.

> Bear in mind, someone who becomes so distressed over a situation and strongly reacts to it has lost control. Once a young person gets the feeling of having some power over a situation, they are able to feel less angry.

"Where do you think you can go outside of your home when you want a place to hang out where nobody will bother you?" is one question to ask. A relative's or friend's house, a youth center in a church or synagogue or some other organization like a Y, or even a place like a bookstore, coffee shop, or restaurant can be places a teen may think of. If an adolescent is unable to come up with any of these ideas, let them in on them by saying something like, "Some people go to (any of the places mentioned) for some peace and privacy. See if a young person responds to any of these suggestions. If they don't answer, ask, "Which of these places might be somewhere you can go to get the privacy and the space you need?" If there is still no response, at the very least you have given them some new ideas.

Another possibility to suggest is a "mental escape." (Visualizations are among the Anger Managers that will be explored in more depth later.) Asking, "Do you ever think about a place that you can get privacy and just relax, or a person that makes you smile or feel good?" gets an adolescent started in this direction. You may get a, "Are you crazy," look, a frown or, if you are lucky, a response. If you don't, saying, "Some people see themselves on a beach, or in the country or remember something funny someone did or said," gives them an idea of what you are talking about. You can also tell them to get a picture of a special place or someone to look at or imagine when things are really hectic. Using visualization, whether it's imagining something or looking at an actual picture is a tool that helps many people to calm down. I had a photograph of my oldest grandson, Julian, on my desk, in my office when I was a guidance counselor. When I started to get stressed, I looked at it and smiled. This is something I mentioned to A.M.P. Program participants, who responded with nods of acknowledgment.

For many adolescents, physical activities are important. Whether it's football, basketball, handball, baseball or soccer, these activities are an essential part of a young person's life. In crowded neighborhoods, courts or playing fields are often not available. To a young person who really enjoys any of these sports, waiting or not getting to participate in the sport on a particular day is a source of great frustration. Difficulties also arise when a teen feels others are taking too much time on a court or field, or competition for a particular area between groups or individuals is intense. In any event, the level of dissatisfaction rises, and with it, many times a fight results. Sometimes these delays last over a period of time and the anger over this situation builds up.

These circumstances represent some of the difficulties of living in a crowded neighborhood. Methods for handling these challenges need to be discovered. At this point you can apply a method similar to that used for handling the issues of space and privacy. Asking a teen what ideas he/she has for being able to deal with limited time to participate in a particular activity is a starting point. They may come up with the idea of getting involved in organized team sports that take place in evening centers, in Y's, churches, temples and other organizations as being one way to resolve this problem. If they don't think of this idea on their own, offer this solution to them. Even without being on a team, times can be reserved to use a court or playing field offered at any of these sites is another suggestion that can be made. They may point out that they still won't be able to participate in a particular sport when they want, or that the facility is not close to home. "Isn't it better to be able to know that you can definitely play (whatever sport) and the time is yours, than not be sure when you can participate, or play at all?" is a thought that may make sense to a teen. You never know what will work. In any event, it's a way that can remove the uncertainty of not being able to do something they want to do.

Disruptive Family Situations

As with the other environmental stressors, a disruptive home life is out of a teen's control. It is also something that can severely affect their moods and ability to cope. While many of the same approaches can be suggested as they were for other environmental influences, situations where adolescents are in danger require that you call in outside services quickly to help this individual. A youngster's safety cannot be compromised or underestimated.
Living with a Family Member Who Is Unemployed

In homes where this reality exists, whole families are under stress. The people who have lost their job get frustrated with themselves and often feel like failures for not being able to provide for their families. They often have a short temper and may physically or verbally take out their frustration on their spouse or other family members. In turn, others living in this environment may take their frustration out on each other. Without a doubt, much tension exists in these households. This reaction sometimes reaches beyond the family. When it does, it can affect relationships with peers, boyfriends and girlfriends, teachers, or with anyone else teens come into contact with.

Living in families with an unemployed individual, addiction or violence often accompanies this problem and become very much part of the teen's life. These associated problems necessitate additional tactics. For an adolescent, dealing with a parent's or other caretaker's loss of income, requires an understanding of what this condition means, not only to the young person and other family members, but also what it means to the individual who no longer can provide for the family. This kind of awareness requires a willingness to look at things from their parent's viewpoint, have empathy (another anger manager to be explored later) for them. Granted, adolescence is usually a time when young people primarily focus on themselves. Use this phenomenon to help them understand the frustration these circumstances bring to the unemployed adult. Remarking, "Now that this has happened, your (father, mother, grandfather, aunt) knows that without money coming in, you and the rest of your family are going to have a tougher time and is really upset about that" and then asking, "How has your father (mother, grandfather, grandmother) reacted to losing their job?" becomes a way to have an adolescent start to see things through their parent's eyes. "My (dad, mom) yells a lot," or relate any number of other reactions, including getting physical with family members.

The next question to ask, is, "How does this make you feel?"

"Scared."
"Angry."
"Worried."
"Like I want to hurt, punch, my (dad, mom, uncle)."

are some possible responses youngsters may have. Keeping these feelings in mind, ask, "Do you see a way for you to keep the other person from making you feel uncomfortable?" They may shrug, look at you with that glazed, "I have no idea," look, shake their head, or even come up with an answer. If they have some idea of what to do, find out what it is. An adolescent may say:

"Stay away from my (dad, mom) until they calm down."
"Leave the house."
Not say anything when they are yelling."

Avoidance is one way these types of reactions can be managed. For a youngster who has no idea, stating, "Some people walk out, don't answer back and let the other person finish yelling" and adding the question, "Which one of these do you think may work for you?" can be helpful.

"What kinds of other things shouldn't you do to stop your mom, dad, from getting on your case?" is another approach to take with a teen. If they can't think of any ideas, ask, "What happens when somebody who has little or no money is asked to do something that may be fun, or get clothing that friends think are cool?" Adolescents may respond, "They feel bad," "Get angry at the other person who knows they don't have enough money and still asks them to do or buy something." By following this train of thought, they can understand how another person feels and reacts, and are able to develop empathy for their unemployed family member's state of mind. By doing so, teens can also learn what needs to be done to keep this situation from escalating, and avoid having more problems with the person that lost their job.

Living with a Family Member Who Has an Addiction

Many of the behaviors evidenced by a family member who has suffered a loss of income are present in addiction situations. Much of the avoidance advice is similar. Violent or aggressive behavior that may take place against family members when an abuser can't get drugs is one source of anxiety for adolescents. The addicted individual may also take money or other possessions from family members to feed their habits. Either of these behaviors threatens a youngster's safety and security. Another stressor for families with addicted members is hiding the addiction. They fear the embarrassment and shame that can come to them if this problem is made public. There is also the concern that the abuser may try to hurt others, or commit a robbery in order to get the money they need to buy drugs. These behaviors may land an addict in jail, or result in their injury or death.

Once a teen has revealed having an addicted family member living at home, different elements of the situation need to be clarified. The behavior of the substance abuser and how it impacts on an adolescent and other family members need to be addressed. The question, "What does your (father, mother, uncle, brother) do when they come into the house?" starts this information-gathering process. A young person may describe a situation where the abuser is high or hasn't gotten drugs. Yelling, throwing objects, taking their anger out on the nearest person, or at the other extreme, goes into a room, shuts the door and cries, describes this state of affairs. "When your (father, mother) acts like this, how do you feel and what do you do?" gets to the impact of an abuser's behavior on a teen.

Once this information is gained, the focus of the remaining part of this discussion becomes what can be done to help the young person and the rest of the family handle this situation. Finding out what attempts have been made to prevent an addict's behavior from escalating is a good starting point. These efforts can include:

> Leaving the house when a teen knows the person will be coming home.
> Being quiet when the addict is yelling.
> Leaving the room when the abuser's negative behavior starts.
> Going to a friend or family member's house or participating in extracurricular activities.

In other words, avoiding the person. With some individuals this method works, with others it causes an addict to escalate his/her behavior. If an adolescent hasn't mentioned talking to other people, find out why. Most often it is either because they are too embarrassed, or afraid the abuser will find out. Having a youngster expressing these feelings is a way for them to limit the effect of these emotions. "What was it that allowed you to feel it was okay to speak with me?" is a means of having a teen feel talking about a family member's addiction is something that can work for them. Trust in an individual is the main reason an adolescent may feel comfortable enough to reveal private situations. It is one of the most important goals for any one working with young people to try to achieve.

A problem arises if you are in an educational or social service agency setting. As a counselor, social worker or youth worker—you often don't have the time to consistently talk to a youngster. There is only so much time in your schedule, and obviously, their case needs more attention. This is also something to discuss with a teen. You don't want to have them feel abandoned or that you are not concerned with how they are coping with having an addictive family member. Having some kind of support system is helpful. To have others who they trust and know will be there for them, is something helpful to an adolescent going through this kind of problem. Isolation, the feeling that they have to live with this circumstance alone often creates depression or anger. Find out who else they can you trust to talk about their (relative's) addiction?" is a helpful step to take. If a young person can't think of anyone to speak with, telling them "Sometimes, people who have some sort of difficulty in their lives find it helps to talk to someone about it, like a close friend, someone in the family, or to a girlfriend or boyfriend" begins to can open a teen's thinking in this direction. "When someone talks about a situation, it is no longer a secret that is bothering him or her and making them feel uncomfortable," reinforces the reason to talk to someone else.

> Keep in mind that if a teen reveals an abusive situation in their family it is information that needs to be reported to the proper authorities. This is something that should be told to an adolescent for the reasons mentioned earlier in the "Building Trust" part of this chapter.

There are other kinds of support systems available. Often these kinds of organizations offer a response to, "No one else can know what I am going through." Some of these support groups include: Families Anonymous, Al-A-Teen, Al-Anon, Phoenix House, and Narcotics Anonymous. All of these groups have websites to provide contact and general information to those in need of their help. You can make the suggestion that there are different organizations that can help them and their families deal with the abuser. Once this thought is expressed, you can give them the names of these or other organizations that offer this kind of support.

Letting a teen know that people in these groups do not provide names of their members to outsiders, noting the word, "Anonymous," can overcome a resistance they may offer to joining such a group. In addition, the idea that these organizations keep outsiders from knowing the names of those people that come to them for help is something that can build their trust in them. Young people often are reluctant to seek outside help. They can check these organizations out online themselves or with family members. "You trust me. So you know I wouldn't tell you to do something that would embarrass or hurt you," is a remark that can help them to decide to contact one of these support groups, then add, "After checking them out you can choose to go to a meeting or not." Part of empowering a teen is providing resources for them to decide to use to deal with a variety of problems that underlie their anger. If and when they take advantage of your suggestions, is up to them. At the very least, you have added some more choices for them to make.

Living in a Violent, Unpredictable Family

This kind of atmosphere is a more obvious threat to an adolescent's need for safety and security:

> "What's going to happen next?"
> "What's (the household member) going to be upset about today?"
> "Where can I go to stay away until he or she is in bed (or goes out)?"

are questions that express this source of stress.

The approaches to helping youngsters and their families deal with violence, follow many of the same remedies for addictive families. Using different types of avoidance and having mandated reporting of physical or emotional abuse follow this pattern. Speaking with friends, family members, girlfriends or boyfriends, is another way to relieve some of the pressures that are caused by the secrecy that surrounds abuse. A great start-ing point for help in the area of family violence is the Domestic Violence Hotline with information attainable online or by telephone, 1-800-799-SAFE (7233) or going online to discover local, city and state mental health agencies. The experience and resources these kinds of organizations provide are essential to an adolescent's physical and emotional safety. Sometimes, situations have to reach a crisis point, or sometimes people have to feel that they endured enough to seek help. Providing young people and their fami-lies with resources is often the greatest assistance that they can receive.

Often, staying away from home and avoiding the people or situations that are unpredictable in a family works well for a teen. Some of the ways to meet the need for security for an adolescent were pointed out earlier in this chapter and can give more ideas on how to help them to deal with the instability that occurs in their household. Getting a handle on coping with this source of stress will help a young person to feel that they have some control. Once this occurs, the level of anxiety, and reactions to other things that normally wouldn't affect them are reduced.

Chapter Summary

Many of the whys of teen anger—the kinds of things that lie beneath their angry faces, constant fighting, cursing, or their need to be alone—have been presented in these three chapters. Symptoms of these causes and adolescent reactions were described. Sources of frustration and their effect on young people were explored. Different ways of gathering information and using it have also been brought to your attention. In addition to a general information gathering process, different tools to help young people to feel free to describe these underlying reasons for anger were provided. Among these were the use of ways to build trust, objectification and under-standing what teen are communicating beyond the words they speak. This information has been presented to help create an awareness for you as to the reasons they may experience this feeling. This knowledge represents the first step to helping them find healthy ways to express anger.

Some people can feel overwhelmed by having so much information. Remembering so many things and techniques for getting information and using it with a teen can explain the reason for this feeling. There are a few hints to help reduce the level of anxiety for those of you who feel this way.

- One of the purposes of giving you information on the causes of anger is to help you and an adolescent become aware of the kinds of things that can create this emotion.

- Consider the many causes described in these chapters as a menu of ideas to choose from.

- When working with teens, their behavior and conversation offer clues as to the causes that are most relevant to situations they find themselves involved in and which techniques to use with them.

- There is a subject index at the end of the book from which you can choose ideas to revisit.

Chapter Five

Challenges in Working with Teens

Effectiveness Blockers

Before taking this process further along, your readiness to handle an angry adolescent's needs must be addressed. Being prepared for this task requires an "attitudinal check-up" that can turn up conditions that need treatment. The judgments you make and the different feelings you have about a young person's behavior may turn up during these examinations. You may think how a teen acted was just plain dumb, made absolutely no sense, or was a deliberate attempt to hurt other people. "What was that kid thinking to get themselves (suspended, into a fight) over this stuff?" sums up these kinds of evaluations. You may find an adolescent's reactions disappointing, annoying, or just unacceptable. They also may occur repeatedly. No matter what you have tried to do to influence him/her hasn't worked. You may feel like writing this youngster off as incorrigible, and not worth the effort. It is easy to become irritated or tired of being involved with a difficult teen. You have your own life, and this type of individual tends to take up too much of it. These sources of dissatisfaction are important to know as a parent, teacher, counselor, social worker or youth worker. Your goal is to help the teen manage anger in ways that won't be harmful to them or to others. Letting your emotions override your ability to help an adolescent work through Anger Management issues is not helpful. Maintaining your objectivity in working with a young person is crucial. Getting yourself to step back takes a real effort. The "How To" of developing this skill will be discussed shortly.

Your readiness to handle a teen's anger also involves knowing some of roadblocks that can be put in your way. Becoming a victim of "contact anger," is one obstacle that can occur. This is a condition that is developed when you experience the same feeling toward whoever or whatever caused the anger in an adolescent. This is similar to what happens to individuals who get caught up in a group's emotions over an issue. Whether it's being on one side or the other of news events, pop culture, religion or politics, groups of people develop a "mob mentality" and tend to create emotional states that are more heightened than if one individual felt these passions alone. In the same way, you lose the ability to use reason, and instead emotionally unite with the angry young person. In this case, both you and a teen have allowed yourselves to let anger take control. Being aware of the possibility of contracting contact anger is the first step in preventing it from happening to you. Once you find this reaction starting to surface using self-talk (an Anger Manager to be explained in more depth later) can be helpful. "I am not getting caught up in this teen's anger," "I am in control," or "I am here to help this individual deal with his/her anger and not in it," made silently to yourself, illustrates this tool.

Sometimes an adolescent will say something negative about you. These remarks may be about your appearance, your role in their lives or your ability to be helpful. "You look crazy (sick, sloppy, fat)," "You are a lousy parent, teacher, counselor, etc.," or a statement like, "You don't really think you know how to get me to stop fighting (or any other negative reaction)," are remarks that exemplify this tactic. A youngster's goal is to upset you. Somehow they know just the right buttons to push if you allow them to. If the adolescent is successful in distracting you this way, any efforts you make to change their behavior gets sidetracked. Once again, keep your mind focused on helping the teen manage his/her anger.

There are different strategies to use to avoid these setbacks. The first of these "focus protectors" involves letting adolescents know that you are aware of their game and don't want to play it. "You are trying to keep us from dealing with your anger. Let's stay on track," illustrates this approach. You can also take deep breaths, or use a self-talk phrase like, "I will remain focused" or "I am going to stay on track" to prevent yourself from colliding with these obstacles.

With this knowledge of the roadblocks that can occur when dealing with a young person you can learn to take whatever steps are necessary to remain calm and keep them and yourself a focused on the behavior. Some suggestions on how to accomplish this goal have been made, others will be described.

Additional Techniques for Staying on Target:

- Counting forwards or backwards, to or from any number.
- Saying, "I am a calm person," "I am the parent/pro-fessional person." These are called self-affirmations and describe your qualities rather than your behavioral goals.
- Thinking of something funny or about something pleasant experienced with the adolescent.
- Silently chanting a phrase repeatedly "Woo-sah" (from the movie "Bad Boyz II," suggested by a high school student) or something like, "Needles and Pins, Pins and Needles"(a phrase recommended by an adult participant of the A.M.P. Program) represent two of these mantras.
- Speaking to someone who can be objective in helping you to address the thoughts and feelings you experience over teens and their behavior.

Additional ideas on reducing the intensity of anger will be presented later on. Although these methods are explained for an adolescent, they also apply to overcoming the obstacles mentioned above.

Is Third Party Intervention Needed?

Once a young person has described past incidents and the effects they had, an important decision needs to be made. Two factors are significant to consider. The first deals with the ability to serve the best interests of the teen. The next choice focuses on whether or not the trust that you have gained with the adolescent can be taken to another level. The question, "Does what the youngster described to me require assistance that goes beyond my expertise and experience?" sums up these concerns.

Several factors need to be taken into account to address these uncertainties. The first involves knowing whether or not you can be objective enough to help a teen fully understand and handle the situations that were described. Can you prevent the feelings that you have for a teen from getting in the way of being helpful? If you feel their pain too strongly, relate too closely to the situation, or develop a strong negative attitude toward the individuals who were involved in particular incidents, then you cannot be as helpful as you may want to be.

Another area that needs to be taken into account is your ability to help an adolescent understand the meaning of present situations, and connect past incidents with their recent behavior. The problem becomes whether or not you know what to look for when events are described. Besides the obvious reactions young people show through the words they use, asking yourself the following questions is helpful.

> Can I recognize other feelings that may be expressed by
> their body language or tone of voice?
> Do I have ideas on what to look for that may not have
> been expressed?
> Do I know how to get beyond any roadblocks a teen may
> put in my way that can prevent me from understanding the impact incidents have on them?
> Do I have the knowledge, experience and expertise required to help an adolescent manage his/her anger?

This mental soul-searching calls for complete honesty.

Another area to consider is your ability to help a teen to move passed the effects of earlier incidents in their lives. This part of the helping process necessitates having a repertoire of ideas and the skill to use past experience with these tools. It makes use of an individual's instinct, to take a specific action, along with the faith and confidence to use it.

Additional factors may also come into the picture in making the decision to involve a third party. Some of the hidden causes of anger explored earlier concerned different forms of abuse and other kinds of trauma. Some require mandated reporting. For those that do, the answer to the question, "Is some kind of therapy or follow-up provided by the agency when a report is filed?" is important to know. If it isn't, there may be other referral sources that the organization can recommend that are available to help a mistreated youngster. In addition, siblings or other family members may have been mistreated or witnessed the abuse. This dynamic can call for knowledge of group or family treatment methods and may also require more expertise than you have.

Finally, your comfort in dealing with depressive or violent behavior, or any of the subjects that a teen may describe is important for you to consider. If a particular topic makes you feel uneasy, for example, rape, extremely violent episodes, or gay relationships, either because you feel ill-equipped to handle it, is something that you personally experienced, or is an area that makes you think, "This is something I really don't want to deal with," then it is time to seek out someone else's help.

The decision becomes, "Does this adolescent need someone who can give them more help than I can?" If your response to this question is, "Yes," then reading the next section will be helpful. It describes ways of assisting the adolescent see the benefit of speaking to another person. If you feel comfortable continuing to help a young person, then skip to the "Setting Behavioral Boundaries" section of this chapter.

Helping a Teen to Accept the Idea of a Third Party's Help

Once you have made the decision to seek the help of a third party, the challenge becomes to convince an adolescent to accept this idea. There are several ways to approach this challenge. The first involves taking the trust that a young person has developed with you one step farther. It requires a teen to believe that you, the person who they were able to share their up-setting experiences with, would only suggest something that was in their best interest. This is an idea that can be difficult for an adolescent to understand.

Providing the reasons for bringing in another person to speak with is the first step in this process. One approach involves using yourself as a role model. This becomes a "teachable moment." This is the time when you acknowledge having limited experience and knowledge in dealing with the situations the teen has described. The message being conveyed is, "When I need help in doing something I haven't really dealt with, I ask someone who has experience working with this kind of situation or knows how to handle it" This admission shows that you are not afraid to show you don't know something, or are weak in one area. It's not just words, and the tone of voice, but your behavior that carries the strength of this message. It can be an ego-shaking admission to ask for help, but one that can pay great dividends in getting an adolescent to agree to speak to someone else.

Without allowing too much time to elapse (a brief pause of about a minute), whether or not a youngster has asked about it or not, the reason why another person can be more helpful to them than you needs to be addressed. "This individual (social worker, therapist, psychologist, counselor, priest or rabbi) has worked with many other people your age who have gone through similar experiences. He or she can give you the best chance of really understanding what happened to you and help you to find ways get past it," addresses this concern.

A teen may strongly resist this idea. They may walk away, start cursing, slam doors or show some other strong sign of disapproval. These are common responses. At this point, leave this suggestion alone. An adolescent needs time to calm down and think this idea over.

Reasons for a Youngster's Resistance to Working with a Third Party

There are many reasons a teen resists this idea. The first is that they find it difficult enough to tell you about their experiences. Now, they are being asked to tell their painful or embarrassing story to someone else, most likely a complete stranger. This discomfort needs to be acknowledged. "I think that it was hard enough for you to tell me about what happened. Now, you are being asked to tell someone you don't even know about it. I can understand that this makes you uncomfortable" addresses this resistance. If this is the case, the next step to take is to try to explain the benefits of retelling a youngster's story. One explanation is that the first time people speak about something difficult is usually the hardest. Reminding them that this is something that they already did with you may soften their opposition to describing events again. A second reason for taking this step is that by taking another look at a situation they can remember details that were left out the first time. Telling about the situation to other people can also offers an adolescent the opportunity to look at what happened in a different light. By getting different viewpoints they may be able to get some more ideas on how to better handle a similar situation in the future.

"Before, when we first mentioned speaking to someone else, I pointed out that this person knows more than I do, and has experience with other people your age with the situation we talked about" takes you back to the place you were before the teen reacted to this idea. They may remember this part of their discussion with you or not. An adolescent may respond with a nod, a "Yeah," or that glazed what-are-you-talking-about? look. Regardless of their reaction, continue to follow this train of thought. It is at this point you can explain that people who work with a specific organization (child protective services, victims assistance agencies), or who specialize in the kinds of situations that they experienced offer the best source of help. If you know that other adolescents have spoken to a particular individual and felt good afterwards, let a youngster know this.

Another objection that a teen may have in talking to someone else may take the form of "image busting." They may feel that by speaking to another person their peers will view them as a person who is really incapable of handling their own problems, or as an individual who is unable to be in control of their own life. "Sometimes people think if they ask for more help they look weak or stupid. Is that what you think?" addresses this idea. A positive response to this thought lets you know that you are on the right track. If this is the case, you can again point out that you are seeking another person's help and ask, "Do you think I look stupid or out of control?" It gives the message that you are "walking the talk," doing what you are telling them to do. They may still be opposed to talking with someone else. However, you have given a young person something else to think about.

"I don't want to go to a shrink. I'm not crazy!" describes another reason for a teen to object to this kind of outside intervention. Questioning the reason they think only crazy people speak to "shrinks" (using their words shows a willingness to try to understand their perception) directly addresses this point. After hearing their responses, (which incidentally may even include an admission that "Not only crazy people go for counseling") find out if they know people who weren't "nuts" and went for help. If this is something they can think of, find out the reason the individual needed to speak to another person. If a youngster doesn't have an answer, gives you a, "You've got to be kidding" look, or offers no response at all, bring in the idea of people going to specialists to help with different problems. "Who do people go to when they get sick?" or, "If someone doesn't understand something in school or something happens there, who do they go to for help?" illustrate this approach. This method focuses the spotlight on other people, rather than on the teen, and provides a greater likelihood that these questions will be answered. "Have you ever gone to a doctor when you were sick or gotten help with something that happened in school from someone else?" is a more direct approach to use. When positive responses are given, the idea of seeing a third party is reinforced. A youngster may or may not admit they have gotten these other kinds of help. Regardless, the thought is expressed for them to consider.

After making these connections, "So!", "What's your point?" or "Going to these people isn't like seeing a shrink?"are possible teen reactions. Whether these kinds of responses are made or not, the point to be stressed is that whatever kind of help people need, going to someone who specializes in some particular area offers the best chance of fixing what's wrong. An adolescent may still remark, "I don't need anyone else's help," "I'm the only one who can make this right," or, "I've told you about my problem. No one else can do anything else about it or me." If they do, leave this idea alone. You have taken them as far as they can go at this point.

Another reason a young person may be reluctant to speak with someone else is that they may feel rejected. This is a feeling that a teen may have already experienced and were hurt by. It may be the underlying cause of their anger. If it was something that was described, it needs to be addressed as soon after the suggestion of speaking to another person is made. An adolescent may verbally lash out by saying, "You're like my dad. When things get tough he has someone else take care of it." At this point you need to do two things. The first is not to react to this tirade, and let it run its course. Once they have calmed down, they need to explain the similarities and differences they see between this situation and those they experienced with a parent or other individual. Using this approach demonstrates that their views are taken seriously and not being judged. It also provides information that may help you convince an adolescent that you are not rejecting them, as some other important person in their life did. One difference that can be pointed out is that you have limited knowledge and ideas of how to handle this problem. This may be in contrast to an experience where a parent or someone else connected to them just didn't want to be bothered

One of the other objections that have already been raised, is the thought that no one else can solve a young person's problems for them. Defining the role of the helping person is a way to change a teen's thinking. This explanation view's this professional as a person,

- Who is not there to tell them what to do,
- Who looks at the situation and can suggest different ways of viewing it, and,
- Who is there to help a youngster come up with ideas that may never have been thought of, can be used to overcome this doubt. The point that it is a teen's decision as to what solution, if any, they want to use is something to be emphasized.

An adolescent may also be afraid that the other people to whom they speak might find something really "wrong" with them, or bring up things that create more discomfort. This fear may or not be expressed. If it isn't, it can be directly addressed with the remark, "Sometimes people think another person is going to find something really wrong, or make them feel bad," quickly followed up with, "Do you think either of these things?" In this manner, you are checking two other possible sources of resistance to a third party's involvement. If they acknowledge the idea that something may be really "wrong" with them ask, "What do you think this person will find out about you that is so terrible?" Responses can vary. These can include revealing embarrassing or harmful things that they may have done to themselves or others. They may feel their behavior can show some sign of weakness to others. Their involvement with drugs, acts of vandalism, violent behavior shown toward others, or attempts to take their anger out on themselves, describe some of these sources of discomfort. These kinds of behaviors, according to an adolescent, can indicate that there is something really wrong with them, rather than being reactions to actions taken by others who created their pain or fear. Describing the youngster's actions as responses to circumstances, rather than character deficiencies, in other words, changing their perceptions of themselves, offers another way to break down the resistance to speaking to a third party.

The idea that telling what happened is often a very difficult and painful for many people to do can be brought when the question, "Why don't you want to talk about it with someone else?" is asked. If a teen is able to answer this question then the issue can be addressed. If they don't or can't describe the reason for resisting a third party's involvement, the remarks, "When someone hurts another person that person doesn't want to feel this pain again and buries it. If someone brings up the incident that caused this pain, they feel it again and sometime it hurts more," may bring this fear to the surface. Once this feeling is in the open, take a minute to let this thought sink in. After taking this time, adding, "Talking about experiences becomes less and less of a hardship the more it is done. Does this seem to make sense to you?"can open the door to having an adolescent discuss this possibility and have the opportunity to work this fear through.

These guesses, trial balloons that you launch, can help discover the reasons behind a young people's reluctance to speak with other people. They can be productive tools to use with a teen to help stimulate additional thinking. After making any of these suggestions, wait for a response. If there is one, you can explore it. If there isn't a reaction, there may be one sometime later.

Another direction to take is to find out what previous experiences an adolescent had with seeking help. Questioning, who they went to for help, and the reason they did, becomes a starting point for this process. A memory of a situation involving a problem with a peer in a subject class will be used to illustrate this approach. In this particular circumstance a young person went to the teacher for help and the difficulty was resolved. After discussing this experience, making the remark, "You were able to deal with your friend better after you spoke with your teacher" can show how going to a third party for help can be useful. If a teen won't admit to seeking assistance, ask about other people they have seen go for help. Let them describe the reasons and results of these individuals' efforts. Following this path can furnish a way to make the idea of getting help more relevant. The role of experience will be explored in more depth in a later chapter.

The time and effort that you expend addressing the idea of working with a third party is an indicator of the value you place on it. By trying many different tactics, you will find one that will influence the teen. You never know what and when something you've mentioned is going to work.

The maxim, "Try, try, again," is something to bear in mind when working with adolescents.

In some instances, usually those that arise infrequently, a young person may readily agree to talk to someone else, although their reasons for doing so may not appear sound. "I'll go to this person if you want me to," or "I'll go just to prove that the shrink can't help me" illustrate these explanations. Some may go under specific conditions they set. "I'll go two or three times," illustrates this idea. Whatever "reason" they give, or conditions they make, doesn't matter. These assertions represent a means of showing some control over what they are being asked to do, and also serve as face-saving gestures. Acknowledge their decision, and then see what happens. It's up to both the helping individual and an adolescent to determine how far their relationship will go. You've led the horse to water.

The idea of seeing someone else may take some time for a young person to accept. If he/she decides to take this step, whenever possible, offer to go with them the first time. By going with them you are physically and psychologically supporting their decision. By helping teens decide to take this step, you bring them closer to ridding themselves of part of the past, and providing them with the possibility of moving toward a more peaceful future.

Setting Behavioral Boundaries as a Way to Overcome Some Obstacles in Dealing with Teens

Developing behavioral guidelines for young people to follow is one of the hardest tasks for an adult to undertake. The example of this process used in this chapter is intended to serve as a model of a behavior modification method that can be used with teens. It can be applied, modified or completely changed to fit different situations that arise. The "dialogs" that are presented provide a way to more fully understand this process. They represent different approaches to use with this method. They are illustrations of what can be said, and how they can be communicated in a way to motivate an adolescent to change his or her behavior.

One of the sources of anger in young people was explored in Chapter Three. It dealt with the frustration of emotional needs. One of these desires was to have the freedom to go where they wanted, with whomever, wherever they chose and whenever they wanted. Challenges to this goal are often met by yelling, cursing, slamming doors or even running away. The question arises, "How can limits be placed on an adolescent that they will be most likely to follow?" The description that follows will provide an answer to this question.

The Initial Approach to Working With Adolescents and Their Needs

Having different restrictions placed on an Anger Scale allows you to see how frustrated young people become, when particular limits are placed on them. Another way to get this information is to have them list three to five restrictions that bother them, and rank them in the order of their effect, going from the restrictions that upset them the most to those that have least impact. Once this information is gathered, you and the teen will look first at the limits that cause the least amount of frustration. These particular boundaries are the easiest to work with because they have the lowest emotional impact. They also provide the greatest opportunity to develop a structure that an adolescent will be willing to follow. They become a model for dealing with more difficult limits to their freedom. Once the least bothersome is chosen, the next step is to develop an "adolescent friendly" plan to deal with this restriction. Keep in mind that part of this plan should include ways for teens to avoid, remove or diminish the length of time particular limitations are placed on their freedom.

Guidelines can be discussed before or after an incident has occurred. During this conversation, the pros and cons both parties see to having this limit imposed are discussed. This information-sharing process allows each viewpoint to be expressed and recognized. From this point, ideas can be exchanged, and a plan can be jointly developed.

Guideline-Setting Conditions

Let's get to the "How To" of setting behavioral boundaries. There are two conditions that are necessary:

Condition Number One: The Timing of the Discussion: Readiness, in this case, doesn't mean trying to use this method at a time when the atmosphere is charged with hostility. The first part of this process requires a young person to have time to calm down after a situation has occurred. This is a must before a particular behavior can be addressed.

> To express their feelings without hurting others or themselves requires teens to be calm. This state is necessary to accomplish any task that necessitates accomplishing any goal rationally.

Condition Number Two: Have an Adolescent Help Create the Guideline: Keep in mind that one of the things that brings about miscommunication and conflict between two people is that specifics on what is wanted, needed or expected from the other, is not clear. The active listening skills of paraphrasing and clarifying haven't been used. A phrase like, "What you are saying is you feel confined," or asking the other person to describe more about what he/ she means, were missing. Assumptions were probably made. Once they are, relationships almost certainly, head in the wrong direction.

Let's add another reason for being specific. Many young people have a knack of manipulating what is said. To illustrate this point, let's use the example of, "The Case of the Nonspecific Rule."

The Situation:

Parent to Teen: "I want you in at a reasonable hour."
Adolescent response: "Okay," with his or her own idea of what is "reasonable."

This is a school night. The young person strolls in at midnight. The parent had the idea that 10:30 was more than a fair time. The parent waited up and had to get up for work at 6:00am.

The Result

The parent was enraged at the child and yelled as soon as the child entered the house. The idea of what is a reasonable hour became the subject of a much-heated and lengthy battle. The parent "grounds" the youngster until they decide differently. The teenager storms out of the room mumbling "I'll show you!" The next night the he or she stays out until 2:00 a.m.

Summary

This example illustrates what often becomes a source of conflict and anger between parents and adolescents. It shows how the lack of specifics in rule setting leads to the frustration of the needs for both freedom and structure. Be very specific in setting parameters for the rules you want to establish with a youngster.

A curfew-setting situation will be described to illustrate the how to put together effective behavioral guidelines with a teen. Before starting this process, keep in mind that:

- This approach can serve as a model for developing other guidelines.
- Whatever behavior needs to be improved should involve measures that are the easiest to implement. That is to say, for both adult and child this plan is

something that involves simple steps to follow and monitor. Success is a great motivator. Working this way provides the opportunity for an adolescent to experience a sense of accomplishment in setting up a structure.

- Being part of the planning process empowers a young person to "own" the results. This idea takes into account that by helping develop this idea, they feel an obligation to see it through.

An Illustration of Establishing Guidelines

The reasons for establishing a guideline are essential for teens to know and accept. This is starting point for this process. It is the time when the basis for and against a curfew is discussed.

Among the most common reactions adolescents may have for resisting this limit is that they view themselves as responsible, trustworthy, or old enough to know when to come home. The question, "Why do I need to have a time to be home?"expresses a youngster's attitude. There are two possible replies that you can make. The first details all the things a teen has done wrong: poor grades, calls about attendance and homework, and hanging out with peers who get into their share of trouble fall into this category. This approach may escalate the discussion into a full-blown conflict, because an adolescent feels attacked, gets more upset, and reacts accordingly. Having freedom restricted, while being labeled irresponsible at the same time, is similar to feeling stabbed twice. This is often the way many issues were handled before, and describes one reason why youngsters resist having limits set. Who wants to get repeatedly hammered about what they do wrong? The answer is, "No one," particularly

This is not to deny that a young person hasn't been doing the wrong things.

teens. Many times, adolescents are well aware of these failures, and feel bad enough.

The second approach deals with a teen's difficulties differently. Using this method involves an adult listening to what an adolescent has to say and accepting these views—not meaning that they agree with them. Once this step is completed, the question, "What do you do with this information? can be answered. A way to deal with a youngster's lack of achievement in school, is by:

- Expressing your concern: This is something that can be described in different ways:
  "I am concerned about school."
  "I noticed the low grades on your math tests."
  "You passed four out of seven subjects on your report card, (accentuating the positive, passing four classes, while letting them know you are aware of the three failures)."
  "Mrs. Jones called to ask that you get some help in algebra,"

show your uneasiness without making any judgments. Once this has been done, you have laid the groundwork for giving reasons for thinking that a curfew may be helpful. "I know you are capable of doing better. I think time is a factor. This is why I think we need to look at the time for you to be home more carefully," describes this rationale.

- Safety is another area that may enter the curfew picture:
  "I worry about bad things happening to you out there. I know you are a good kid, but there are some others who hang out looking for trouble. A lot of things happen later at night when there aren't many people around" express this cause of anxiety.

With both of these sources of concern, it's not what is said, but how something is said that often makes the difference between being heard or being ignored by an adolescent. This approach emphasizes reason over hostility. Without the emotional interference that results from the feeling of being verbally assaulted, a teen is more capable of understanding and addressing your concerns. When this state of readiness exists, a productive discussion is more likely to occur.

Benefits of Curfews for Teens

Once an adolescent hears the reasons for setting a curfew, the "What's in it for me?" factor has to be considered. The most convincing answers to this question come from a youngster. If they have a response to it, it's time for the next step in this process. If they can't see any benefit to having this limit placed on them—a more common answer—making some suggestions is helpful.

Try to think as a teen does. An adolescent doesn't like to be hassled. "Wouldn't you like it if I didn't have to argue with you, and we both were cool with each other?" takes you in this direction. The answer to this no-brainer is undoubtedly a "Yes." However, raised eyebrows, quizzical looks, frowns can also take place, or the question "What does this have to do with a curfew?" may follow your remark. The response to an adolescent who has doubts about this idea is that they would have time to complete what needs to be done without being hassled and be able to do what they want when things were finished. Typical responses to this rationale include:

> "I can get these things done when I come home from school."
>
> "I'll do it when I come back." (Often when they give the "I'm too tired" excuse.)
>
> "I'll do it before school tomorrow." (Often done in a rush.)

"So far this year, you haven't been able to do what needs to be done at any of these times," gives a youngster something to think about. Assuming that they haven't taken a mental leave of absence, have them attempt to see a curfew as something that hasn't been tried, that might work, and can get them what they want. No doubt the question, "How?" may be raised. Patience is required, and a lot of it. Take a deep breath, and then continue this tennis-match like exchange. Besides avoiding the "hassle factor" (using the example of improved grades), they are told that by getting better marks (whatever both you and they decide this means, whether it's achieving a specific grade in a subject or passing all of their classes), they are showing they can be responsible. Once this happens they have given themselves the opportunity to do more of the things they want: have more time to hang out with friends, play video games, go shopping, play basketball or any other sport or go to the movies. Once these benefits are described, how successful this rationale was, will be determined by an adolescent's response to, "Wouldn't these things make a curfew worthwhile?" If it is, move on to the next step, setting the time. By accepting the idea of having this time limit, a young person has become part of this process and "owns" it. It becomes a joint venture that gives you and them the opportunity to reach your goals. Before going down the road to setting up a curfew, it is important to have them see what has already been accomplished in this process. They have:

- Accepted the idea of a curfew.
- Agreed to it as a means of getting things done.
- Given themselves the chance to be seen as responsible.
- Seen a curfew as the means for gaining more freedom.

The idea behind this pause for reflection is to show an adolescent that they have been successful using this method so far. "Success Breeds Success" summarizes this idea and is something young people, as well as most other individuals, need to experience.

Setting the Curfew

The first step in this process requires trusting a youngster's ability to make responsible decisions. The why and how you are going to do this involves two ideas. Allowing the "power of positive expectations" to enter the picture is the jumping off point. "I am counting on you to come up with a time that will allow you to do what you agreed to," describes this leap of faith. Here they have a chance to prove that they can act responsibly. This step is not being taken in isolation. While you are letting them think of what they need do to strengthen this belief in them, you have already created a time-frame for this curfew in your mind. In this case, having a specific time to work from will act as a reasonable guide for this process. At this point your "positive belief" is being tested. Keep in mind the goal in this case is to see an improvement in grades, something that hadn't been accomplished in any other way. As with some of the other things discussed earlier in this book, you don't know if something will work unless you try it.

With the idea of having a particular time set in your mind, let's use an example. The curfew you have come up with is somewhere between 8:30 and 9:30. If an adolescent's idea of a time to be home coincides with yours, there is no further discussion. If it is within fifteen minutes, depending on your thinking, this curfew time can work. If a youngster's idea of this limit is a half hour or more later, ask them if this schedule will allow enough of a chance to do what was agreed needed to be accomplished and done well.

However, if there is big difference between the time you feel will work, let's say, 9:30, and a teen thinks that 11:00 will be okay, other strategies need to be employed. These ideas can be useful whether an adolescent agrees to have a curfew or not.

The idea of taking some length of time, perhaps a week, might enter the conversation to "test market" the later time suggested by an adolescent. If this is something that you believe is worthwhile to consider, it should be incorporated in the curfew agreement being put together with the youngster.

> By appealing to a youngster's reason, you'd be surprised how much more willing they may be to reconsidering the idea of a curfew or a particular time for it. This idea requires you to have another leap of faith.

A teen may try to bargain with you. They may tell you that they will be able to do what they have to without a curfew and then plead with you to give them a chance. "If I don't get better marks by Spring semester, then I'll come home earlier" illustrates a not so unfamiliar adolescent strategy. Making this deal may avoid further resistance to a curfew if this idea doesn't work. It gives a youngster the opportunity to help his/her own situation, or to see that their way isn't getting results. Whether it is setting a curfew, or avoiding one by using other means, specific details need to be part of a plan for them to get better grades.

Components of the Curfew-Setting Process

In this example, having homework completed will serve as the means for an improvement in grades and the reason for having a curfew. Setting this limit involves:

- Elements Involved—all assignments are written down, work is complete, the times to carry out these actions, which should not be before bedtime or going to school, and the methods for monitoring these behaviors.
- A teen should leave the work to be completed in a specific place (a kitchen table or a person's desk in

an office), which will be checked daily by a specific person (parent, guardian, staff member) who must be responsible for consistently carrying out this process. If an adolescent is aware that these steps are being consistently taken, they will be less tempted to avoid meeting their responsibilities.

These steps indicate the responsibilities both parties agreed to in this jointly developed plan.

- This method should include ways of evaluating its effectiveness. For example, an improvement in grades must be accomplished over a defined time period. In this case, this might be after exams, a verbal report from a teacher in a given week or two, a month after the agreement is put into place, a marking period, a report card, or after a term.
- Specific behaviors must be emphasized throughout this entire process. The involved parent, counselor, social worker, youth worker and a youngster must clearly understand the rules and expectations of the curfew, as well as the positive and negative consequences of a teen's behavior.

Results of the Curfew-Setting Process

Opportunities for expanded privileges when the adolescent meets his/her commitment, or negative consequences if they don't must also be spelled out. If the system is working consistently, then a young person is establishing a positive habit. By doing so he/she is exhibiting a sense of responsibility and earning the opportunity to do more things and go more places. Their need for freedom is being met, while your desire to see the right things being done is being satisfied. In this way a win-win situation is created.

Dave Wolffe

Fine-Tuning the Behavioral Guideline Process

This process doesn't happen in just one sitting. Allow multiple meetings to establish the guidelines between you and the teen.

Ideas should be written down, so those involved can view them, have a chance to think things over, and understand what has been discussed. This document can take the form of a single page, easily readable and understandable by using short sentences, and bullet points.

Once the whole process is completed, both an adult and adolescent sign this agreement, indicating they agree to its terms. By spelling out these conditions, there is less of a chance for misunderstanding its terms, and preventing accusations and denials from taking place. It is also easy to refer to in times when there may be a misinterpretation over how things are to be done. In this way, an "official "document is created to be followed by both parties.

Times for evaluation of this agreement need to be made. This allows for either positive or negative adjustments to its terms.

This process takes time and effort. It is something that allows both an adult and a teen to work on collaboratively. It is a way for having adolescents feel their opinions are valued and they are capable of working together with someone older in a responsible way. The benefits of using this method, in this case for a youngster to improve grades are summarized below.

- A teen is part of this process, making the agreement that is reached more likely to be followed.
- Reason, rather than emotion, dominates this approach.
- Decisions are not forced, or arrived at hastily.
- The needs for structure and freedom are both being met.
- An adolescent has a chance to show that they have a sense of responsibility.

- Both parties agree to specific behavioral guidelines and consequences. Everything is clear to both the teen and the adult.

This process serves as a model for establishing other guidelines. Its benefits and influence on a young person and to your relationship with them can be tremendous.

Chapter Summary

In this chapter many of the roadblocks that are faced when working with a teen were explored. How making judgments about a teen's behavior can interfere with understanding, and helping them see other points of view, describes one of these obstacles. Other barriers included the ideas of contact anger and personal or professional attacks against you. In addition to exploring these difficulties in working with an adolescent, ways of avoiding them, and maintaining your objectivity, were also explained.

One of the decisions that need to be made is whether or not to involve a third party. Reasons for taking this path were explored. The resistance a teen may offer, along with ways to deal with them, were also noted.

The final area discussed was setting behavioral boundaries with an adolescent. The goal of this method is to find a win/win situation, in which a youngster is able to obtain freedom, and make the right choices. This process was described in detail. The dos and don'ts in setting guidelines were presented. Establishing a curfew was used to illustrate this approach.

Chapter Six

The Effects of Anger

Knowing the effects that anger has on teens can be a means of empowering them to handle this emotion differently. In a conversation with an adolescent who "lost it", the idea of being in control of his behavior was presented to him in the question, "When someone says something to you, or does something to get you angry, and you hit them, who is in control, you or the other person?" He thought for a short time, nodded, then replied, "I never thought of it like that." This is one way to have a young person understand the effect of reacting to a person who tries to push their buttons.

In this chapter, the different effects that anger can have on a teen will be examined. There are three categories that will be described. The first covers the body's reactions to this feeling. The next views other emotions that are connected to anger. Finally, there are the thoughts that a youngster has about the people and situations that cause this feeling.

Physical Effects

Why identify physical effects? The first step in answering this question involves explaining what happens to a person's body when anger is experienced. "When people start to get angry, they feel things happening to their body. There is a force that starts to build up inside of them that needs a place to go. Their heart starts beating faster, muscles begin to tighten or they feel their face begin to flush," describe some of these reactions. As these effects keep building, the more intense this feeling becomes, the quicker people will reach a level of 8 to 10 on the Anger Scale. When someone reaches that level it can cause him or her to explode, OD, go ballistic, go nuts, or whatever other term an adolescent uses. The remark, "This is like a person who has been under water and feels they need to let the air out of their lungs or their lungs are going to explode," explains this idea. "For a youngster who doesn't get the picture, another approach to use is to describe a part of a situation, and have them fill in the blanks. Using a balloon as an example, begin with, "When you start blowing up a balloon and you keep putting air into it, what happens when it gets too much air?" Describing the effects of too much pressure building in a water pipe, or what happens when steam builds up under a manhole cover, provide other examples of situations to use. Once this idea is understood, and the question, "What happens when these things build up so much force and it has nowhere to go?" is answered, a parallel is drawn between rising anger and other kinds of pressure building that needs to be released. A teen can respond in several ways. "The person will yell, curse, hit someone or something," describe some of these answers. In this way an adolescent is able to connect the increasing intensity of the anger with negative ways of releasing it.

Once this effect is understood, the next step is to help a young person to build a bridge between knowing these effects and learning how to control this feeling. In other words, if a teen can find a way to chill out before their body gets to the blowing up stage, they can prevent themselves from doing something that results in negative consequences. Giving a young person reasons for learning how to prevent themselves from reaching this level of anger effectively answers the questions, "Why should I know what my body does when I get angry?" or "What's in it for me to know this stuff?"

The question "What happens when you go nuts?" takes this process further along. You can expect a variety of answers. These may include:

"I feel better,"

"Whoever bothered me knows to stay away."

"People think I am nuts."

"I get grounded."

"No one wants to deal with me."

"I hurt someone and then the cops or other people get involved and I get hassled."

Keep in mind that some of these results can seem totally wrong to you. However, these are responses an adolescent can make.

> Being non-judgmental and accepting what a young person thinks and feels, keeps the road to hearing what you have to say open.

Once a teen expresses these outcomes, the next thing to do is ask, "Which of these things don't you like happening?" One response may be "I don't care!" If this is the case, it is important tp find out why he/she feels this way. If they just hold up their hands or say, "I just don't!" Accept it. Your conversation with them has come as far as it could for the time being. The remark, "If you decide that there might be things that you don't want to happen when you explode, we can talk about them some other time," leaves the door open. It also provides the opportunity for an adolescent to make a choice, that is, be in control of when or if they want to continue this conversation.

Other replies can focus on specific negative consequences blowing up can have to a young person.

"I don't like getting hassled by my parents!"

"I don't want to have to look behind me wherever I go."

"I don't like people thinking I am crazy, so they stay away from me."

describe some of these responses. The question, "So why should I know about what happens to my body when I get I get mad?" indicates a teen's curiosity. Whatever the reason is for an adolescent to discover ways to calm down before exploding; it enables you to take them down this path. How this is done will be discussed later in this chapter.

Some Teen Physical Reactions

The next stage of this process has a teen identify physical reactions to anger. The question, "What happens to your body when you get mad?" leads the discussion in this direction. If there isn't a response, sharing what happens to your body when you experience this feeling can be a conversational jump starter. Once this step is taken a young person may think, "If he or she is willing to share something personal with me, then I can tell them something personal." It may also contribute to strengthening your relationship with the teen who sees this sharing as a way to trust you. "Another way an adolescent can look at your behavior is, "You don't know anything about what happens to me!" This response is typical of a young person's resistance to adult suggestions. Like many other things, describing physical signs of anger building in you is worth a try.

Another way to help a teen answer this question is to mention some of the physical effects other adolescents have described. Some of the responses offered by young participants in the A.M.P. Program were:

- My heart beats faster.
- My face feels hot.
- My body shakes.
- I cry.
- Veins start to show in my face.
- My muscles get tight.
- I scream.
- I feel my blood pressure rising.
- I start to make a fist.

- My breathing gets faster.

Pointing out peer responses is often the convincer. Whether or not a young person outwardly acknowledges any of these effects, it offers a menu of choices of anger de-escalators. Finding out more about their reactions to anger, or at the very least giving a teen something to think about, makes this information useful.

The next path leads to an explanation of how to prevent the adolescent from letting the physical effects of anger get them to the point of losing it. Knowing how important control is to an adolescent provides one way to make this connection. The question, "What would you think of having the power to keep your cool when someone tries to get you angry?" makes this point. "When people go nuts, they are out of control and the person who got them that way has shown they have power over them" emphasizes this thought. If a young person sees this connection, as the young man at the beginning of this chapter did, then go right into exploring ways they can calm themselves down. One approach to reaching this goal is to have a teen try to think of something that he or she has already learned to do to calm themselves down. If they have shown this ability, this behavior needs to be recognized. An adolescent may remark, "Everyone knows how to do that," or in some other way try to diminish the importance of this positive behavior. If this happens, point out that they did something to handle their anger that worked. In other words, they knew what to do, did it, and can do it again. The power of positive reinforcement works wonders with a young person.

If a teen's response is a shoulder shrug, an "I don't know" reply, or dead silence, there are two other approaches to take. The first is to ask them to think about other people they've seen successfully calm themselves down. They may describe a family member, friend or teacher who they saw get angry, yet kept their cool. If they did observe this behavior, have them describe what this person did to remain calm. If an adolescent is still unresponsive, relate the idea of remaining calm under stress to baseball players or entertainers who have to be cool before getting up to bat, or going out on stage to do a concert, and see if this approach gets some reaction.

Another way to illustrate the relationship between mind and body is to use a visual tool. This method is illustrated and explained below.

The Anger Scale and Control

Body Up: Muscles tensing, heart beating rapidly, face turning red. By using the Anger Scale, you can show a youngster that the stronger their physical reactions become—that is, the tighter their muscles get, the faster their hearts beat or the redder their faces get—the angrier they are becoming, and the closer they are to losing control.

I am losing control

1 → 2 → 3 → 4 → 5 → 6 → 7 → 8 → 9 → 10

There are different ways to use this tool. The first involves having a teen describe a situation or choose one of the "Ten Causes of Anger in Teens." After they do this, have them tell you where this cause of anger puts them on the Anger Scale. If they aren't able to or are unwilling to come up with a reason for experiencing this feeling, describe a general situation that can occur. "For a person who was lied to, some people your age feel this situation would put them at a six or seven on the scale. When they feel this way, their muscles start to tighten up. About a minute or two after the incident is over, they start to feel angrier. As this feeling starts to get bigger and bigger, the person's muscles get tighter and tighter, and begin to hurt. This individual cannot hold this feeling in any longer and goes all the way up the scale to ten. They lose control and start yelling or hitting the other person," illustrates this progression of events. If there still isn't a response, use the idea of the rising anxiety levels an athlete or entertainer can have before they do their thing by asking, "What would happen if David Wright or Derek Jeter came up to bat really uptight before a game about getting a hit because he was in a long hitting slump, and isn't able to calm down? or, "If Kid Rock started a song when he was nervous about appearing in front of a group he never played before?" If a young person was familiar with these two public personalities, he/she would say, "They'd strike out" or "He'd sound bad." If they didn't know of these individuals, have them come up with some famous personality they can relate this idea to.

Keep in mind, a teen can learn in different ways. Some understand things when they hear them. These kinds of learners respond to discussing ideas. Others comprehend things when they see them. For a visual learner the Anger Scale is helpful. Being aware of the way an adolescent can best understand ideas is helpful in getting ideas across to them.

"When someone says something to you, or does something to get you angry, and you hit them, who is in control, you or the other person?" was a question that was posed to the young man who was mentioned at the very beginning of this chapter, as well as to different groups of young people. Some snickered; others said that they were in control because they hurt the other person, while still others saw the other individuals, the instigators, as getting what they deserved. To the young man mentioned above, as well as to other teens, this idea made an impression, and gave them something more to think about that hadn't crossed their minds. For others, depending on their maturity level, their unwillingness to handle anger in ways differently than those necessary to survive in their neighborhoods or dictated by peer and family expectations, this idea was useless. You never know what is going to appeal to teens.

Anger De-Escalators

Once adolescents see different ways anger can affect them, and realizes that having the power to deal with people and situations calmly is in their best interest, finding additional tools to de-escalate the intensity of this feeling becomes the next road to travel with them.

Some of the ways A.M.P. Program participants described keeping this feeling from taking control of them included:

- Counting (up or down).
- Taking deep breaths.
- Writing a letter or e-mail, or keeping a journal.
- Talking to someone (family, friend, teacher, etc.).
- Removing themselves from the situation.
- Listening to music.
- Playing a video game.
- Physical activities (exercise, sports, running, walking, etc.).
- Going shopping.

The Body Down illustration shown below describes to the effect of being able to calm one's self down and remain in control.

I am in control

Being lied to is the situation that is being used with this visual tool. This cause of anger, is being rated as a six or seven on the Anger Scale. Referring back to the example of David Wright, Derek Jeter and Kid Rock, asking the question, "If these three people were able to do things to chill out enough to bring themselves down to a two or three on the scale, what would happen?" gets teens thinking about ways to remain cool. "David Wright and Derek Jeter would have a chance to get a hit and break out of their slump, and Kid Rock can have his audience applauding and cheering," are possibilities teens may express about the results of these individuals' ability to remain calm. Following this response with, "Someone who was lied to will find if they are able to get themselves to feel calmer, their muscles will relax, and they will stay in control" brings this idea back to a teen's reality. After a brief pause, a weird "So what's your point?" look, or raised eyebrows, making the remark, "There are different ways you can try to help yourself chill out," will give an adolescent an idea of the road you are going to take with them. Ways they can think of for calming themselves down should start flowing. If they come slowly or not at all, saying, "Many people your age have said taking deep breaths to calm themselves down has helped them relax. Others count to fifty or any other number. Some others take themselves away from where the other person is," is a useful approach to use.

Some situations call for using more than one of the anger de-escalators. This idea, as well as others, will be explained in more depth later on in Chapter Eight devoted to Anger Managers.

"How can knowing these ways to chill out help me?" moves the conversation further along. The analogy of blowing up a balloon, and connecting it to having a teen feel muscles tightening up, provides a way to use this information. "Think of a balloon being blown up. Air is being forced into it to make it larger. When you are angry your muscles feel pressure, like the air going into the balloon, and start to tighten up. If they get too tight they hurt and you have to do something. If there is too much air in a balloon, it bursts. If you can find a way to prevent the pressure that anger brings from making your muscles hurt, by doing something like counting, you will be able to stop this force from building up inside and you'll remain calm, rather than blow up. Does this sound like something worth doing?" takes this knowledge one step further.

Feelings Related To Anger

The feelings that accompany, underlie, or contribute to anger, are often those that aren't readily expressed. Fear, hurt and disappointment fall into this category, along with frustration, anxiety, stress and depression. These emotions can also be described as aftershocks or by-products of the situations that evoked anger.

Some of these feelings were described earlier, as the causes of anger. Looking at these emotions as effects offers another perspective for understanding a teen's reactions to situations.

Why know about these feelings? One explanation for acquiring this knowledge is that it helps adolescents become aware that there are a variety of other feelings that can accompany or describe anger, and that experiencing these feelings is okay. They are not weird or stupid to have. Another reason to know about these feeling is that some of them, like hurt and fear are often viewed as signs of weakness. The fact is that most people who care about youngsters, find this knowledge helpful in their relationship with them. If other people know how certain things they do, or comments they make hurt adolescents, they may stop these actions, refrain from making hurtful remarks, or do these things less frequently. Finally, knowing about these other feelings provide young people with another way to describe how anger can affect them, and provides an additional way for them to better understand and handle this feeling.

Thoughts Connected To Anger

Different thoughts that accompany anger describe the final effect you will be exploring. Some of the more common ones expressed by A.M.P. Program participants were:

- I want to kill the other person.
- I want to hurt them badly.
- I want to see what they did to me done to them.
- How can I hurt this person (the way they did me)?
- Why did I get angry over this stupid thing?
- How could I be dumb enough to let the other person get me mad?

As with the feelings related to anger, these ideas can be used as a jumping-off point for discussion, or as a way to give a teen more to think about.

Thoughts and Managing Anger

One reason that an adolescent can refuse to discuss feelings or thoughts related to anger is that this subject falls into the "unmentionable category" when talking to adults. Other topics in this group include sex and drugs. They fall into this off-limit area for many reasons. "These are things that are not discussed in families, or by "good" (religious) people." "These are not things teens should know about until they are older," are two of these explanations. Anger often becomes, like so many other subjects, something that is never spoken about. It can also be a topic that many people find awkward or uncomfortable to speak about. This uneasiness is telegraphed to a youngster in different ways. Adults sometimes talk about these subjects in ways that teens know aren't true. Adolescents are often made to feel guilty about bringing these experiences and feelings up. These reactions are obstacles that often get in the way of working with young people. Add to these ideas the reality that much of what teens learn about these "forbidden subjects" comes from peers, their "street professors," who are seen as cool and as experts in these areas. With these avoidant approaches and information sources, the subject of anger takes on a sort of mystique. It becomes an area for an adolescent to handle in his or her own way. Needless to say, their actions can result in negative outcomes, as they often do with other "unmentionable" topics.

When young people can openly express and discuss their thoughts about anger they are given freedom. This choice allows the subject of anger to be something that is okay for them to think about. It is also a topic that can be openly discussed with an adult, who can offer information that goes beyond that provided by street professors. With this openness comes the opportunity for adolescents to discuss the consequences of any actions they may think of taking. In addition, openly expressing their thoughts when they experience anger gives young people the opportunity to release the negative energy that comes with experiencing this feeling.

Chapter Summary

In this chapter, three possible effects of anger were described. These were: physical effects, other feelings that accompany or underlie this emotion, and thoughts related to it. A process was described for identifying what reactions the body has to anger, and ways to reduce the intensity of this feeling. Different feelings, such as hurt, fear and disappointment that often lie below the surface of anger were described. Reasons these feelings are not discussed with many adults, and explanations of why they are important to talk about were presented. Thoughts that accompany anger explain the third effect of anger. Reasons why ideas connected to this emotion are not discussed, along with ways of opening this feeling up for discussion were explored. The responses of adolescent A.M.P. Program participants were added to provide you with an additional perspective. Knowing these effects offer another road to understanding this feeling in teens and helping them to find ways to handle it in more positive ways.

Chapter Seven

The Role of Experiences with Anger

Past Experience → Present Situations → Future Experiences

Adolescents' past experiences with Anger Management, both positive and negative, can provide ways for them to handle present and future situations. This concept builds on the connection with the causes and effects of anger discussed earlier. The role of previous incidents and other influences on a young person will be expanded in this chapter.

There are many influences a teen has in his or her life; family, friends, peers, the neighborhood they live or hang out in, and the schools they attend are among these. Many of the thoughts an adolescent has, and the things that they do, stem from these sources. The words, "Children learn what they live" summarize this idea.

The Influences of Media and Technology

What young people see and hear from other sources, also plays a large role in their life. Two major influences in a teen's life are the media and technology. Through these "authoritative" sources come stories and accounts of people doing all kinds of things, both positive and negative. The heroic efforts made by people to save lives, or attempt to help others fall into one category. Unfortunately, these kinds of events don't appear too frequently. Those limited exposures provide a limited influence on a young person. Instead, stories involving conflicts, violence, sex, criminal and unethical activities dominate radio and television coverage, and are posted on the Internet on a daily basis. They often relate to incidents involving athletes, movie and television personalities and music or other media artists. These well-known people often serve as role models to teens. Similar kinds of situations involving the not-so-notable also appear in the media. They deal with people living or working in an adolescent's neighborhood or going to their schools. Most of these reported incidents reflect the negative ways people handle different situations. Throwing phones, jumping into fights with other athletes or fans, robberies, murders, and other criminal actions become "worthy" of time and space on television and radio, in magazines and newspapers and on the Internet. The message to an adolescent is, "People notice you when you do something violent, dramatic or dangerous." Music and YouTube videos they see, blogs they read, things shared on Facebook and Twitter, websites they browse, video games they play, stories from friends, neighbors, classmates and relatives add to the list of negative influences on a young person's behavior.

The question to answer is, "With this barrage of negative input, how can I help a teen look at and manage incidents in their lives in more positive ways?" Getting an adolescent's perceptions of these realities of modern life furnishes a starting point. What they think of the people and events they witness and entertainment they enjoy are areas to explore. It also provides some idea of how these things influence their behavior. A young person often remarks that actions taken by someone, or events that have taken place, are "cool." Asking "What makes a professional basketball player getting into a fight with a fan cool?" is one approach to take. "He didn't look soft and beat the guy up who yelled that he sucked," illustrates one response a teenager can make. Asking an adolescent, "What happens to an athlete after he gets into a fight with a fan?" can help them move in another direction. An adolescent's response to this question tells you whether or not he/she is aware of the fines and suspensions that accompany these kinds of incidents with athletes. If a young person doesn't know what happened as a result of this star's behavior, let them know. In this case, telling a teen that a professional basketball player did something that kept him from playing in many games, and also cost him a lot of money, describes the consequences of an athlete's actions. Immediately after describing these results, ask, "How cool do you think having these things happening to him was for this basketball player" A teen may say, "It was worth it!" or look puzzled. Whatever the reaction is, the idea that some acts of "coolness" aren't worth the results they bring, gives an adolescent something to think about.

Young people receive additional kinds of messages from the Internet. There are different forms of entertainment found on it. Some exhibit pornography. Sex, for many teens when viewing it, is something they do regardless of whether the other person consents or not, without any thought of consequences, or consideration for the other person's feelings or reputation. Other websites offer boxing, wrestling and war games aimed at destroying something or hurting another person. Games showing different forms of combat, hurting others, violence and destruction are viewed as, "okay." "These things aren't real," is one possible response a youngster can make. The reaction of some adults is, "This is a way for my son to let off steam. Watching things on the Internet doesn't hurt anyone." This adds additional justification for a teen to view different videos and video games on the Internet. Admittedly, some games do allow an adolescent to let off steam without bringing harm to anyone. However, some young people become so involved in this world of Internet activity that they feel that what's done in it is what they can and will do, without thinking twice. It becomes reality. Think of incidents where two youngsters wrestle and do things they've seen on a video or on television. One of them breaks an arm, something they don't see happening in this form of entertainment. What about sex? Thinking that is okay for someone to force another person to perform certain acts because they are what the other person really "wants" according to what is seen and heard on the Internet, is another message a young person can get from this source of information. The pain from either of these forms of violent behavior is genuine. It is certainly not just unreal or about letting off steam. Getting an adolescents thoughts about what they see and hear over the Internet, and discussing other possible consequences that can result from taking actions described on the information superhighway is another way for them to see how taking some of the actions shown as Internet entertainment can be harmful to others.

For a young person who believes that anything done on the Internet is fine—and there are many individuals who do—the result of this belief needs to be discussed. Particularly in the realm of cyber-bullying, where an individual can be stalked and harassed on public sites such as Facebook and through instant messaging (IMs), a teen is at risk of constant persecution. "What do you know about cyber-bullying?" starts the conversation ball rolling.

> Much information on cyber-bullying can be found on the Internet and through other resources. It is important to learn more about this subject to understand what and how this kind of abuse occurs, and to prevent a young person from becoming victims of this treatment or using it to harass others.

If a teen understands what this behavior is and does, ask, "Do you know anyone who was bullied over the Internet?" If they don't know what it is you can explain, "Some people threaten to do something or tell about a person if they don't do what the bully asks." After offering this explanation, ask an adolescent the same question. If he/she doesn't know anyone, ask, "What would you do if this happened to you?" and "How would you feel?" If a young person is resistant to personalizing cyber-bullying happening to them, objectify it by remarking, "Suppose someone was doing this to your sister, brother or someone else close to you, how would you react?" "I'd go after them", "I'd be really mad," "I'd do the same thing to them," describe some possible reactions. After the teen has responded, ask why this treatment to their sister would make them feel this way?" "My sister would be scared, embarrassed, hurt, lose sleep, cry a lot," describes the thinking. By taking this route you are allowing an adolescent to see how this cyber action can affect someone. "Some people see someone on YouTube pushing someone around and think doing this is okay," describes another use of the Internet and the effects it can have on others. Wait for a young person's reaction. If there is none, at the very least, they have some other things to consider about another form of Internet abuse.

The same pattern of discussion used for cyber-bullying can be applied to posting nude pictures of another person on YouTube, "sexting"—that is, sending sexually explicit pictures of themselves or others—or posting personal information about another individual on cell phones. The influence of the subjects found, and actions taken on the information superhighway, and other forms of modern technology can be damaging to others or to a teen. The influence the Internet and these other sources can have on an adolescent's behavior and thinking makes it something to be concerned about and understood by both you and them.

Positive Experiences in Handling Anger

Having a teen remember a time when anger was managed in a positive way, either personally, or by people they observed, takes you both in another direction. This knowledge becomes necessary and helpful for adolescents to manage this feeling in future situations. Pointing out that their success in handling their anger before will allow them to handle it well again, or that because they saw the way someone else managed this feeling in a positive way is something that they can also do, are ways to make this connection.

Some teens simply haven't had any positive experiences with anger. They have not seen other people manage their anger well, or don't remember themselves ever handling this emotion other than by reacting aggressively. An adolescent not only may not have had this experience, but he/she also feels that there is no way to handle this feeling except with hostility. This is one reality that you may face.

Another approach is comprised of four components. These elements can be expressed as questions or as parts of the conversations that you have with a young person. Finding out what teens want from the other person in a particular situation describes the first step in this process. Usually they are looking for some sign of respect from the other party, whether it's in school, on the street or in any other public settings. Did they want an apology? Were they looking for an acknowledgement that the other person, for example, understood that yelling at them or calling them names embarrassed them in front of their peers? In most cases, the cause of adolescent anger or outright hostility results from the other person's failure to apologize or recognize that they had been hurt or embarrassed by their actions.

The next step is to find out what a teen thinks they got by reacting the way they did. Common responses made by adolescents are: they showed they aren't weak or soft, didn't take any kind of (expletive) from others, or showed the other individual that they couldn't get away with certain behavior.

These reactions lead us to the next, and probably most crucial part of this method: having youngsters decide whether or not their response to the situation was worthwhile. A follow-up to these strong remarks is to explore the results of their reactions. One outcome is that nothing else happened and the other person left them alone. In this instance, the actions were worth it and there isn't much else to say. However, if a teen responds that they got some sort of payback from relatives or friends of this other individual, they were physically or verbally assaulted, ignored by others, they were suspended or received punishment from their parents or school, then the consequences of their behavior merits further discussion. The remark, "It certainly seems like what you did wasn't worth it," sums up this idea. However, don't be surprised if they answer that their actions were worth the consequences. Leave it alone. This is often a show of bravado, a way to save face. The point is still made and in some way this idea may influence their thinking and future behavior.

Exploring what teens could have gotten without creating any more hassles for themselves brings you to the final stage of this process. Whether adolescents respond that their actions were worthwhile or not, this step allows them to consider other alternatives. If they are resistant to this idea, ask, "If there are some other ways of dealing with situations without opening yourself up to being hassled, wouldn't it be worth looking into?" There still can be some resistance. Two choices exist. The first is to let this part of this process go for the time being and let them know that this part of the discussion can take place at another time. The second approach points out the idea that finding other ways to handle situations can be useful in preventing future problems from arising. This suggestion might be rejected. If it is, be confident that other roads have been opened, and some will be taken at a later time.

For teens that want to continue this discussion, have them think of alternatives to handling the situations in ways that wouldn't cause them grief. One way is to remain in control of anger, that is, to calm down, so that they don't lash out at the other person. Another alternative is to encourage them to evaluate a past incident objectively by getting some information about it. Answering the questions, "Did the other person mean to embarrass you? and "What caused the fight in the first place?" can be helpful.

Dealing with past incidents also involves accepting a young person's perceptions of these situations, without making any judgments. Keep this thought consistently in mind. It enables both you and a teen to continue discussing this subject.

Exploring Recent or Familiar Situations

The situations to try to explore first with adolescents are those that have occurred most recently. However, if they seem reluctant to use personal incidents, describe more generic ones, those that seem to be common to many youngsters. We used the "Objectification Method," in an earlier chapter. It takes the spotlight off the teen. Being "dissed," that is, not being respected or valued by someone else, falls into the general situation category. The event described below illustrates one way an adolescent can experience this offense.

The Event: Someone bumps into you in the school hallway and keeps on walking, without looking back or saying anything.

Before furnishing any more details, ask a young person what they might do in this situation. Teens are often eager to give their opinions, something many adults don't often allow to happen. Their responses set the stage for using the process described earlier in this chapter. Whatever answers an adolescent provides are helpful. If they don't know what they would do, or shrug their shoulders, add the information described below.

Additional Details: You go after him and say in a loud voice in front of a whole bunch of people "Hey, why don't you look where you are going? What are you blind or something?" At this point he starts toward you and your hands go up. Next thing you know you are fighting.

After describing these particulars, you can move forward with your conversation with a youngster.

Step One: What does a teen want from the other person in that situation? Responses from adolescent participants in the A.M.P. Program centered on getting an apology from the offending individual. With this act, respect is shown, and the offended young person is able to save face in front of friends.

Step Two: Find out what a teen thinks they got by reacting to the situation the way they did. The A.M.P. Program respondents said:

> "The other person got what he deserved."
> "The guy who didn't take being bumped did the right thing."
> "The guy's friends would be glad he did something about being disrespected."

It is important to understand these perceptions. It is a matter of accepting—not agreeing—with what they have to say, without judging them, that helps keep the discussion open for the teen to at least be able to hear other possibilities for dealing with this kind of an incident.

Step Three: Ask an adolescent if there might be other ways, besides fighting, to resolve this problem. By recognizing their opinions, you open up another approach to dealing with anger, and a young person is more likely to give some thought to your question rather than feel they are being lectured to. Some A.M.P. Program participants replied that there aren't any other ways to handle it. However, a number of them started thinking about other ideas. Some came up with alternative approaches. These included:

- Take the other teen aside calmly and ask him or her if they bumped into you on purpose.
- If the other person didn't realize he did, move with him or her away from their peers where he or she might apologize or the guy who was bumped can ask if the other individual was sorry.
- The person who was bumped may just realize that in a crowded hallway things like this happen, that it was accidental and is nothing to get upset about.
- The guy or girl who was bumped might have taken deep breaths or tell himself or herself it is nothing to get upset about.

Step Four: Looking at whether the behavior to save face was worth the consequences it brought leads the conversation in another direction. Adolescent participants in the A.M.P. Program responded differently. Some said it wasn't worth the hassle people get from their parents, missing school and trying to catch up, or having to watch their backs—that is, wondering if someone will take revenge for hurting the other individual. Others said, "Yeah, that kid got what he deserved," or, "If he was my friend I'd respect him for not taking being dissed."

After the consequences and their value to a young person have been discussed, have them consider other ways to save face without getting into a fight. A teen may give you a disbelieving look or answer, "There is no other way." You may get the famous shoulder shrug, an "I don't care," with a few expletives thrown in, or just silence. Keep in mind adolescents have many different causes of anger. They often distrust adult motives and have learned that the less information they reveal, the less their chances are of getting hurt again. However, they often consider these ideas privately without letting an adult or their peers know. A.M.P. Program participants often indicated that certain ideas were valuable to them on the anonymous feedback survey given at the end of a presentation, illustrates this point.

Alternative Methods of Handling Situations

Directing teens to come up with ways that would allow the person in this hypothetical situation to save face without fighting starts you and them in this direction. Right after you make this suggestion, let an adolescent know that whatever they say is okay, nothing is stupid, and that taking guesses is something to do to try to solve a problem in new ways. This makes use of the idea of brainstorming, a way to get ideas without judging or discussing them, a worthwhile technique for solving problems. The thoughts that young people provide are noted, verbally or on a piece of paper, chalkboard, or chart and not discussed until after a number of ideas have been suggested. The more alternatives that are suggested, the better the chances are of finding one that can work in this situation.

If there is no attempt to come up with suggestions to resolve this problem on their own, there are a few ways to stimulate teen thinking. One path to take is to find out if the person who bumped into the other individual was aware that this incident occurred. To find out the answer to this question, include the idea of having them look at ways to approach the other person without coming at them loudly.

Another way is to deal with this situation is to have an adolescent judge how angry it can make people. Using the Anger Scale gauges the intensity of anger a person can feel over this situation. By doing this, the question, "Is this situation worth getting really upset about?" can be answered. One adolescent may see this incident as making them really angry, while another may see it as annoying, but not enough to get into a fight over.

From these approaches, ideas to resolve this problem peacefully may occur to a teen. One thought is to let the situation go; the thinking being that he/she being bumped into really could have been an accident since the other person did not look back or laugh once they moved down the hall. Another possibility is to go up to the person and ask the other individual if they knew that this happened. The way this could be done, without escalating the situation, is for the individual who was bumped to ask if it was an accident, using a low tone of voice and not getting in the other person's face. If you are unable to draw out these ideas from a youngster, suggest them.

It is also effective to tap into young people's creativity to come up with alternative solutions. Using this resource can be accomplished by having them act as movie or television directors, or put together something on YouTube where the "Bumped in the Hallway" incident has a different ending. This approach also gives teens the opportunity to be in control of the outcome.

The Past-Present Connection

After exploring past experiences and discussing how they may have been handled differently, the next step is to have adolescents establish the relationship between recent situations and similar ones that occurred in the past. They may or may not be willing to discuss these incidents. If they are willing to talk about these related events, asking how they handled both situations is useful. Find out what happened between them and the other individual involved makes a good starting point. If you get a shoulder shrug, or an "I don't know" response, try objectification, using other people's experiences, either those a teen personally witnessed, or characters seen on TV, in a movie or from another entertainment source.

If the results in both incidents were negative, have an adolescent think of a time when anger was expressed in ways where both people didn't get hurt, either physically or emotionally, or in ways that relationships weren't damaged. Even if a young person doesn't come up with any answers, a connection between past and present experiences has been made. At the very least, another possible tool has been added to a teen's Anger Management repertoire. In addition, by focusing on other people's lives or situations, you give an adolescent space—that is, a chance not to feel as if he/she is on the "hot seat." By using this method, the chances of them becoming defensive or escalating the anger is minimized or avoided.

Ways to Promote Adult Effectiveness

Repeating the words "Patience, Persistence, Determination" to yourself may be a helpful bit of self-talk, or a chant to remember when experiencing frustration with a youngsters' behavior. Keep your mind focused on the goals you want to achieve no matter what obstacles teens try to throw in your path.

Unfortunately, there is no magic formula to foster trust and cooperation from an adolescent. Ideas on how to gain these objectives have and will continue to be presented throughout this book. These objectives are musts in being effective with a young person.

Chapter Summary

Experience is another great teacher. The form that it takes varies. In this chapter you have seen how television, radio, magazines and the Internet can influence a teen. In addition to these sources were those that come from an adolescent's personal life, those that he or she may have witnessed, or from general knowledge that comes from being a part of the peer culture. A four-step process for understanding a young person's perception of a situation and the means of creating alternative means for resolving it were provided. What a teen wanted from the other person involved in the situation, what their reaction to this incident brought for them, looking for alternative ways to handle it, and finally examining whether the outcome was worthwhile, describes this method. A situation was provided to demonstrate this process, along with teen A.M.P. Program participants' responses to this particular incident. The information provided in this chapter, as well as the knowledge that came before, provide stepping stones to understanding things that influence an adolescent and approaches to use to empower adolescents to handle their anger more effectively.

Chapter Eight

Anger Managers

Twenty-one Anger Managers will be presented in this chapter. There were chosen from a larger list, found in the "Information Booster" section of this book, by teen facilitators and participants in the Anger Management Power Program who felt these methods would be the most likely to be used by their peers. Some of these methods for controlling this emotion were mentioned in earlier chapters. All of these tools will be described in depth along with suggestions on how you can use them effectively. As you become more familiar with this list of Anger Managers, no doubt other ideas on how to use them will occur. Jot them down as you think of them, without making any judgments. One thing that I've learned from some of my experiences with teens is to go with your instinct. Rather than hesitating to mention a particular Anger Manager because you are not sure it is the right thing to try or will work, just use it. Something inside of us—call it a still, small voice—tells us to take a particular action that often turns out to be the right thing to do.

Before these techniques are explored there are some ideas that need to be considered. The first is that many of the methods used to manage anger can also be used to handle anxiety and stress. The next thought to bear in mind is that adolescents need to know that before they can express their anger in a positive way, they have to calm down after an incident has taken place. Some ways to de-escalate the intensity of this emotion, and create this state of readiness, were described in the previous chapter when the physical effects that anger stirs up were discussed. These Anger Management tools will be brought into focus as we explore the first of the anger managers, "Physical Outlets," as well as many of the other methods. What is useful for many people is to categorize the anger managers into two groups, one known as "Anger-De-Escalators," the other called, "Anger Expressers." The second group describes techniques for a teen to use to tell other people about their anger in a positive way.

Physical Outlets

Explanation: Exercise of any kind (sports, walking, running, aerobics, dancing), counting forwards or backwards (to or from any number), or taking deep breaths all fall into this category.

The following illustration provides a way to understand their use.

Illustration: A teacher puts down a teen in front of his classmates for coming late to class. His face starts to redden and the muscles in his arm begin to tighten.

Without Using This Anger Manager: He reaches a point where he explodes, and yells at the teacher. As she approaches him, the student tells her to get out of his face before he hits her. His behavior results in suspension from school and a long, loud lecture from his parents.

Using this Anger Manager: The adolescent takes several deep breaths, and then feels his body calm down. After class, he explains to the teacher that his mom was taken to the hospital and he was very upset. The teacher apologizes for scolding him in front of his peers.

Depending on where an incident takes place, or with whom, a young person may avoid blowing up by walking away from the person, or becoming involved in a sport or other form of exercise. At home, or with friends outside of school, a teen may be able to do these things to let off steam caused by the anger.

Precaution: When leaving the place where a situation occurred, it is important that an adolescent be told to let the other person know he/she wants a chance to calm down before they can deal with the incident. The

139

remark, "I need some time to chill out and then we can talk about this stuff," is an example of how this walk away can be accomplished without creating more difficulty with the other person. This behavior is also part of another method that is described later in this chapter.

Is It Worth It?

Explanation: This idea takes into account a teen's thoughts about the consequences of their reactions to anger-provoking situations. Having an adolescent think of a light bulb or a buzzer going off in their mind connects this image with the question, "Is It worth it?"

Illustration: Another way to describe this tool is to call it the A-B-C Anger Manager. With this approach, you first look at the causes of anger that get a youngster into trouble, or an incident that describes this feeling as being high on the Anger Scale.

If a teen is reluctant to respond to either of these ideas, use the following example and go on from there.

A: Anger Activator (cause of anger): A general situation can be used. For example, another adolescent says something nasty about a person's family.

B: Behavior (the reaction): Have a youngster describe what he/she would do. In this case, they may say:

- "Tell the person to shut up."
- "Punch the other person."
- (in rare cases) "Walk away."

C: Consequence (what happened): A variety of responses may be offered. Among these are:

- "The person yelled back."
- "We both kept yelling."
- "We fought."

- "We got suspended."
- "My parents grounded me for a month."

The next step after analyzing the situation is to ask the question, "Was it worth it?" This is the key to this Anger Manager. Regardless of the consequences, an adolescent may still answer "Yes," and think the reaction was worth the cost. In addition, many young people do exactly the opposite of what adults think they should do, part of the rebelliousness that is equated with being a teenager. However, if exposed to another approach in dealing with these sorts of situations, they may consider using it sometime in the future. Who knows?

When exploring specific situations with an adolescent, find out where an incident took place and who observed it. If, for example, an event took place in school, peers were probably around to see it, so saving face becomes a factor in handling this incident. Under these circumstances, explore ways the consequences could have been avoided without "looking soft" to peers.

The issue of control is another approach this Manager suggests. Many A.M.P. participants were asked, "Who is in control in a conflict: the person who says things to get you mad—and you do; or you, when these people try, and fail to get you angry? Many youngsters responded with the latter. This is often a good time to offer the observation that many people who try to start trouble are the first ones to run away from it. For a young person this idea may make sense, and they see it as a way to save face, while preventing themselves from getting into more trouble.

This Anger Manager can also be used as a preventative measure. Looking at the result of a teen's actions, and the grief it brought them, may stop an adolescent from doing the same thing the next time they face a similar situation. This is something that adolescent A.M.P. Program participants saw as possible.

Self-Talk and Affirmations

Explanation: These are two similar methods. When someone uses self-talk, they speak to themselves—not out loud—as a means of calming down after a situation has occurred. Such phrases as:

"I am calm."
"I am in control."
"I am not going to lose it."

describe this method. A teen literally talks him/herself down the Anger Scale.

Using an affirmation has the same goal as self-talk. It describes the qualities people have that keep them from reacting to the anger-activating situation or other individuals. Such statements as:

"I am a peaceful person."
"I am a calm person."
"I am a problem-solver."

illustrate this Anger Manager. Both of these methods are aimed at reducing the intensity of the anger a teen experiences.

Illustration: Darlene sees her boyfriend Devon with his arm around a girl outside of school. She feels her heart begin to beat faster and her face start to get flushed.

Without this Anger Manager: Darlene explodes at Devon and doesn't give him a chance to talk. He says that he's had it with her short temper and doesn't want anything more to do with her. The relationship is ended.

With this Anger Manager: Darlene decides to wait and then approach Devon. While she takes this pause, Darlene says to herself, "I am in control, I am cool, I am a trusting person." As she does this, she feels her heart slowing down and her face not feeling as warm as it did. She approaches Devon calmly. He reveals that the girl he was holding just found out that her dad was in a bad car accident and adds, "She is someone I've known since elementary school." The three of them walk away together, with the Darlene holding Devon's hand.

> Knowing that this and other Anger Managers can prevent a teen from damaging important relationships is something that needs to be repeatedly communicated. It is a way for adolescents to make sure that their needs for belonging and recognition are being met. Being part of a relationship satisfies the first desire, acknowledgment for having this close bond with another person satisfies the second.

Repeatedly Chanting or Saying a Phrase or Word

Explanation: Many of the Anger Managers that have and will be explored safely channel the energy resulting from experiencing anger. In this case, repeating a word like, "Woosah" (taken from the popular movie "Bad Boyz II,") suggested by a high school student, provides an angry youngster with a way to "let go" of the pressure they feel from a situation. They are able to "come down" the Anger Scale. This is a variation of self-talk and affirmation anger manager described above. It creates a mantra, a sound that a young person can make repeatedly, to calm down.

Often creating a funny sounding name or word can motivate using this Anger Manager. "Gobbledegook," or some other ridiculous word you and the adolescent can create, serves this purpose. This allows a young person the power to choose his or her own nonsense word and "own" this anger manager.

Illustration: A teen loses his cell phone. He is about to pull out all the draws of his dresser and throw things on the floor or kick his furniture. He decides instead to use this Anger Manager, and repeats the word, "gobble-degook" several times. He calms down and is able to find his cell phone.

Listen to Music, Play an Instrument or Sing

Explanation: This method takes into account the idea that certain activities, such as listening to music, can calm an adolescent down. Playing an instrument or singing also serves to divert the energy generated by anger into another activity, releasing it before it becomes destructive. The thought to keep in mind is there are many different activities (some that you may find on this list, others that you've come across earlier in this book, or some others that you know a youngster likes to participate in) that can help a teen release the energy that accompanies this feeling, and allows him/her the chance to calm down.

Anger Journal

Explanation: Many young people like to write. This journal is similar to a diary; however, it deals specifically with anger-producing incidents the writer encounters. It allows a teen to deal with the situation quickly, without directly confronting the other person involved in it. It is also a way for an adolescent to look at the entire situation and decide how to try to resolve it.

This method contains three components:

The first describes the anger-activating incident. It specifically tells what happened, who else was involved, where it took place, and how angry a young person felt. The intensity of the emotion can be described using metaphors such as, "As mad as someone who got punched in the stomach for no reason," or as a point on the Anger Scale. It is an analytical way to look at anger and put it into perspective.

In the second part of this method, a teen creates a plan to resolve the situation. It answers the question, "What solutions am I going to come up with to end this problem without bringing myself more hassles?"

The final section describes how an adolescent plans to handle similar situations in the future.

Precaution: The idea of writing other information besides the causes of anger must be emphasized. Going beyond only noting the incident allows the writer the opportunity to become a problem-solver, and offers a preventative measure to similar future incidents. It also avoids repeatedly revisiting the cause of this feeling and prevents the possibility of escalating the anger felt by repeatedly going over the situation, in other words, not dwelling on it. When this Anger Manager was discussed with young people during the A.M.P. Program, they themselves expressed the negative effect that just noting the incident can have on a person.

Illustration: Two close friends, Sue and Beth had an argument. Sue was really angry because Beth seemed to be ignoring her and not spending time with her because she had a boyfriend, Marty.

Without this Anger Manager: Sue confronts Beth and yells at her, saying that she cares more about Marty than her and that she is a really a [expletive] friend. Sue does this in front of Marty and some other friends. Beth yells back and tells Sue to go to hell. The friendship ends.

With this Anger Manager: Part I: Incident Description: I got mad at Beth because she used to spend more time with me, before Marty came along. Now she almost totally ignores me. I cursed at her and she yelled back at me. It makes me feel like I was being left on an island by myself.

Part II: Resolving the Situation: I can call Beth on the phone, or when I see her talk to her in private. First, I can apologize to her for yelling and cursing her in front of Marty and those other people. Then, I could tell her how I felt and see what she says. If Beth says she doesn't care, that's it for her. If she is sorry, we can talk about how we can fix this problem.

Part III: Preventing Future Problems: Try to handle a situation just between me and the other person and talk about our relationship and how we both feel.

This method is similar to a dress rehearsal for a play. It allows a young person to read the script and know what is happening, to play out the situation, and then see how to improve their role in future performances.

It also provides time to release the energy a teen feels and channel it into a constructive problem solving activity.

Talk It Over With Someone Not Involved

Explanation: Adolescents can avert acting on anger if they just discuss the problem—in other words, vent—to a friend, relative or counselor.

Precaution: Talking it over with an objective person is the key. If youngsters speak with a person who is going to side with them, it may result in intensifying the anger they are already experiencing and prolong the hostility. For example, teens may ask certain friends or family members, people they know will agree with their side of the situation, and get their opinion on how to handle a situation. Their answers may include, "Let that guy know that you are not someone who takes [expletive] from anyone!" or "Don't let that girl get away with that!' Bottom line, the fires of hostility are kept burning, without a chance to cool them down.

Illustration: Pete's friend John told him that Dan was spreading rumors about him and his girlfriend, Carol. Dan told other people that Carol has sex every day with Pete and with a few other guys behind his back.

Without this Anger Manager: Pete asks John for his advice. John tells him not to let Dan get away with this [expletive] and punch his lights out. Pete is really riled up and goes looking for Dan. After their fight, both boys are bruised and both get suspended. Carol starts crying and wants Pete to leave her alone and ends the relationship.

With this Anger Manager: Pete goes to his guidance counselor, Mr. Dominick, and tells him what John revealed and asks what he should do. Mr. Dominick asked, "Do you know for a fact that Dan actually said these things? Why would he say these things about you and Carol? Is there a reason why John might tell you this stuff?" and then adds, "If it isn't true, then leaving it alone may just end it right there." In this case, Mr. Dominick provided Pete with ideas to think about, rather than giving him the go-ahead to react to the situation. By talking to his counselor, Pete also had time to chill out, and get some ideas on how to deal with the situation. Then end result for Pete was that he prevented himself from creating more hassles than this "He said, she said" situation was worth.

Accept Differences

Explanation: This Anger Manager reminds teens that they can't control others. This idea can be expressed, "Thinking differently, feeling differently or acting differently than other people is okay."

Precautions: Keep in mind that adolescents often think in terms of absolutes. For example, how they dress, who they associate with, the music they listen to, are usually linked to the belief of a like-minded peer group. Their way is "Right" with no room for differences. This is the reason that there are different peer groups. Jocks, Nerds, Metal Heads describe some of these. These beliefs, like a religion, are non-negotiable. When a young person is asked to look at and understand that other beliefs are okay, they don't buy it. It's their way or no way. This is something you need to be aware of and accept. Teens look at adults' thoughts, as well as those of other adolescents who are members of other groups, as foreign and suspicious. If any person tries to discuss other ways of thinking to a member of a particular group, it becomes a war of the beliefs, which ends in a lot of frustration for both sides. To this way of thinking, differences set two people apart, creating a distance between them. This kind of mindset may lead to heated verbal attacks, or in some cases, the use of physical force to convince the other person to see, feel or act in one particular way. "You cannot be part of my life, have a relationship with me, or live in my house unless you think, do, feel, the way I do" expresses this idea. In some cases it can be called "emotional blackmail."

Accepting youngsters' differences in thinking does not mean agreeing with them, only that you recognize them as legitimate or okay. Listening and hearing teens' viewpoints and then enabling them to be open to what you have to say are key ingredients to moving forward in your relationship with them. The main idea is that by accepting differences between your thinking and adolescents, the need to have their thoughts valued is satisfied and you have helped create a closer bond with them. Regardless of what they say (often face-saving or bravado for them), becoming more connected also helps to meet their desire to be part of a relationship. It is certainly a goal worthwhile achieving with a young person.

Other than the areas of strong beliefs previously mentioned, a teen can look at other things to learn to accept differences. These may include physical differences between people, such as those involving height, weight, a person's complexion or those of people coming from other ethnic backgrounds reflected in their language, dress and customs. These are often things dealt with by ridicule that often result in conflict. The idea of acceptance can be pointed out by having adolescents see similarities between themselves and these other "different" individuals. Membership on school teams, participation in the same sports and extracurricular activities, attitudes toward teachers or parents, boredom with some subject classes and rules they are made to follow, illustrate some of the things that can be used to demonstrate these similarities. Pointing out likenesses in people, lessens the degree of dissimilarities between them, which creates a bond is an idea that can be emphasized with this Anger Manager.

Illustration: Tom, who is on the football team, sees Carl, a short, thin boy, being bumped in the hallway by another student. Carl looks at the person who bumped into him and does nothing else. The other student walks on without saying anything about this accident. Tom comes over to Carl, who is also a friend of his and asks why he didn't at least say something to the other guy, and tells his friend, "I would have stepped in." Carl looks at Tom, and says, "Do you think someone my size could do anything to that guy? Besides to me, something like being bumped accidentally isn't worth the hassle it can cause." Tom shakes his head, and says, "I understand what you are saying, but if it were me, I'd have made that guy apologize."

As you go through more of this list, you will see similarities between different Anger Managers. Often the same thing can be expressed in many ways. Our goal is to enable young people to pick methods that appeal to them. "Whatever works" is a philosophy I believe in. Applied here, what is understandable and acceptable to a teen is the goal to strive to reach. Presenting variations of different Anger Managers often accomplishes this task.

Treat Others with Respect

Explanation: Being respected by others is something really important to teens. To be disrespected or "dissed" is one of the worst things for them to experience, especially in front of peers. This is the cause of many conflicts. This idea is something for adolescents to be reminded to consider when they speak to others or by the behavior they show toward others. Young people often just think of respect only as something to be felt from others and forget that it's a two way street, particularly in situations with adults. This idea may be summed up by the question, "How do you feel when someone doesn't show you respect?" or in the statement, "You know how it feels not to be respected."

Illustration: John is waiting for dinner. His mom is usually home and has dinner ready when he comes home at 5:30. It is 6:30 when his mother comes home. John is really upset.

Without this Anger Manager: John yells at his mother, telling her she is a lousy mom who doesn't care about him. Before she is able to say anything, he keeps up this tirade with more insults. His mom turns away from him, tells him to make his own food, and yells, "Because of your big mouth you can't go out this weekend!"

With this Anger Manager: John sees his mom come in the door, out of breath. He asks, "Hey, Mom, are you okay?" She tells him she got stuck on the subway train for almost an hour and then apologizes for being late with

149

John's supper. John says, "Don't worry, I am not starving to death," smiles and lets his mom settle down.

Tell Others What Bothers You. Be Direct, Specific and Polite

Explanation: This Anger Manager involves the use of direct communication. This is something that can be done in contrast to teens' rolling their eyes, "staring daggers," slamming doors, mumbling under their breath, talking in a loud tone of voice, giving the silent treatment, or cursing. These indirect means of letting adults know they are angry, does little else. The source of adolescent anger, and the possibility of preventing the situation that caused this feeling from occurring again, are left undetermined. Statements like, "You should know why I am angry," "This is something you do over and over again" don't really get into the specifics, they make assumptions, a source of frustration for both parties. If you are on the receiving end of the anger, getting to its source becomes your objective. The "how to" involves calmness, sincerity and patience. This approach will serve as a means of helping young people learn how to use this method in a way that benefits them. By applying this method, their thoughts and feelings will be understood, and this cause of anger can be avoided in the future.

The following situation demonstrates how to use this Anger Manager. Two reactions are described. The first shows how this incident can escalate; the second describes how using this tool can produce a positive result. If an adolescent can't—or won't—provide a response to questioning the consequences of their behavior, then describe both approaches. Once this is done, give a young person the opportunity to judge whether they would use this Anger Manager with their parents or other adults. The reasons for this decision are worth discussing. This is another information gathering process that can be helpful in understanding a teen's thinking.

The Situation: A daughter brings home her report card. Her mom starts to tell her that once again her grades are disappointing.

Without this Anger Manager: The daughter says "No [expletive]! Like it's something I don't know!" She stomps out of the kitchen, goes to her room, mumbling some other barely audible four letter words, and then slams the door.

With this Anger Manager: The girl tells her mom, "I'm already upset with myself over these grades. When you shout at me that I'm not doing well in school it makes me feel ten times as bad, like being hit over the head again." (Direct) She adds, "Instead of just looking at my poor grades, look at the passing grades or those that have shown improvement and maybe I'll be encouraged to find ways to pull up my marks." (Specific)" The daughter said what she needed in a calm way, without cursing or slamming doors. (Polite)

Ask the adolescent who you are working with, "What did the daughter gain from acting the way she did when she didn't use this idea to handle her anger?" Possible responses can include.

"The girl let her mother know she was mad."
"She got her feelings out."
"The girl didn't change anything."
"She didn't let her mother know why she was mad."

Without making any judgments or comments, ask the same question, this time focusing on when the girl used this Anger Manager. Once a youngster has answered this question, find out which way he/she thought worked better and why. After having this discussion ask, "Would you use this Anger Manager?" Depending on their reply, find out the reason for this decision. Whatever result you get doesn't matter. At the very least you provide a teen with another tool to use to manage anger.

Another way to avoid escalating a situation involving an adolescent's lack of progress in school is to say, "We need to talk about your grades. Let's decide on a time we can both discuss this." It's not only what you say, but also how you tell a young person about some negative behavior that can keep things calm. By taking this approach, an undesirable conflict is avoided, time is allowed for a teen to keep his or her lack of progress from getting them more upset, and the subject will be discussed, and not avoided or forgotten. When this discussion is to take place is a joint decision made with an adolescent, who, by being part of it, has a feeling of some control, something that also helps to keep this situation calm. Saying, "Sit down, young lady! We are going to talk about your grades here and now!" that is, making it a demand, is more likely to cause a negative reaction. Your goal is to resolve a problem, not create another one.

This approach can accomplish a couple of things. For one thing, it can be used as a model for a youngster of how to deal with an issue when they are upset. We, as adults, model much of what a teen learns and does. Expressed another way, if what you say and do is consistent, your credibility with an adolescent is certainly going to be strong. As a person who deals with teens on a regular basis certainly knows, consistency is a key to credibility and influence. A youngster may think, "My mother is not going to make me feel like I'm being attacked, so maybe things can get better," when you use this method. This is the kind of reaction that you want from a teen. It is a goal that to reach to eliminate some of the hassles that can occur in your relationship.

Using this Anger Manager can prevent, in this case, the daughter, from becoming defensive and reacting in such a way that makes this situation even harder to deal with. It removes a roadblock to dealing with her grades constructively. To say that the daughter's falling grades don't have any consequence is not a possibility. The results of certain kinds of behavior, in this case, a young person's grades, may have been discussed previously. This is something mentioned earlier in this book, when behavioral guidelines were presented. The discussion the next day will reiterate these consequences. At this point, the situation is over and the results of this behavior will be dealt with. This is not to say, in this case, the daughter, might not try to plead, "Give me one more chance to get better marks," or start her statement with, "But." Patience is definitely required. After doing whatever it took to keep this situation from getting out of hand, the girl should be reminded that this subject was discussed before, along with its effects on her. If consequences weren't previously discussed, after a situation occurs is a good time to discuss what the results of her efforts can and will "earn" her. In this case, the girl's frustration over her grades has not been elevated and she is in a calm state, ready to rationally deal with the subject of her grades.

Keep in mind: there are certain predictable behaviors that teens exhibit. For example, yelling back when someone yells at them or coming up with excuses for poor grades, only help to escalate feelings between an adolescent and a grown up. It is worthwhile for both of you to deal with these possibilities before they occur. The remark, "I know your grades are upsetting and you may feel like yelling when we discuss them, but if we're calm you won't find yourself getting more upset" can produce a positive effect. In the case of excuses, "Let's look at what can be done about your grades, rather than blaming them on a teacher or something else. It takes a lot of energy and only takes us longer to get through," can also help to keep this situation from escalating. Using these tactics and understanding their effects, can prevent an adolescent from taking these actions and creating more hassles for themselves with an adult. Yes, this takes time! Yes, you are the older, more experienced person, and they are the children. However, isn't the ounce (maybe ten pounds) of prevention worth the pound (maybe ton) of aggravation for all concerned? Here again, it's your choice to decide if using and showing a young person this anger manager is worth the time and energy for both of you.

The "I Statement"

Explanation: This Anger Manager is a variation of the above. The "I Statement" does two things: It tells others how a person feels, that is, people take responsibility for their own feelings without saying something like, "You made me feel ___!" It also avoids blaming other people, a real anger-provoker. It removes the "you always/you never" accusations that set off many conflicts. It focuses on the behavior that created the angry feeling in people and not on the other person's character. It is a way for adolescents, as well as adults, to express their feelings without causing more hostility or harm. This idea is also applicable to other emotions (happiness, sadness, fear, pride, etc.). It is expressed in the following way:

The Feeling: I feel angry (any feeling can be used)

The Behavior: ... when you yell at me in front of my friends

The Reason: ... because it embarrasses me (made me feel little, etc.).

This statement can also be used with the behavior expressed first and then the feeling "When you yell at me in front of my friends, I feel angry." Some people omit the reason, something that adds more to the meaning of the behavior, but isn't essential in using this tool. Many teens felt that this is a useful Anger Manager. Some have reported using it effectively in different kinds of close relationships.

Precaution: This Anger Manager is useful in close relationships. Many young people understood why this idea wouldn't be helpful in situations with someone on the street or people they don't really know. The remark, "I could care less how they feel," sums up the reaction of people who are not close to an individual, and the reason for not using this method with them.

Give the Other Person Space

Explanation: Some people don't want to be around others when they are mad and know they need to cool off. This requires them having time and space. In the case of a teen involved in a situation in which his/her emotions run high, your discovery of how they meet this need is important. "How do I know an adolescent needs space to calm down?" and "Where is a good place for them to go?" become your concerns. The first matter often comes directly at you with direct remarks, "I need to be by myself" or in a stronger, not so gentle, statements, such as:

"Get out of my face!"

"Don't bother me!"

"Leave me alone!"

This knowledge can also come from observations of a young person's previous responses to being around others when they were upset.

Another form of space is personal space. One thing a teen does not like is for anyone to be two feet or less, about an arm's length, from him or her, particularly when they are angry. It is breathing room and provides some distance from others. This is also a factor for victims of abuse who see people getting too physically close as a threat to their safety.

The next part of this plan involves an awareness of places where an adolescent can calm down. In some places that are familiar, in school, at home, in the workplace, certain areas where a youngster can take some time to calm down are known. In other unfamiliar places restrooms, empty offices, open spaces (inside or outside of a building or room), may offer this kind of "chilling out" area. Previous discussions with a teen may have also produced places that provide this space when the need arises. In many educational facilities and social service agencies, this subject is discussed and plans are made to handle an adolescent who becomes really upset. In families, this might also be something worthwhile to have members discuss. It could be as easy as having individuals go to their room or to a bedroom, bathroom, hallway, or some other empty, space when an incident occurs.

Illustration: Sean has just come home. As he opens the door, he shouts, "That [expletive] girlfriend of mine. She can't leave her friends for a second when I want to talk to her," then slams the door.

Without this Anger Manager: When he slams the door, you come up to him and tell him, "You'd better watch your language and calm down right now!" He glares at you and goes to his room and slams the door. You follow him and he starts yelling, and cursing. You wonder if he'll ever calm down, but you aren't about to put up with this nonsense and ground him for the next two weeks. He goes past you and out the door.

With this Anger Manager: You see how upset Sean is. You tell him that he looks upset and ask if he needs time to calm down. He frowns and stomps to his room and slams the door. About an hour later he comes out and says, "Darlene is so inconsiderate, I really can't stand her sometimes." You ask what happened and so he describes what got him so mad.

A youngster may not come to you that day, that week, or at all to discuss a situation. However, he has seen he is able to get the space and time he needs to be able to calm down without creating a problem at home.

Give Others a Chance to Express Their Thoughts without Saying Anything

Explanation: This for many is just allowing the other person the opportunity to vent their thoughts and feelings. Many of the high school youngsters I have worked with just needed someone to hear them out, and commented, "All I wanted was for my (Mom, Dad, brother, teacher) to hear what I have to say." The importance of just listening can't be stressed enough.

Precaution: Adults too often feel they need to voice their opinion, or help adolescents by judging their actions and putting them on the right road. Asking young people "What do you want me to do?" or being more specific, "Do you want me to just listen, or do you want my opinion?" allows them to decide what is appropriate to their needs. Jumping into the situation often leads to "telling" teens what you think they are feeling. This idea was mentioned earlier when the importance of meeting an adolescent's need for recognition was explored. In this case, by asking youngsters what they want, you are letting them know that what they want from you is important. Having teens aware of this prevents frustration and gives them the message to hear what other people want from them before they react.

Illustration: Tony comes into his house and remarks, "My so-called friends really suck." His dad hears this and goes over to his son to discuss this issue.

Without this Anger Manager: Tony's father remarks, "Don't let them get to you. It isn't worth it. Even friends sometimes screw up."

Tony looks at his father and walks out of the room muttering, "Why can't he just listen. I don't want his damn advice."

With this Anger Manager: Tony's dad asks, "What happened?" Tony tells him the whole story. After he is through with it, his dad asks, "Do you want my advice about handling this situation?"

Tony replies, "No thanks, Dad. I just wanted to get it off my chest. I'll deal with them myself."

Dave Wolffe

Stay Calm When Another Person Is Angry

Explanation: Many times when people are upset, whether it is due to anger, stress, anxiety, or disappointment, others often get "caught up" in the moment. They react with a similar feeling and get agitated as well. This can be described as a kind of "contact feeling." To avoid this reaction with angry individuals, show teens how to deal with others who are upset. Suggest that they try a few of the following steps:

- Take slow, deep breaths.
- Relax jaw, neck muscles and body.
- Maintain a healthy attitude by creating a calm atmosphere

This behavior requires the teen not to be defensive. Angry people often take their anger out on those close to them. It also means being confident about understanding the reason for the anger without acting as if you know more than they do, are cooler, or as teens often say, act as if they are "all that."

Finally, don't take a person's anger personally because their judgment is impaired by the emotion they are experiencing. In this Anger Manager you are giving the other person the opportunity to vent their anger by just listening, giving them space, and providing yourself with ways to maintain your own cool. By keeping in mind that you are not the source of the anger and need to keep an emotional "distance," you are eliminating the possibility of adding more fuel to an angry person's emotional fire.

Illustration: Doreen has a big argument with her friend Kathy. She is really upset. Another friend, Alba, sees how upset Doreen is and approaches her.

Without this Anger Manager: Alba goes over to Doreen and asks, "What happened?"

Doreen starts yelling, then tells Alba to mind her own [expletive] business!"

Alba responds, "Who do you think you are! Don't dump your [expletive] all over me!"

Doreen turns around and walks away. Alba says out loud, "No wonder you don't have too many friends."

Doreen responds, "Who do you think you are, Miss Popularity!" and leaves, cursing under her breath.

With this Anger Manager: Alba goes over to Doreen and asks, "What happened?"

Doreen starts yelling, then tells Alba, "Why don't you mind your own [expletive] business!"

Alba takes a couple of deep breaths, and says, "Listen, sometimes, when people are angry, they need to talk about it. If you want to, I am here for you." She stands there, with a smile on her face and her hands at her side.

Doreen, responds, "Hey, I am sorry I told you to back off. I'm really upset. Right now I need some more time to chill out. Maybe we can talk about this later."

Catch a Breeze

Explanation: Have the teen go somewhere isolated, where he/she can be alone, a private place. When an adolescent gets to this place, they can sit down and feel the wind blow against their face and the warmth of the sun. The young man who suggested this Anger Manager described his place as sitting on an abandoned car, somewhere on a quiet street.

Stress Putty

Explanation: Have something in hand to manipulate. Here a young-ster can squeeze this object, or use something else, like a ball, that fits in the hand. As with many of our other Anger Managers, energy is diverted into something that cannot harm an angry teen or others.

Illustration: Fred had a fight with Louis. He is told to try to resolve the situation by talking with Louis in the dean's office. As he is about to enter the office, Louis turns around and makes a fist. His back is to the dean, who doesn't see this gesture. Fred is feeling his anger resurfacing. He puts his hand in his pocket where he has a rubber ball. He opens and closes his hand around it many times and feels himself start to calm down. Fred enters the office, sits down, gets comfortable in the chair, smiles and says, "Let's talk about ways for me and Louis to squash this problem." Louis frowns and then both young men discuss the situation.

Take a Bubble Bath or Shower

Explanation: With this Anger Manager, a teen can use the warmth or coolness of the water in a bath or shower to help relax his/her body, creating a feeling of calmness.

Look at Your Angry Face in the Mirror

Explanation: An A.M.P. Program participant who was told by her boyfriend to take this action suggested this idea. When this young woman did, she found herself smiling at this image. This is something many young people asked to have explained, and once it was, they saw its value. Try it yourself and see if you crack up when you see this image.

Think How Someone You Care About Would Handle the Situation

Explanation: Using this idea relies teens on having calmed down after an incident has occurred. In the chapter on past experiences, adolescents were asked to describe how others reacted in similar situations that had positive results. You use the same idea with people youngsters respect and have spoken about. They are role models to teens who they respect and feel know the right things to do.

Visualizations

Explanation: There are a variety of visualizations that have been used and suggested. These can occur in two forms. The first is as a mental picture. However, for some adolescents this is something they cannot do. The second method is for young people to have actual pictures of whatever or whomever can help them remain calm. These are more concrete images. They may be personal photographs of special people, places or events, or pictures found in magazines, on posters or drawings they themselves have made. These tools are another way to help teens dissipate the angry energy they experience.

Illustration: Mark had a big fight with his girlfriend, Jessica, over her wanting to spend more time with her friends. Nasty things were said between them and they both walked away really upset. When Mark got about ten blocks away from where the argument occurred, he began to smile. He stopped, reached in his pocket for his wallet, and pulled out a picture of himself and Jessica. They were holding each other and smiling. This is the way he realized they had been throughout their relationship. With this image and thought Mark decided that he would call Jessica later on.

Visualize Anger

Explanation: Adolescents are told to describe what anger looks like. They are told that this image not only is something they see, but also feel, smell and touch. Some of the images that were described by young people who experienced this method as a group activity were volcanoes, bombs going off, the Hulk, a boiling pot (pressure cooker). To start young people thinking in this direction use the illustration of a fire. Have them tell you its color, size, how it feels, the heat coming from it, even seeing the devastation it causes when a building is ablaze, something that makes this image sharper and more recognizable. The more vivid the description the easier it is to see.

This particular visualization can be used as a preventative tool. Whatever image of anger adolescents participating in the A.M.P. Program developed, they didn't want their anger to reach the point where they became the person, place or thing that was pictured.

Illustration: Frank had been speaking with his mom about being able to go with his friends clubbing. She didn't want to hear about it and left the room. Frank began to feel his anger building. He went to his room. He couldn't calm down. As he was about to come out and verbally charge at his mother, he imagined the Incredible Hulk, all green and big, with his mouth wide open. Frank shook his head and thought, "If I get that angry I won't get a chance to go to a club until I am fifty." He decided to wait a little to calm down and then try to approach his mom about this subject.

Visualize the Outcome of the Behavior

Explanation: This idea is similar to envisioning the devastation that occurs before a severe rainstorm takes place, which is, picturing flooded homes and roads and fallen trees. The idea of this Anger Manager is to have teens create a picture of what would happen once their anger is released. This approach is a variation of the Is It Worth It? method, or as another way for adolescents to view the consequences of their behavior. It requires youngsters to be calm enough to be able to use before reacting to a situation. This idea can also be used as a preventative measure once a situation has gone badly.

Illustration: Joey's guidance counselor, Mr. Donaldson, told him that he didn't have a chance to get into his first choice college. Joey knew that many of his friends were planning to attend this school, and he would be the only one who wouldn't be able to go there. He felt as if Mr. Donaldson didn't really care about him or how he felt because Mr. Donaldson didn't give him an explanation or bother to know how Joey felt. His anger was beginning to build. He decided he was going to let Mr. Donaldson know how lousy a counselor he was without holding back any feelings. He was about to go to his guidance counselor, when a picture of how this situation would play out came popping into his mind. He saw himself coming into Mr. Donaldson's office, slamming the door and starting to yell, using whatever language came out of his mouth, and then get right into his guidance counselor's face. The next thing he saw was some security people coming through the door, grabbing him and bringing him to the dean's office, where his mother would be called and he wouldn't hear the end of it. It would also mean he might be blowing his chance of graduating, which would get his mom even crazier.

He decided to approach Mr. Donaldson on another day, when he was calmer, and maybe the guidance counselor had more time to talk.

Visualize a Calm Scene

Explanation: In describing a calm scene, as we did earlier in picturing an image of anger, have a young person use as many senses as possible.

Illustration: In describing a beach, use the warmth of the sun on a person's face and the sand underfoot, the sounds of the waves softly breaking onto the beach. Add to this picture seagulls flying and the sounds they make. You may wish to throw in, as some young men have indicated, a young woman, with a nice figure wearing a sexy bathing suit, or for the young ladies, a "hunk" of a guy, and you have a completed picture.

This technique can also be used to describe another peaceful scene, a place a teen went on a great vacation, pictures of someone special, a brother or sister, a grandparent, niece or nephew, girlfriend or boyfriend, or someone who they shared some pleasant experiences. I remember telling some young people of the picture I had on my desk in my office of my oldest grandson that I looked at many times when I was upset.

Pretend to Blow Up a Balloon

Explanation: Have a young people imagine that they are blowing up a balloon, or have them actually force air out of their mouths as if they are really inflating a balloon. Here we are attempting to have teens divert "angry energy" into a non-harmful visualization.

Illustration: Angie wasn't chosen as a cheerleader. She was really upset and felt that she performed better than some of the other girls who were chosen. Seeing this, a teacher who was the assistant cheerleading coach went over to her. She knew Angie and told her to try something different to get over this disappointment. This teacher told Angie to close her eyes and pretend she had a balloon in her hand and needed to blow up this balloon for one of her best friend's birthday, only it was a really hard thing to do. She knew that her friend was coming and the balloon needed to be filled to give to her with some presents. After Angie did this, she smiled and said, "Thanks Ms. Taylor, I feel a little bit calmer and didn't let making the team make me as upset.

Imagine the Anger Draining Out of Your Body

Explanation: Earlier, we discussed, the physical effects that anger has on a teen's body. These included facial muscles tensing, faces feeling flushed, blood pressure rising or heart rates increasing. Taking this idea one step further, let's look at the physical site of the anger as the starting point for draining this feeling out of an adolescent's body. For this exercise have a young person close their eyes and begin the process.

The first thing that the teen is instructed to do is to see anger as a foreign object that is going to be leaving their body by following a specific exit route. Have him/her describe the size, color and shape of this object. One object to use is a red ball, the size of a handball.

Once this is done, describe several ways an adolescent can have the anger exit his/her body. The journey may go down through the stomachs down the legs and out through the toes. It may go up through the chest, out to the arms and leave the body through the fingers, or out through the butt. It may also go up and out through the top of the head or through the ears. The road taken does not matter.

For some teens their imaginations are strong and vivid. For these adolescents this Anger Manager can work really well. For others, drawing a map of the path this object is going to take is another way to use this tool.

Visualize Pleasant Experiences

Explanation: This involves having adolescents think of specific times that brings a smile to their face. Some of the A.M.P. Program participants described swimming, riding in or driving a fast car, hugging someone special, or shopping in an unusual place, such as Paris. Try to have young people describe other people involved, sights, sounds and physical sensations to make this experience really clear.

For teens who find mental imagery hard to do, suggest that they look at pictures from scrapbooks, photographs they have taken, those that they appear in, or others found in magazines, or from other sources like travel brochures, videos or posters they have.

Caucus

Explanation: This particular Anger Manager involves the use of one or more third party who is not part of the situation. It is a method for teens to enlist the aid of peers to prevent situations from escalating. These helpers can be friends of the individuals involved in the conflict or people who don't want to see a situation getting farther out of hand, resulting in extended hostilities and severe consequences.

Young people who were peer mediators suggested this Anger Manager. A mediator's job is to help other adolescents work out their problems without taking sides or making judgments. This is a structured process facilitated in a particular setting, such as in an office or special area set aside for performing this task. This kind of third party intervention can also be done in less formal ways in different places that are convenient at the time. These may include stairways, hallways, empty rooms or deserted areas in playgrounds.

Explanation: During the course of a conversation between two young people, one of them starts to get more upset. This escalation in feeling is noticeable by one of the teen's loud tone of voice, reddening face, clenched fist, or movement closer to the other person. Once this behavior starts to take place an adolescent has to be removed from the area to have a chance to chill out. During this time, the third person goes out with the individual whose anger is rising to try to find out what is causing this reaction. Time and space is provided for this person to calm down, with the opportunity to talk about what's happening with them. This alone time with someone who is upset and removed from a situation is known as a caucus.

Illustration: Pat and Dave are arguing in the hallway in school. Dave's friend James saw this going on and heard Dave's voice getting louder and his face turning red. James knew that the next step to come would be a fight. He takes Dave into a nearby stairwell and starts to find out what is going on. Dave tells him Pat keeps going on and on about being a better athlete and how great he is and tells James, "I had enough of his bragging. Then he started pointing at me to his friends who began to laugh. That was it. I was about to make him shut up when you stepped in." After a few minutes Dave calmed down. Most of the crowd had dispersed. Later on that day, knowing that Dave and Pat had been good friends, James told Dave to try talking to Pat, and let him know what was going on. James added, "He probably thought he was just joking and didn't realize how seriously you took it until you started getting heated. With other people around he knew he would have to do something if you kept up yelling at him. That's the reason I wanted you to come with me."

Chapter Summary

Many of the Anger Managers that have been described are variations on a theme. The different kinds of visualizations fit this category. Another idea for you to keep in mind is that some of these tools can be used in combination with others. For example, deep breathing, self-talk or counting can be used to calm adolescents down, and then methods such as, "Is it worth it?" the "I statement," "Tell others what bothers you. Be direct, specific and polite" can be used to express a teen's anger without creating more hassles. What Anger Managers to use with a specific adolescent is your decision to make. The methods described above came from adolescents who participated in the A.M.P. Program, some of whom facilitated peer workshops. Peer endorsements and experiences with these tools make them more appealing to a young person. They can be influential in having them try some of these tools. Your knowledge of a teen is also something to take into account when suggesting different Anger Managers. There may be some of these ideas that you know in advance get the "No Way!" response, or are things you have tried without success. There are others you aren't sure will work, but have the feeling that they might work. Try them! You may also have your own ideas on how to use some of these methods. Follow your instincts!

The explanations that were given described what the Anger Managers did, along with precautions to be aware of when using them. The illustrations that were given described situations using particular methods, and provided ways to explain how they worked to a teen.

There is an expanded list of Anger Managers in the Information Booster section that can be found at the end of the book. This larger list is overwhelming for many people to try to absorb at once. Young people pared it down to include only those methods they felt their peers would be more likely to use. The bigger document is something that initially has to be skimmed over. As this is being done, try to locate additional anger managers that you feel can be helpful in working with a particular teen. Once you have chosen these, look at the explanations. The better you understand them, the easier it will be for you to describe them to an adolescent.

There is another "Tool Kit" that addresses Anger Management for adults, found in the "Information Booster" section of this book. Whether you are a parent or responsible for an adolescent in some other way, it is easy to get drawn in, or let your own feelings get the better of you. This list of Anger Managers will help you cope with your own hot buttons.

Chapter Nine

Matching Anger Managers to Situations

This chapter focuses on applying the Anger Managers that have been explained to situations that take place in different settings, involving different relationships. Keep in mind that these scenarios can be done with individuals, groups or classes of teens. The events that are presented come from participants in the Anger Management Power (A.M.P.) Program and involve real-life situations that have occurred. The adolescents who described these incidents were instructed that they had to have been personally experienced, or witnessed, so that they could see the applicability of the different Anger Managers to situations that actually took place. The events that these young people noted cover many important parts of teen life. These areas include, the need for recognition, belonging, security, safety and freedom; values they have; expectations of and from young people; respect, relationships, and the treatment many youths feel they are not getting or don't deserve. Some of the incidents described may be familiar from your personal experiences with teens, while others were chosen because they were common to this age group. The more adolescents can relate to these situations, the better chances are that they will be willing to work with them.

The first step in this process is to choose the Anger Managers that can work best in each of six categories of conflict. This decision is based on the knowledge of a teens' responses to some of the approaches you've already used, on ideas you think will work, or on their own decisions as to which of these methods they feel would work in the incidents and relationships that are described. There are six categories of situations that are going be used with this activity. These include incidents that occur in families, those involving peers and close relationships, and those found in neighborhood, school, and work settings. By providing these "dry runs" you are giving adolescents the opportunity to test ideas for handling situations that can arise in their lives before attempting to use them. This is a step that can give youngsters the confidence that certain methods have a chance of working with similar events that occur.

How to choose which of these groups to use, can be determined in several ways. This decision represents the second step to take in this part of the learning process.

Choosing Categories of Situations to Use

One way to find out the kinds of situations young people are willing to look at is to give them a list of categories to choose from. This method was used with groups of teens in classroom settings. These students were asked to come up with authentic incidents that took place with particular people in whichever area they chose.

Another approach to use is to have teens select the environment in which they encounter the most difficulties. This choice can be based on their need to show strength, that is the need to prove to others that they cannot be taken advantage of. These incidents can occur in their homes, schools, neighborhoods, or in places where youngsters find the most difficult people to deal with. Wherever this situation is found, respect is often the hot button that is pushed.

A teen's choice of a particular area can also be based on interest. Two of the most popular of these groups expressed by the A.M.P. Program participants were intimate relationships—that is, those involving boyfriends or girlfriends, and those dealing with family members. Having conversations centering on adolescents' interests becomes one of the most productive ways to get them engaged in this activity.

Some groups of A.M.P. Program participants were given a specific area to focus on. This method was more expedient with young people who were either undecided or unwilling to participate in this part of the experience.

Another possible way to select a situation category to use with teens is to have them volunteer a situation that they wrote down on a document known as the Situation Description Recorder (SDR). This tool contains three elements:

> The situation that caused the conflict,
>
> The people involved in it—that is, their relationship to the adolescent—parent, brother/sister, friend, associate, girlfriend/boyfriend, teacher, co-worker, boss, or manager,
>
> The setting—where the incident took place.

A copy of this tool is found in the Information Booster section at the end of this book.

Another way to use the SDR is to have teens write any situation that comes to mind. Once this is done, the categories can be placed on a board, chart, or as part of a Power Point presentation, with the adolescents choosing the grouping that fits the situation.

A final method for using this tool involves young people orally describing something that comes to mind, using the format of the SDR. This alternative is used without listing the categories. It also can be used with groups where time is limited, or when a teen is resistant to writing.

The application of Anger Managers to real-life situations is the primary goal, not the form that these methods take.

Deciding Which Anger Managers to Use with Specific Situations

The next step to take is to look over the two lists of Anger Managers. Deciding which ones to expose a youngster to is based on two suggestions. One choice is for you to read the specific situations and determine which Anger Managers you think are most applicable. Once you have these methods listed, have the teen choose which one he/she thinks is applicable to the situation you are analyzing. Another way to make this decision is to expose an adolescent to the entire list and have them pick the methods that they think would be useful.

There are two lists. The first, shorter one, was developed by other teens, who felt these methods would be most acceptable to peers. The second document contains over forty more anger managers. This list, also found in the Information Booster section of the book, can be used when youngsters cannot find methods to use with specific situations, or when you feel the need to expose them to additional ideas.

After deciding which method to use, the next task is to know how to explain the Anger Managers that are unclear to a young person, or those that you feel need clarification. The Anger Journal, I Statement, Self-Talk and Affirmations, Pretend to Blow Up A Balloon, Look at Yourself in the Mirror, are examples of Anger Managers that need further explanation. With teens, as well as many adults who I've given this training to, asking to explain different Anger Managers was a sign that they were dumb. You can try to put aside this idea by saying, "Smart people want information, like finding out what Self-Talk is, and ask it to be explained." However, even with this kind of positive rationale for asking a question, some participants still remain uninformed. For these individuals, explaining the methods listed above is helpful and warranted.

If you aren't sure how to describe some of these methods to adolescents, don't try to bluff your way through an answer. If you do, it can cause irreparable damage to their trust. If this happens, an unnecessary roadblock to this process is created, and whatever progress has been made can be brought to a screeching halt. The point of this warning is to see how important learning to correctly describe each Anger Manager is. If you are unsure, simply don't choose that particular method, or be honest, and tell a youngster that you are also unclear about it, and find a different Anger Manager to use. You can also contact me for further clarification of any of these terms at peacefulyouth422@yahoo.com.

Noting the Settings, Relationships, and Levels of Anger to Use Within Situation Categories

When dealing with the categories of situations, it is important to note the settings in which they occur, the kind of relationships that exist between teens and the other people, as well as the level of anger that these incidents create. The first two elements provide clues to what Anger Managers to use. As an example, in a situation that occurs in front of peers in a public setting, such as a school, a basketball court, a mall, or in front of family members, face-saving needs to be taken into account. The question you should ask yourself is, "How can adolescents in these settings, with these people around, find ways of handling a situation peacefully and still protect their image?" This a common need for a youngster. Time and thought must go into solving this puzzle prior to working with teens.

The last factor is the intensity of anger created by a situation. This can be determined by asking how angry specific situations would make them. The Anger Scale ranging from a little upset to really angry can be used to gauge their reactions. The higher the intensity of this feeling, the more beneficial it is to explore particular situations.

Another approach to use with knowing the strength of the anger felt by teens created by individual situations is to view those that yield the least intense reaction first. By doing this, adolescents are able to find success more easily in applying Anger Managers to incidents. From this point, young people can work their way toward finding similar results with more difficult situations. Being aware of these variables creates a better chance of using this process successfully.

With groups of teens, these scenarios can be acted out. When they are, the actors are told to choose Anger Managers to use in their scenes. Their peers are asked to identify which tools were used in the role-plays, and offer suggestions of what other methods they think could have been used to resolve the conflict. This is something many adolescents really enjoy seeing done and is a great educational tool. It's a form of entertainment, something many youngsters find helpful to the learning process.

However, many times young people feel too embarrassed to act out these scenes. If this is the case, incidents can be analyzed and treated the same way as they may have been if they were acted out. The format of the Situation Description Recorder becomes useful with this kind of treatment.

You can use the scenarios dealing with family relationships, as well as those in the other categories as trial balloons. They are objective means of exploring the kinds of situations in which a youngster often finds himself or herself involved. They can also be used as away to understand the types of things that arise with a teen, and to help him/her see how these incidents can be handled in positive ways.

Explanations of approaches that can be used in situations occurring in families are given after each of the first three incidents is described. Don't be concerned with going through every situation in every group. Focus on the categories and incidents that you think are most relevant to an adolescent.

Situations within Families

Situation 1: Samantha wants to go to a party. Her mother says "No," because her room is not clean and she always comes in past her curfew. Samantha tells her mom she doesn't care about her happiness, so she makes up different [expletive] excuses for her not to go somewhere to enjoy herself. Samantha's mom says, "You can add disrespect to my list of reasons for you not going places you want to go," and walks away from Samantha.

People Involved: Mother and Daughter
Setting: Inside their house

Approaches to Resolving this Situation Peacefully

One approach to use with this situation is to ask an adolescent, "What does the mother want from Samantha?" Some possible responses are:

"She wants her to be the perfect daughter."
"She wants Samantha to know that her mom's the boss."
"She wants her to remain a virgin."

With these replies, acceptance of these remarks (not agreement with them) is important. Once you've said, "These could be reasons for Samantha's mom to prevent her from going to the party." Add, "What are some other reasons her mom won't let her go to the party?"

Other possibilities include:

"Samantha needs to know what she has to do to be able to
    go places and do the things she wants."
"Her mother wants her to show she can be responsible by
    telling Samantha two ways she can prove this to her."

If they can't think of any, providing other choices for them to consider is helpful. One theme to follow through with, whether it was the reason given by a teen, or your suggestion, is responsibility. Discussing its role in helping Samantha get to the party is one approach to take. If cleaning her room and coming home when her mom asks are the reasons for her mother's response, then ways of showing that Samantha can do these things is a path for her to take to get to what she wants.

Another area to explore is to find out what additional information is needed that can be helpful in dealing with this situation. For example, knowing when the party is taking place can be important for Samantha. If the party is some time away, weeks or a month, she may have an opportunity to prove by her actions that she can be responsible and offer her mom the chance to change her mind. If a youngster doesn't see the timing of the party as something that can be helpful to Samantha, asking, "How could knowing when the party is work for Samantha in dealing with this situation?" can help him/her become aware of this point.

The main focus of this discussion is to have teens get the full picture of the situation. This global view takes into account the perspectives of both parties involved in the situation. By exposing the different elements that can be involved, you are giving adolescents some additional ideas on how to resolve conflicts. It is a way for them to think beyond their own perspectives. Whether it is in this example, or any of the others that are provided, be confident that by giving a young people the opportunity to gain enough experience and knowledge about conflicts, they can learn to deal more effectively with them.

Before having a teen try to apply a method he/she thinks is useful in this situation, have them consider who is the most upset in this conflict. After making this decision, they can decide how to prevent the mother or Samantha from getting more upset, and describe why this needs to be done. An idea worth repeating is that when people are upset, they first have to calm down before they can deal with a situation. With this thought in mind, the first step in dealing with this incident is to have a youngster come up with ways for Samantha and her mom to calm down, or at least not get more upset. If the situation is acted out, some of these tools may have been used and observed. Depending on whether a teen viewed Samantha as the one more upset, or her mother, several different Anger Managers can be used. These include:

- Taking deep breaths.
- Counting.

- Giving the other person space.
- Staying calm.
- Listening to music.
- Chanting a phrase.
- Asking them, "Is It Worth It?"

In this example, have an adolescent try to see things from the mother's perspective. This goes beyond the idea of responsibility. The question, "How do you think the mother was feeling?" makes this point. The use of empathy, a method described in the larger list of Anger Managers, that is, putting yourself in the other person's place, is one possibility. It is often a real "mind-blower" for a young person when they are asked to reverse the roles of a parent and a child, or for that matter, with any adult. Often, when people who are upset are shown that others understand where they are "coming from," the intensity of the situation is decreased. In this case, having Samantha try to understand the frustration her mother has of seeing the same things happening over and over again, or the feeling that whatever she tries is just not helping Samantha, are things that can show that the daughter understands why her mom is upset. This is not an easy thing for a teen to do, and often isn't something they want to do. However, it's worth a try.

The next step is to ask, "What do you think Samantha could do with this information to help change her mom's mind?" As a rule of thumb with close relationships, the "I Statement" can be used. Samantha's feelings can be expressed as, "I feel angry when you tell me I can't go somewhere, because I am not a little girl or someone you can't trust." Here a dialogue can develop as the mother describes when she lost her trust and how her daughter can earn it back. Allowing Samantha to go to the party may not be something that can happen, but it leaves the door open for her to attend other activities and have the freedom to do other things. It takes a lot of work and a willingness to let reason and understanding take a front seat, along with the desire to strengthen the relationship. It also takes persistence and a readiness to believe that a relationship with parents is something many adolescents really want to have, in spite of bravado, or statements like, "I don't need her/him/them!" Trying different things and making changes is uncomfortable and awkward. If this is something different than what has not worked before, there is nothing to lose, and a stronger relationship to gain.

Situation 2: Steven gets home late after a day out with his girlfriend and hanging out with some of his friends. Once he gets home, his father begins to argue with him without letting Steven explain why he was late. Steven yells back, "You never want to hear what I have to say! All you want to do is yell at me! Then he walks away muttering a bunch of expletives at his father.

People Involved: Father and Son

Setting: Inside their house

Approaching the Situation: As we did with the first scenario, having a young person look at the teen's behavior from the parent's perspective can be helpful. Asking, "Why do you think the boy's dad is so pissed? serves this purpose. You may be surprised at some of the reasons adolescents come up with. See if any of these remarks are among the responses that you get from them. From the predictable:

> "He has to be on his son's case about something."
> "He doesn't care about anything the boy has to say."
> "He is just an [expletive]."
> "He has a date and that [expletive] is more important than his kid's safety."
> "When he has to do something, or go somewhere, it doesn't matter where or when, he goes and does what he wants. It is always more important than what his son wants to do."

Other statements may include ideas such as:

> "He's scared something happened to his son."

"He thinks his son just doesn't care."
"He's worried that he'll get blamed if something happens
        to his kid."

These kinds of statements provide insight into youngsters' perceptions of their fathers or other males in their lives, in addition to their ideas about this particular situation. Using objective means like these scenarios often has the effect of getting teens to relate to similar things that happen in their lives. Whatever their response is to seeing the father's side of this situation, you can get some ideas about adolescents from it.

Keep in mind the greater the number of views that can be brought into a particular example, the broader the understanding a youngster can develop, the greater the chances of succeeding in handling situations in positive ways.

Bringing techniques that are important for Steven to get control over himself, before responding to his dad's behavior, is important. These can include, deep breathing, counting, or any of the other tools that help de-escalate the strength of this teen's feeling. The idea is to have adolescents see ways to stay in control of their feelings, and empower themselves to be regarded as responsible problem-solvers. This is also one way to increase young people's self-esteem.

Finding Anger Managers that can be used to express feelings without, in this case, damaging the relationship between Steven and his father, or escalating the situation, becomes the next task to accomplish. Asking teens how this can be done starts the conversation in this direction. Have adolescents come up with ideas on how to prevent the situation between Steven and his father from getting out of hand. Youngsters might shrug their shoulders, or use the famous, "I don't know." Don't be tempted to give your thoughts just yet. Use the pregnant pause—that is, let the discomfort of silence do its job. If you don't want to take this path, give some clues. One way to do this is to use previous situations or experiences a youngster has dealt with or described. You can brainstorm possibilities, or have teens choose Anger Managers from the list you have put together, or from one they might be developing. Other ideas that have popped into mind during this kind of discussion can also be used. Try them.

Knowing that the father keeps going on and on without letting the son explain himself, ask, "What can Steven get out of it if he lets his father finish saying what he is going to say?" By doing this, you are letting adolescents know that Steven can gain something by doing this. At this point, ask which Anger Manager uses this idea. One response can be, giving people a chance to express their anger without saying anything, in other words just listen to what people have to say (an anger manager found in the larger list), or any other ideas a youngster feels would work. It is good to have responses to questions you ask in mind, in case they don't have, or want to give any of their own answers. The question, "How can not trying to explain his lateness until his father is through yelling be helpful to the son?" brings us back to the idea that there's something beneficial to Steven by hearing his father out. If you don't get any answers, "What would happen if the Steven continued to try talking and his father kept on going on and on, and didn't want to hear anything his son had to say?" One possibility they may see is that if Steven tries to tell his father the reason, knowing that the father will go on anyway, he won't be heard and will wind up angrier and more frustrated.

After this response, ask, "What question might Steven ask himself that might be helpful?" Whether a teen can come up with it, totally has no clue, or doesn't make an attempt to answer even after a long silence, continue keeping them going this way by using the idea of the consequence of being frustrated and getting angrier. After this discussion, whether it's one-sided or not, suggesting the "Is It Worth It?" Anger Manager is one idea that an adolescent may find useful in this situation. Discussing how it can be helpful to Steven takes you one step further.

Two ideas may come into play, whether they are from a response to this question or after more discussion with a youngster. The first has to do with finding out what's bothering the father. By doing this, Steven can show that he is trying to understand his dad's concern. The second thought takes into account that people who are able to express themselves without interruption are more likely to listen to the people who heard what they had to say. In this case, Steven listened while his father let his feelings out. Once he felt that his son listened and understood what he was talking about, he would be more likely to hear what Steven had to say.

Some of you may not think that young people are capable of understanding this idea. To make sure they do, turn the tables around and ask, "When someone hears you out, and shows they understand what you are saying, how do you treat what they have to say to you?" In other words, "Do you want to listen to them?" then ask, "Why?"

If there is a negative response, toss this idea out and go to the next possibility. Focus on Steven again and ask, "If the father finishes yelling, without his son getting into it, what can Steven get out of it?" Peace and quiet is one possible response. If not, add, "Wouldn't having his father off his case without any further hassle be worthwhile to Steven?" This statement illustrates your ability to try to see things through a teen's eyes, demonstrating empathy. Although this idea may not elicit a response, it is another way to help adolescents see advantages in not reacting to particular situations. The Anger Managers "Avoidance" (another found in the larger listing) and "Is it worth it?" are also useful in this case. Avoidance is a temporary measure. Situations sometimes require both parties to have time and space in order to deal with them productively.

Finding out what a teen thinks Steven wants from his father is of great value. Responses may range from:

> The different reminders that are being provided throughout this book need to be repeatedly stressed. They are ways to make sure ideas are communicated clearly. As an educator, I believe the more someone hears and sees things, the better the chances are of these ideas sticking in his/her mind.

"He may want his father to hear why he was late."

"He wants his dad to give him a chance to explain himself," (recognition for his thoughts and actions are things to bring out).

"He wants to apologize," (being responsible enough to realize he was wrong for being late and not letting his dad know).

Being Direct, Specific and Polite, is another method that can be used in this situation. One way to start using this approach is by asking the question, "What do you want?" Whether it is Steven in this situation asking his father this question, or directed toward other people who show that they are really upset, it is something that can be an invaluable and expedient tool.

How the "What do you want" question is asked is important. Whether it's in the tone of voice, (calm or loud, honest or sarcastic) or in the body language, (with arms folded, and glaring eyes, or with a relaxed body posture, where face muscles are loose, and eyes have soft gaze), will determine the manner this question will be answered, and the direction a situation will go. Knowing about non-verbal communication is something that can greatly benefit young people. Being aware of how it can affect others or themselves in difficult situations is an important skill for them to have. It is not easy to learn, but worthwhile to teach.

Situation 3: Tara took her sister Toni's jeans without asking. When Toni was about to go out, she wanted that particular pair of jeans. She couldn't find it in her closet. The next day she saw the jeans on Tara's bed. Toni flipped out and started yelling at Tara, calling her a thief and a selfish [expletive].

People Involved: Two sisters

Setting: The girls' bedroom.

Resolving the Issue: Start with Tara's reason for not telling that she was borrowing Toni's jeans. Many times there is only one side that an adolescent sees in a situation—theirs. Some reasons for this behavior are expressed as:

"She was afraid her sister wouldn't give them to her."
"Her sister is a mean and selfish [expletive]."

"She borrowed other things before without asking and was
threatened and told if she did, she'd catch a beating."
"She didn't think her sister would mind or care."
"She thought her sister wouldn't find out."

Exploring these possibilities may also give a young person more clues on how to deal with this situation. Bringing up the fact that Toni was upset when this happened and asking a teen "Why?" takes them in another direction. This question sounds really simple to answer on the surface, but it's not. "Because Tara took her jeans without asking," is the most obvious and probably the simplest response. However, there's more to the meaning of this behavior than meets the eye. Asking an adolescent, "What is Toni really mad about?" or "What other reason can you think of that can cause Toni to be really angry at Tara?" may start them thinking of more "important" causes of anger. Privacy, trust and honesty may be among the responses they give or ideas you may present as this situation is explored.

> Privacy, trust and honesty are at the root of many conflicts that occur in different relationships. By understanding that these values may be at the heart of many situations, and by using the appropriate Anger Managers for expressing this feeling, closer bonds between people can be created.

Empathy is one of the tools that can be used in having a youngster try to see this situation from both sisters' points of view. Here you can have him or her put themselves in either sister's place and try to see the situation from that person's point of view by coming up with a statement that shows they understand the other person:

Tara: "By taking your jeans without asking you, it was like I was not someone close to you, someone who cares about you, stealing from you." This illustrates how empathy can be used to express Toni's point of view.

181

Now, let's look at it from Tara's perspective "You thought I'd get mad at you like I did when you wanted to wear my bracelet," or "You know that I don't like to share any of my stuff with you," are two remarks that Toni could make in trying to understand Tara's side. In addition to using empathy, have teens come up with other ideas on how else the two sisters could explain how they felt about this situation.

Different ways of having them calm down before dealing with the jeans problem may be suggested. Asking adolescents whether or not they felt Toni and Tara were ready to discuss this situation is the first step to take. If they answer, "Yes," the question, "When something like this happens, can people deal with it when they are both upset?" opens up another avenue of exploration.

Follow this by asking, "What can be helpful to getting them to calm down?" Once some suggestions are made, ask, "How else can Toni and Tara let each other know how they felt?" Each hearing the other out can serve as one method. Using the I Statement would be another way. In this case, ask, "What would each sister say?" For example:

Tara could say, "When I borrowed your jeans, I was afraid to ask you, because you yelled at me when I asked you to lend me something last week."

Toni could say, "I felt angry when you borrowed my jeans without asking, because it was dishonest and I have always been able to trust you before."

Situation 4: Jacqueline comes into her house after she had a fight with her boyfriend, slams the door and starts cursing. Her mother tells her not to make so much noise when she comes into the house and to cut out the swearing. Jacqueline starts yelling at her mother and tells her, "I'll slam the door if I feel like it! This is my house too and I'll do what I feel like. What's the matter, you never heard those words?" The mother starts yelling back and telling her daughter that she'd better show her respect if she knows what's good for her.

People Involved: Mother and Daughter

Setting: Living room in their house.

The Elaboration-Demonstration-Practice (E-D-P) Method

Now that you have been guided through an analysis of the first three situations involving family members, this last scenario will be left open for you to analyze. As a guide to accomplishing this task, a step-by-step description of the process used to explore other situations will follow. This particular method is known as the Elaboration-Demonstration-Practice (E-D-P) process. It is something that will lay the groundwork for you to deal with the remaining categories and situations as well.

In the final situation involving family members, the elaboration phase takes place as elements that come into play for Jacqueline and her mother are discussed. It is during this first part of the method that the perceptions of the parties' behavior and concerns are brought up. This is done through questioning. Asking, "What did the mother think of Jacqueline's behavior? How did Jacqueline see her mother's behavior?" illustrates this point. When no or minimal responses are given, offer some possibilities that may be on the mother and daughter's mind. "Do you think the mom felt disrespected? Do you think Jacqueline felt her mom didn't care what was bothering her?" describe some conversation jump-starters.

Before moving to the next stage of this process, having teens look at where situations take place is especially important. The events described in the family category all took place in the privacy of the home with no other family members present. The setting had no bearing on these particular situations. However, if they took place in a more public setting, that is, one where others witnessed the conflict, then other factors come into play and need to be considered. For adolescents, the idea of not appearing soft, weak or as a person others will take advantage of, is something to discuss. Their desires to be recognized as capable, strong, intelligent, or any number of other attributes have to be met. If a situation makes them look weak, stupid, or feel as if they are being put down, it often causes them to react strongly. The question of how to get someone out of a situation so that they don't lose face—look weak, dumb or incapable of handling the other person's attack on them has to be answered. Ways of helping a youngster to calm down and then resolve a situation without causing damage to their image enters the picture. It is something to be considered as part of the demonstration phase of this method.

The demonstration part is the application of different Anger Managers to the situation. By choosing different ways the mother and Jacqueline can handle this feeling, teens demonstrate that they understand the situation and have a sense of what might work to resolve the problem. Focusing on having both parties calm down, find an approach that will help them understand each other, and then discover a way to resolve the issue, helps youngsters demonstrate the knowledge they have gained.

The final stage of this process—practice—involves teens applying the information and skills they have acquired. It occurs after you have worked with them at home, in an office or other setting, and new situations arise. Adolescents can either show they can handle these more recent episodes in a positive way, or they need to look at what went wrong. At this point, it's back to the drawing board, with a review of the situation with ways to come up with additional methods to handle it. These skills take time for teens to learn and try. They require patience and a willingness to try, try, again. A teen will express their frustration by commenting, "I tried, it didn't work, and so what's the use? To this response, asking them, "When you tried to do something new like ride a bicycle, drive a car, learn something different in school, did you quit?" can be helpful. This point is made for them to accept or reject. If they say, "Yes," then talk about how they finally overcame their earlier frustration. Prior to letting them practice their skills in this area, you can remind them that sometimes something doesn't work when people first try it. Sometimes what was tried wasn't done correctly, or wasn't something to attempt in a particular situation. Teens need to know that if something doesn't work, they can come to you to try to figure out what went wrong.

This is the method that has been used with the first three scenarios, and can be beneficial to use with the events described in the remaining categories of situations. The E-D-P process is something that is used to train A.M.P. Program facilitators and is an effective training strategy.

The remaining categories of relationships and situations represent areas that have been described by adolescents as conflicts that have occurred between themselves and others, or have occurred in places where they or their peers have gotten into the most trouble. They give you ideas of areas of difficulty for many youngsters. Based on your personal knowledge of what kind of relationships or situations a particular teen finds the most trouble, or on their preferences of subjects they want to discuss, help determine which of the following groups and events to explore.

Situations with Peers

Situation 1: Gail is upset that her best friend, Doris, who now has a boyfriend and doesn't spend any time with her.
People Involved: Two female friends
Setting: Outside a classroom in school.

Situation 2: Two best friends, Mike and Chris like the same girl and argue over who should have her. (This is a common situation for both sexes)
People Involved: Two best male friends.
Setting: School Cafeteria

Situation 3: Two close friends, Pat and Chris, are hanging out with some other friends, who are part of the "in crowd." This group of youngsters is passing around a joint. (This could be any kind of situation involving peer pressure.) Chris takes the joint. Pat doesn't want to smoke pot. Chris repeatedly tries to get Pat to smoke it. He keeps pushing and pushing Pat to do it, and threatens that their friendship is over if Chris doesn't smoke. At this point Pat is really angry at Chris.
People Involved: Two best friends and a small group of their peers.
Setting: Schoolyard.

Relationship Situations

Situation 1: Denise suspects her boyfriend Ted is cheating on her because one of her friends told her that she saw Ted with his arm around another girl.
People Involved: Girlfriend and boyfriend.
Setting: In a hallway in school.

"He Said/She said" is a common cause of conflict with teens.

Situation 2: Pete is mad at his girlfriend, Renee, because she hangs around with her "backstabbing" friends who cause her to be mad at them and take her anger out on him.
People Involved: Boyfriend and girlfriend.
Setting: Outside of school as they are walking home.

Situation 3: Patty is at a club dancing and sees her boyfriend Eddie there. She goes over to say "Hi." Then Patty notices another girl "wrapped" around her boyfriend.
People Involved: Boyfriend, girlfriend and the other girl.
Setting: A club.

Neighborhood Situations

Situation 1: While playing basketball, John deliberately hits Darnell in the face with the ball.
People Involved: John and Darnell who are on different basketball teams and six other players, one of which is Darnell's brother.
Setting: Basketball court in a neighborhood playground.

Situation 2: Larry turns his bike around and accidentally hits Steve's leg with the back tire. Larry apologizes, but Steve starts cursing at him.
   People Involved: Two teens
   Setting: On the street.

Situation 3: Janice has a party. There is a lot of loud music being played, with her many guests' voices contributing to this disturbance. Some of her neighbors complain, but Janice's party keeps going on with the same level of noise.
   People Involved: Janice, her friends and neighbors
   Setting: An apartment building.

School Situations

Situation 1: A student yells at the teacher because she told him to raise his hand after he already shouted out the correct answer.
   People Involved: Student and teacher.
   Setting: Classroom

Situation 2: Laura, Joan, and Shannon are talking about Sherry—who hears them and gets mad.
   People Involved: Three girls in a group and Sherry.
   Setting: In the girls gym locker room.

Situation 3: Maria, who is normally quiet and calm, comes into class in a bad mood because her mother is in the hospital. During class, another student, Olga says something, but the teacher, Ms. Calderon accuses Maria of talking. Maria becomes angry at Ms. Calderon's accusation, and starts yelling at her.
   People Involved: Two students and a teacher.
   Setting: Classroom

Work Situations

Situation 1: A customer in a fast food restaurant doesn't get what he ordered. One of the food servers doesn't want to deal with the customer's problem. The customer gets really angry and throws the cheeseburger he was given down on the counter.
People Involved: Customer and employee.
Setting: A fast food restaurant

Situation 2: An older co-worker, Denise, gives many of her responsibilities to a younger co-worker, Geri, who feels stressed out and explodes.
People Involved: Two workers.
Setting: In an office.

Situation 3: A customer comes up to a cashier. The cashier doesn't acknowledge him because she's too busy talking on a cell phone, (brushing her hair, talking to a coworker). Customer explodes.
People Involved: Customer and Cashier.
Setting: Any kind of store (students didn't specify for this scenario).

The goals in presenting these scenarios are to have teens relate their perceptions of the people involved in them, to look at factors that can occur, and then to give ideas on how to resolve these situations using different Anger Managers. You have been given situations involving different kinds of relationships occurring in a variety of settings. They can serve as a springboard for discussion with adolescents who may relate to these specific situations, or to similar ones they've experienced. Feel free to use any other scenarios youngsters think are useful, or those that you think would be appropriate. Whichever situations are chosen, explore them with confidence. You have the knowledge you need. Before trying to explore situations with a youngster, go back over the first three situations that were presented to you in depth, and then look over the list of Anger Managers and categorize them as de-escalators or positive ways of expressing anger. Finally, view other factors (needs, causes and effects) that can affect the way a teen handles anger.

Chapter Summary

This chapter was intended to incorporate all the elements of Anger Management that have been presented up to this point. The causes and effects of anger, the previous experiences that an adolescent has had, and different ideas for handling this emotion, came into play with the situations that were provided. The Anger Management Power (A.M.P.) Program, on which *Peace: The Other Side of Anger* is based, was designed to create a developmental method to explore this feeling. My goal in writing this book has been to provide information and ideas that can be helpful in understanding this emotion in young people, and provide the tools to empower them to handle this feeling in positive ways. Whichever ideas and suggestions are most helpful in fulfilling these objectives, are yours to choose from.

One of the things that frequently happen with many worthwhile programs is that their effectiveness is not checked. Once a teen has experienced this Anger Management training, a follow-up should be scheduled to see whether or not it has been effective. For the parents who are reading this book, you often find out the result of this kind of work with your child when he/she does something wrong. For educators and other people who work with youth, this is also often the way you find out about adolescent's behavior. Perhaps in the absence of any reported incidents comes the thought that a young person must be handling his/her anger more positively or you would have heard about it. Perhaps with all the other things going on in your personal life or profession, time to follow up, just isn't available. Whatever your thinking and circumstances are, the idea of checking on a teen proactively, that is, not waiting to hear about any incidents that may occur with them, is something that can be worthwhile and productive. For this reason, following up on work with in an adolescent in this area of their lives will be the focus of the next two chapters of this book.

Chapter Ten

Following Up on
Anger Management Training

reating awareness of the "whys" of anger, providing teens with ways of understanding the effects of this feeling, and being able to present ideas on how to resolve anger-provoking situations are all useful. However, this knowledge does no good in a vacuum. Getting adolescents to put this information to work in their everyday lives is the real test of the effectiveness of a learning experience. The "How To" of assessing your efforts with young people in dealing with anger, is the next step to take. After a period of time (around a month or so) has elapsed since you worked on the "Whys" "Effects" and "How To's" in your learning laboratory with teens, it is a good time to see the impact of this kind of training on their lives.

An Introduction to the A.M.P. Program
Feedback and Follow-Up Surveys

There are two tools that are used to gauge the effectiveness of the Anger Management Power (A.M.P.) Program on its participants. The first is "The A.M.P. Feedback Survey." This document is administered during the last part of the training. "The A.M.P. Follow-Up Survey," is the second evaluation tool used for this purpose. It is administered approximately one month after the training has been completed. Both of these documents can be found in the Information Booster section at the end of this book. If you are a parent following this process, or someone working with an individual adolescent, the questions found in each document provide worthwhile ideas for you to use and present orally.

The A.M.P. Feedback Survey focuses on the value of the ideas that were presented during this experience. The responses to the questions on this document indicate what youngsters learned, liked, disliked and how valuable they felt this experience was to them.

The A.M.P. Follow-Up Survey is a reality check. The answers to the questions found on it tell you whether teens used or didn't use the information that was presented during their learning experience on anger and Anger Management. If they responded that they didn't use this knowledge, simply ask, "What stopped you from using some of the things we talked about?" Their responses vary.

"I wanted to get you off my back."
"I didn't want you to feel bad."
"I didn't think they would work."
"I felt like my friends would think I was soft."
"I didn't get a chance."
"I didn't have any problems with anyone."

represent typical answers to this question. Whatever the reason, patience is the order of the day. Sometimes adolescents want to see your reaction, or deliberately try to push your buttons—to find out whether or not you are going to jump on them with a resounding "Why Not?", or they figure out by your tone of voice or body language that you expected more from them. They see this attitude as a sign that you either aren't really going to listen to why they didn't use this knowledge, or they are being judged as incompetent in handling anger in new ways. In other words, not using the Anger Management techniques they were exposed to is often a test of your willingness to listen and not judge them. Taking this thought one step further, if some negative kind of attention is what they expect from you, a youngster may think or feel that they shouldn't try using these tools because they represent something else to be hassled about. The bottom line in working with teens is to, keep trying! Adolescents often act in ways that lead you to believe that whatever you are trying to do with them won't ever happen. Many of their responses are bravado, or "For show." Hear them out, and then continue getting information from them.

Overcoming Adolescent Resistance to Using Anger Managers

There are several reasons why youngsters don't want to discuss their efforts to use particular Anger Managers. One possibility is that they were not used successfully. If you suspect that this is the case, say something like, "Sometimes people try things and they don't work at first," or "Things don't always turn out the way we expect them to," and wait for a response. Teens can respond by nodding, giving some other kind of non-verbal clue, or muttering almost inaudibly, "Yes." You may also get a loud, "Yeah, I tried it and it didn't work. My way of handling stuff works better." Adolescents are often resistant to change, or fear embarrassment. After they attempt to do something differently and it doesn't work, they go back to the ways they are used to doing things because they are easier to do, and are more comfortable. This is common behavior.

Acknowledge these possibilities. One way to do this is by making an attempt to compare Anger Managers to others things that were new to them at some point in their lives. Riding a bike or driving a car, are two examples. The remark, "When you learn to ride a bike or drive a car, you probably found out they weren't as easy as you thought they would be" provides this connection. "When people try doing new things they often experience some success. They may ride a bike a few feet before falling off, or drive a short distance without braking too hard or going too fast or too slow," present two ideas for young people to consider. After these remarks are made, pause to let these thoughts sink in. Regardless of any reaction they make to this analogy, they have been given the opportunity to add more ideas to their mental toolboxes.

Being embarrassed about trying out a new idea that doesn't work can also stop adolescents from trying to use Anger Managers. If you feel this might be the case, acknowledge this fear. Their response can open the way for further discussion about the recent incident that they were involved in.

Young people frequently look for instant results. Patience and encouragement are helpful to successfully use the management skills they worked on in the learning lab, regardless of any setbacks. This means going back to the drawing board with them. The point to be made is that you and they have spent time discovering different ways of handling anger, so why not try finding out why something didn't work, rather than eliminating it altogether. To accomplish this goal, ask them to describe what happened. They may remark, "That was all the time I wanted to spend trying this stuff," or offer some other form of resistance. If this is the case, bring in the consequences of how the teen handled their anger before. Explore what happened when they took care of situations in the ways they wanted. Some of the results of handling incidents their way can include, being hassled by teachers, parents or other adults or receiving payback from peers or their families or friends. If they still don't want to look at the recent situations and their failed efforts to handle them, let this discussion alone for the time being, and tell them you and they can look at it again sometime in the future, if they want. This offer provides a youngster with the power to make the decision as to whether or not to bring up the subject again.

It is also worthwhile to be alert for indirect, as well as direct indications that a teen wants to revisit situations. He/she may refer to a friend's situation and how this person handled it, or to another conflict they had, and leave the subject of handling it open. Discuss what happened and how the people involved handled the situation, focusing on what worked and didn't work to resolve the issue between them. Look with them at what methods could have been used to calm things down and settle the problem. Continue the discussion by indicating that since they brought up these other incidents, you think they might be ready to look at the situation that wasn't previously talked about. With any kind of positive response, look at what was done wrong during the situation and look at what you and the young person think can be done differently to improve the situation. If there is no indication that this is a good idea, leave the subject alone and see if this incident can be revisited at a later time.

Another approach to use in situations where Anger Managers didn't work is to use the Situation Description Recorder (SDR) format described earlier. Using this method requires examining the issue that caused the particular conflict, identifying the people involved, and describing the setting in which the incident took place. If a teen doesn't supply all of this information, simply ask for whatever details were missing, including the Anger Manager that was used, and what happened when it was tried.

Viewing a situation that went south using the E-D-P Method is another road to take. This method of evaluation is the same approach described in the first three family incidents explored in the last chapter. The first step is to elaborate on the situation to be discussed. This means looking at as many factors as possible relating to the event. The perceptions of both parties, the setting of the incident, and how close a relationship a teen had with the other person are some of the dynamics to be considered. The "How To's" have been demonstrated by words and examples used in these scenarios. The final stage is to put into practice the ideas that were discussed. This is where the recent incident that the adolescent has experienced comes into play. Let's look at an incident that occurred that wasn't handled effectively. Situation: Anthony and his girlfriend, Carolyn began arguing because he saw James with his arms around Carolyn, kissing her on the cheek. James leaves and goes down the block and disappears. Anthony starts walking toward Carolyn at a fast pace.

People Involved: The boyfriend, girlfriend and another male

Setting: Outside of school, just after dismissal.

You are speaking with Anthony, who tells you that at this point he started to take some deep breaths and slowed down his pace as he got closer to his girlfriend. As he just about reached Carolyn, she turned away from him and said he needed to calm down so they could talk about it later. Anthony described himself looking at her, shaking his head, and then reaching out for her to try to turn her around to speak with her. As Anthony did this, Carolyn turned around and told him "Get your [expletive] hands off of me!"

A whole group of their peers were nearby when Anthony and Carolyn started yelling at each other. At this point, these bystanders focused their attention on this unfolding drama to see who would win the argument.

Anthony said, "We got to talk about you and James now!"

Carolyn pulled away from him.

He tried saying to himself, "Keep calm, don't lose your cool and screw things up with Carolyn." Then in a rising tone of voice, he demanded, "We gotta take care of this business now!"

It was then that Carolyn said, "No!" and told him to, "Go [expletive] yourself!"

Anthony responded by yelling and described his girlfriend as a whore and added a few expletives.

Both walked away muttering to themselves, with Carolyn screaming back, "I don't need a jealous man in my life!" and Anthony replying "I don't need a two-timing [expletive]!"

After this incident is described, the focus needs to be on what Anthony thought went wrong. "Where did things start to go downhill with you and Carolyn?" takes the conversation in this direction. He may react to this and say, "When I saw her all cozy with James?" Responding by saying, "It certainly started this whole bad scene," shows Anthony that you are accepting his viewpoint. Add to this acknowledgment recognition of Anthony's attempts to try to prevent his anger from escalating by remarking, "You certainly tried to calm yourself down before you spoke with Carolyn when you took deep breaths, and then later when you tried to use self-talk." Then get back to the cause of his increasing anger.

Whether or not Anthony can see where he made things worse, some thoughts need to be addressed. The first involves the point when he tried to turn Carolyn's around to get her to talk things out. However, instead his girlfriend reacted. Anthony responded the same way. Instead of just remaining calm, the situation began to spiral out of control. It ended with name-calling, and both he and Carolyn walked away from each other really upset. This reaction worsened because it also involved face-saving, because the incident took place in front of peers. This is another factor that will also be explored.

> This kind of acknowledgment is something many teens have said they didn't get. In their words, "My (parents, teacher) only looks at what I do wrong. They don't ever look at when I do something right." This is also a way for an adolescents to see that you are trying to understand their viewpoint.

Finding alternative ways to prevent Anthony's anger from escalating, and ideas on how to resolve this situation without harming his relationship with Carolyn, are the next roads to follow. The question, "What other ways can you think of to deal with this difficult situation you had with Carolyn?" moves the discussion in this direction. If Anthony can't think of any ideas, stimulate his thinking, by having him try to,

- Think of ways he's dealt with situations with Carolyn or other young women in the past.
- Think of responses he's made on the A.M.P. Feedback Survey, if he was a participant in the program.
- Think of some of the things he felt might be worthwhile to try in situations that were explored during the training.

If Anthony can't remember, remind him of some of the Anger Managers his peers indicated they would use, or some of those found on a list he was given or developed on his own. Keep these ideas handy in some written form. Whatever shape this resource takes, it represents ways for Anthony to resolve this or future situations.

Refocus Anthony's attention back to the point where things got worse. Have him give reasons why this incident headed in this direction. "When I grabbed Carolyn," or "We were in public," are two reasons that the situation could have escalated. After these ideas are expressed, have Anthony try to see his responsibility in seeing the incident deteriorate. This is a challenging and worthwhile idea to pursue. More often than not, a teen blames the other person, rather than taking responsibility for having a negative role in a conflict. Keeping this idea in mind, ask "What could you have done differently at this point?" A look that could kill, or comments such as, "She's the one who made me react, it's her fault" or a "Get off my back and don't start laying a guilt trip on me!" are typical responses. Take deep breaths, count, think of something that can bring a smile to your face. This kind of reaction is predictable. After you have calmly weathered this youngster's storm with patience and acceptance, explain to him that your interest is in helping him find a way to resolve the situation, adding, that is, if it is something that he wants to do. If Anthony still objects to delving into his part in this situation, ask, "Do you still want to have a close relationship with Carolyn?" If he indicates he does, then the "Is it Worth It? Anger Manager comes into play. This can be addressed by saying, "So the way this situation went is not something you wanted, it just wasn't worth what happened." This tool has a place here, not only as a way of looking for methods to resolve this conflict, but is also something to think about when things get nasty between them again. If Anthony says, "No," take the approach that this kind of thing can happen in the future, in other relationships. This idea provides a reason to find a solution anyway. If he still doesn't want to deal with this situation, leave it alone. It may or may not come up again. Anthony will make that decision.

In the case of the, "Yes" response, suggest that Anthony let things simmer down for a while, allowing him and Carolyn to chill out enough to be able to calmly think enough about this situation to discuss it. Let Anthony know once more that his deep breathing and self-talk did calm him down before and is something that can be helpful when he and Carolyn are able to speak to each other again.

Having a teen carry a list in his wallet or in her bag is one suggestion that can be made. Asking an adolescent for their ideas on how
to remember what Anger Managers they could use in a situation
is something that is worthwhile exploring with them especially if
they can't think of any during this conversation.

Talking about when things escalated offers Anthony an opportunity to
understand why things went wrong, and how they could have been handled
differently. Whether or not he was able to remember when things started
to go badly, review his account of the situation by saying, "If I remember
correctly, you said that when you got to Carolyn and put your hand on her
shoulder and turned her around, that's when things went wrong."

Using a phrase like, "If I remember correctly" allows a teen the
freedom to agree or change some of the details. It also demonstrates a sign of humility, that is, that you possibly did not hear
or remember correctly. This kind of behavior is something adolescents feel adults rarely exhibit.

Whether Anthony can or cannot recall the behavior that set things off,
ask, "Why do you think she got upset when you did this?" Several answers
may come to mind. Among these are, "She thought I was going to hit her,"
or "Maybe Carolyn thought I was going to turn her around and start yelling at her in front of our friends. She didn't want to be embarrassed or look
like someone who would take [expletive] from her boyfriend." If Anthony
doesn't have any ideas, mention these as possible reasons for Carolyn's response. "How else could you have gotten your girlfriend's attention?" offers
another way to take this discussion. "I could have walked around and faced
her and asked her calmly and quietly if we could talk, without yelling that
we had to speak right away," represents one response that he could have

made. This approach uses the "Ask, Don't Demand" anger manager found as an Information Booster in the larger Anger Manager list at the end of the book.

Viewing other responses Carolyn might have made or thoughts she had about the reasons for her reactions is another way to take this discussion. One idea is that Carolyn knew that Anthony was really angry when he saw her with James, and was walking quickly toward her. This behavior suggested that Anthony would be too angry to deal with the situation calmly at that moment. Once again the use of empathy is helpful to a young person. When teens are able to see a situation from another person's viewpoint it can help them understand how someone else could misinterpret their actions. When Carolyn started yelling at Anthony he could have done some deep breathing, used such self-talk phrases as, "I want to stay cool," or "I want to work this out" or thought of a good time he had with his girlfriend. To prevent himself from looking "soft" in front of their friends, (an adolescent who cares about the other person or has a higher level of maturity may add, "And make sure Carolyn also doesn't lose face or get embarrassed"). Anthony, may have asked his girlfriend to go somewhere, without others around, to talk out this situation. When a discussion takes place between him and Carolyn, using the "I Statement." to express his anger over Carolyn's behavior with James can also be helpful. It may be a method that he may recognize as useful in this situation or one that you suggest. "I felt angry when I saw you acting so friendly with James because I always thought I could trust you," is a way for Anthony to express this idea. There are other Anger Managers that could be used. This is something you and a youngster can search for together.

The situation that occurred between Anthony and Carolyn shows how he took the idea of calming down before he expressed his anger and tried it. He was exposed to a lot of ideas, yet when it came to applying them, more work had to be done to help him to express his anger without escalating the situation and damaging his relationship with Carolyn. In this case, Anthony needed to see what he could have done differently and learn ways to remedy the situation with Carolyn. This knowledge can also be useful to him in handling future incidents that occur.

The A.M.P. Program Feedback Survey and the A.M.P. Follow-Up Survey can be used in different ways. The first is in written form. The opinions expressed by peers in these documents can help persuade a teen to try some of the ideas learned in their training. Written responses are also used when there isn't enough time to get each individual participant's oral responses. The knowledge gained can be used as a jumping off point for a group discussion at some later date. Oral responses to the questions found in the survey represent another way of getting information from adolescents. It gives them the opportunity to express their opinions and eliminates the "I don't like to write" resistance.

The oral responses to the questions asked on the follow-up survey can be presented differently. "*What have you tried to use that we spoke about?*" or "*What kinds of situations have occurred since we spent time talking about managing anger?* are useful questions to ask. Whatever open-ended questions you feel comfortable using will serve as a stepping-stone for gathering this information. For other teens, writing down their reactions rather than expressing them openly works best. For these adolescents, not making their opinions public to peers eliminates facing the possibility of looking "soft," "weak" or "vulnerable." The main focus is to have young people react to their experience, no matter what form they choose. Teens may also come to you and talk about an experience they had, initiating the follow-up phase of the training. In other cases, you can pick an arbitrary time for this part of the process to take place. This is something that can be mentioned to an adolescent at any time. When I do this training, participants are told the reason for, and when this stage of the process is going to take place. This idea is explained by telling them that in order to see what things are used, and what ideas aren't, this kind of check-up needs to be done. Along with this explanation, the reason for the timing of this part of the process is described. They are told that if too much time goes by after the training is complete, then many of the things learned, or that they tried, may be forgotten.

A different use for the activities and knowledge gained by some of the adolescent participants in the A.M.P. Program came from their willingness to learn how to create and facilitate workshops for their peers. The opportunity to become a peer Anger Management workshop leader was provided at the bottom of the A.M.P. Program Follow-Up Survey. The youngsters who chose this option decided on which activities to use and which Anger Managers they felt would be most effective with their peers. This is a topic that is discussed in more depth in the next chapter. Samples of the teen-developed workshops appear in the Information Booster section of this book.

> Adolescents empowered to provide information to their peers represents one of the most effective ways of having this knowledge get to young people in this age group.

The Timing of Training Effectiveness Evaluations

Evaluating the effectiveness of the information given to teens can be useful in making adjustments in helping them handle anger, as we saw in the example provided above. For the parents who are reading this book, providing the time and effort—and most of all having the patience—to follow-up on the things you've shared with your children on this subject is an important thing to do. This part of the process will be taking place continuously, over a long period of time. For those of you whose profession is practiced in one location, the possibility of multiple check-ups is slightly more difficult. The likelihood for you to continue this part of the process depends on the time you can devote to it, and the flexibility you have in carrying out this function, along with your other professional responsibilities.

Obstacles to Evaluating Training Effectiveness and Ways to Overcome Them

For the rest of the chapter, we will be discussing methodologies applicable in an educational setting. Parents and non-educational workers should skip ahead to Chapter Eleven.

One of the realities of attempting to follow-up on this work with youngsters in an educational setting was pointed out in a conversation I had with a high school social worker in March of 2008. As a background for this discussion, the "No Child Left Behind" policy, and its effect on the delivery of services to students in many school systems, will be described. To carry out this strategy necessitates a great deal of effort and student and teacher time. Much of these two factors is channeled into the preparation for standardized tests. Achieving a certain level of accomplishment on these examinations enables teens to advance academically, in order to meet the requirements for graduation. The results of these measures of academic performance are often gauged by the percentage of students who receive passing grades. In many cases, achieving this result determines ratings for both teachers and schools and is used to decide the amount of funding schools receive. This, in turn, creates the basis for the decision on which staff and programs will be retained. Taking into consideration this whole process, comes the question, "When can the time be found to follow-up on this and other similar kinds of programs without interfering with administrative goals and requirements?"

In response to this policy, this person shook her head and told me that rather than bring in any of these kinds of programs and presenters, which certainly could be helpful to students, she felt that the time would be wasted. To illustrate this viewpoint, she described how her role as a social worker was limited. Counseling adolescents is one responsibility she has in her job. To be effective, this function needs to be carried out on a consistent basis. She went on to say it was difficult to see youngsters regularly, because they needed to be in the classes that prepared them for the standardized tests. As a result, students who needed or wanted to talk to her could only miss an occasional period of a particular subject. In addition, other duties she had—for example, writing reports or furnishing statistics—further limited the time she could spend providing students with counseling. She was only able to see students in crisis briefly and act as a referral source. In this role, she recommended places outside of the school setting for students and families to get additional help. Whether or not teens and their families went to these agencies was often dead-ended for financial reasons, or lack of trust in other mental health practitioners. This kind of situation describes the frustration professionals working in many educational settings, as well as those working in other environments face. However, don't give up on this part of the process just yet!

Overcoming Limitations

Since this is a "How To" book, let's take some more time and consider how to work with such constraints. The question for people in the educational setting to answer is, "Where can the time be found to follow up on the work done with young people while allowing them to prepare to meet these standards?" Looking back to how you are able to provide a youngster with the Anger Management training is a helpful starting point. In many high schools there are subjects that don't require a standardized examination. Health Education is one of these areas. As part of this course, the area of mental health lends itself to talking about anger and Anger Management. Some high schools offer elective subjects, such as psychology and law. These classes can also lend themselves to this kind of training because knowledge on how to deal with anger is helpful in specific careers. In some districts, different programs and specialty high schools (High School for Teaching and the Professions, Academy for Social Action, High School for Law and Public Service, found in New York) allow this kind of experience to take place. As a teacher, guidance counselor, or social worker in the educational setting, these are the kinds of opportunities you have for exposing teens to Anger Management training. After the initial experience is completed, let adolescents know that you will be following up on the ideas they have been given, on a specific day and date and at a specific time. This should take place about a month after the training is completed. For example, "We will look at what you guys did with this information on Tuesday, April 20th during period 3. If this process involves a written document, it usually takes about fifteen minutes to finish. Depending on the size of the group or with individual young people, when oral responses are being asked for it may take a full period, roughly forty minutes. This takes care of fitting this kind of training in ways that don't interfere with student preparations for meeting standards.

The next consideration is allowing you to be able to fit this training and its evaluation into your limited schedule while keeping this experience within your professional responsibilities. With teachers who have classes in relevant subject areas or are in specialized schools and programs, Anger Management training can be incorporated as part of the curriculum, the time is there to be used. This is for both the training and follow-up experiences. In some cases, teachers may not have the expertise in this area, and have a specially trained guidance counselor or social worker bring this experience to their students. If you are not the teacher of this class, the timing of this part of the training needs be worked out within the classroom teacher's schedule. When I did this training, during the time I spoke with the teacher initially, part of the plan for facilitating this program was to include scheduling this follow-up session.

The availability of this kind of training is something that needs to be made known to the staff. This can occur through individual contacts with colleagues, or through departmental or professional development presentations. When Anger Management training is requested, time frames for its presentation and follow-up need to be discussed prior to its facilitation. Programs that I presented in high school settings ranged from one forty-minute period to about two and one half hours. (This was a unit done over four weeks, one forty-minute period per week). The length of time available to work with a particular group and educator will determine what elements of the training you want to incorporate and what ideas need to be checked during the follow-up session.

No matter how long you have to facilitate the training, the evaluative process should focus on whether or not Anger Managers were used, and if they were, which ones. If they weren't, why not, and the situations that arose since the initial training experience took place. These questions are key to understanding how effective the training was.

Obstacles to having a teen use these techniques and how to overcome them were pointed out earlier in this chapter. The more input you can get from an adolescent, the more helpful you can be to future participants in this training. The elements found in the training sessions created by adolescents provide additional information on what kinds of situations youngsters describe they find themselves in and what would most likely be used. Following this lead, you can find the training ideas most teens found worthy and find out if this knowledge was used when you speak to them during your follow up.

The limited time you may have available to facilitate Anger Management, or any other related service as a guidance counselor or social worker, is the next thing that we are going to look at. In either capacity, running groups usually falls within your job responsibilities. A supervisor often dictates the number of sessions that are required or the time you are given to carry out this responsibility. Keeping this in mind will determine the number of sessions you can devote to Anger Management training. This experience can take place over a period of time, let's say one month. The major components of your program can take place during the earlier sessions, so that the time to check up on its effectiveness serves as the last session of this group. In the school setting, make sure that this training doesn't take place too close to preparation for exams or when they are actually given.

Another challenge you face is to decide how to justify this kind of experience within the framework of your responsibilities. The idea of "Advisory" had been and still is part of the New York City high school service plan for students. Under this function, staff members—including guidance counselors—have a limited number of students to follow. What this means is that ninth grade students or those with a variety of challenges (academic, attendance, behavior, motivation) are given different forms of assistance from staff members. Among these is social skills development training. Something that can fall into this category are conflict resolution and Anger Management skills. In New York State there is a mandate, a program known as SAVE (Schools Against Violence in Education), part of which requires educators and students to have training in violence prevention, including, Conflict Resolution. This policy, or something similar, provides validation for Anger Management training. Once again, finding out whether or not this means of violence prevention works requires follow up. In this case, the use of statistics, relating to number of incidents, suspensions, etc., both before and after this training, is often required. Not only would this follow-up look at these numbers, which in many cases leads to funding of programs, but can also include responses to questions asking about the situations youngsters were involved in and which Anger

---

Variations of the A.M.P. Program have been developed because of time limitations. To give you ideas on what to include with this constraint, look in the Information Booster section of the book for the description of these training formats.

Managers were used. Outside of the educational setting, agencies working with youth often look for programs that can provide additional funding for them and services they provide. Anger Management training may provide a vehicle to acquire additional sources of financial support.

Chapter Summary

This chapter provided an introduction to the ways of gaining the information necessary in gauging the effectiveness of the Anger Management training given to teens. It has given you an introduction to the Anger Management Power Program's feedback and follow-up surveys and how to obtain adolescent responses to the questions and ideas presented in these two documents. It also described the sources of resistance offered by youngsters to using these Anger Management methods or to discussing failed attempts to use them. This chapter also described the timing needed for this evaluation process and provided ideas for getting this task accomplished, even with certain roadblocks thrown in the way.

Chapter Eleven

Adolescent Reactions to Program Ideas with Ways to Take the Training to Another Level

This chapter focuses on the specific information gathered from the Anger Management Power Program's Feedback and Follow-Up Surveys, and ways to use it. The full documents are available in the Information Boosters section at the end of the book. To more fully understand the value of these surveys, an overview of both the feedback and follow-up documents will be presented to you. Conclusions reached and information gained from them will furnish you with ways to better understand and influence adolescents. The generalizations you draw from these evaluations provide a foundation for working with youngsters.

Before getting into these results, there are two thoughts to bear in mind: The first is that teens are unique individuals whose lives may differ in many respects from the individuals who participated in the Anger Management Power (A.M.P.) Program. These differences can result from coming from dissimilar families, living in different neighborhoods, attending different schools, and working in diverse locations. Based on these conditions, adolescents with whom you are involved may respond differently to situations, Anger Managers and adults than those involved in the A.M.P. Program. This individuality can also come about because of differences in personality. For example, some youngsters are more outgoing than others. This characteristic results in differences in the way they handle conflicts.

The second idea is that although teens come from diverse backgrounds and have different personalities they also share many needs and attitudes. For instance, the desire to belong to specific groups, and the need to be recognized for what they think and do are important. Many adolescents regard adults as people who don't know what they are talking about, don't want to hear what young people have to say, don't value teen opinions, and make judgments. Keeping these thoughts in mind you are ready to examine the conclusions drawn from the A.M.P. Feedback and Follow-Up Surveys.

How to Use These Facts

Being able to present the responses made to the feedback and follow-ups in a meaningful way can be of great value. Before viewing the results of these evaluation tools, pointing out to adolescents that the comments made to the questions found on these documents were from people in their age group, or around the same ages as their brothers, sisters, cousins or friends. In other words, individuals whose judgment they respect made these responses. This relationship can open youngsters' minds to the value of the thoughts and opinions expressed on these feedback surveys. Teens are more likely to respond to ideas and comments made by peers than those offered by adults is a truism to be recognized.

Survey Results

The replies to the questions found in "the A.M.P. Program Feedback Survey" represent those most frequently given. The questions found on this document required written responses, since they were used with large groups. Responses to the questions from this survey can be elicited from an individual teen or from small groups either in a written or oral form. Written responses can furnish an adolescent with a way to organize and think about their answers. Others who don't care for writing, simply respond to doing a questionnaire with the "No way!" remark. However these questions are presented, and whichever ones you choose to ask, is your call to make. These decisions are dependent on what elements of the training were stressed. Other factors include:

How much time can be spent on an evaluation,

The attention span of the adolescents you are dealing with.

The ability of teens to understand different concepts.

This assessment can be developed before the Anger Management training takes place, as part of the planning process, or after each topic is covered. For example, if you are discussing the effects of anger and ways to prevent them from controlling a adolescent's reaction, you may ask questions after this subject is discussed, rather than after all the areas are covered at the end of the training. The time, attention and ability a youngster has, to understand and remember the concepts, are crucial factors to consider.

As you take an overview of the responses to this document, thinking of what may or may not appeal to a teen, needs to be taken into account. The conclusions you reach can be used to help develop the elements you want to use and those you want to eliminate from the training. Now that these suggestions have been made, the next step to take is to get into the feedback survey responses.

The first question in this evaluation asks about ideas that adolescents thought would be helpful. One part of the program participants felt could meet this goal was the Anger Managers. Their responses took two forms. The first category of thoughts was expressed in general terms:

"Anger Managers give different ways to deal with anger,"

"Knowing how to control anger better,"

"How to help and understand anger in others,"

"How to prevent anger or keep it from getting worse,"

These choices can be provided as a checklist. Expressing them in this way minimizes the time and effort needed for this evaluation.

The second way adolescents referred to Anger Managers was by pinpointing individual methods. "Is It Worth It?" "Visualizing Anger," and "Deep Breathing" were among the most popular.

The second question in this assessment asked youngsters what activities and ideas they liked. Replies to this idea furnish an understanding of what activities were most popular with them. These tools can be used with an individual or a group of teens. Many adolescents like to be entertained or enjoy doing things that allow them to be more active. Two of the more popular methods that fall into this category were role-plays and the Human Anger Scale. Both of these involved groups of youngsters. Skits that were performed were described as entertaining, or as some participants commented, "funny." This method provides a means of looking at a particular situation objectively, allowing teens to see situations more impersonally.

Your watchful eyes, alert ears and open mind will often lead to more effective ways in helping change the behavior of young people. You may get ideas from this program, use some and eliminate others, or find variations that may work best. If some of the activities listed as being eliminated can work better for a teen you are concerned about, use them.

There are variations of these activities that can be done with individual adolescents or with small groups (three to five young people). Showing a video, often something that can be found on the Internet, under the subjects of "Conflict" or "Anger," offers another entertaining way to explore situations. Instead of using the Human Anger Scale, which was a teen participant's idea, you can have them use the "Top Ten Causes of Anger in Teens," activity, or refer to their own anger activators and then have them describe situations that cause this emotion to surface. With both of these methods, participants are involved in the discussion and have an opportunity to voice their opinion. In the case of group experiences, they can get different perspectives from their peers. These are selling points for using these activities. They are also furnish topics for conversations to have with adolescents.

Question Three asks what activities the participants disliked. As you have no doubt noted, the word, "boring" is a common expression among many youths. It has been used to describe some of the training activities as well as in other kinds of situations. This is not to say that teens have to be constantly entertained, stimulated or otherwise part of the perpetual movement that is characteristic of this age group. However, in some instances, your desire to give adolescents experiences that will open their minds and eyes to this kind of Anger Management knowledge require some type of stimulation.

The overriding concern is to find whatever route you need to take to reach them. Keeping this goal in mind, some modifications were made to the Anger Management Power Program since its inception. These modifications resulted in the elimination of some activities and the addition of others. (These can be found as part of the Statistical Overview of the Feedback and Follow-Up Surveys in the Information Booster section at the end of the book) What is important for you to note, is that experiences involving writing or discussion of ideas, rather than some interactive experience, are regarded negatively by many teens. Knowing whether an adolescent minds writing down comments or would rather talk about ideas will help you to determine whether or not to use particular activities. As with many programs, the opportunity to improve them often presents itself in some way. From the feedback and suggestions given by adolescents came ideas on how to better reach their peers. Suggestions made by youngsters can be helpful for you in making the Anger Management program you develop more effective.

Question Four also deals with Anger Managers, specifically asking which ones teens would be willing to try. They were given choices of different Anger Managers. (The full list of popular responses to these two questions can be found in the Information Booster section of this book.) The list of Anger Managers described in Chapter Eight came from this survey and from discussions with participants. The popularity of certain Anger Managers taken from this evaluation can be stressed. This point may cause reluctant adolescents to decide to choose particular methods because their peers thought they were cool.

As you discovered from the responses young people made to Question One, which focused on what they wanted from this program, many of them listed different Anger Managers that they felt would be useful. Question Four asks, "Which of the ways of handling anger do you feel you would try?" It listed five Anger Managers, along with an "Other" category. This aspect of the program represents the heart of Anger Management training. For specific information on the use of these tools refer to the "Statistical Overview of the Feedback and Follow-Up Surveys" in the Information Booster section. The importance of knowing the more popular Anger Managers makes these ideas more appealing to other youngsters.

The final question focuses on rating the Anger Management Power Program. This part of the evaluation took the form of a scale, with "1" being, "Want Less Time" and "10" being, "Want More Time." It provides a source of validity for the training. It can also be asked orally, with individual adolescents, small groups, or those young people who don't want to write. If participants rated your program anywhere from "1" to "6", ask for suggestions that they have to improve this experience. This kind of information provides an opportunity to fine tune it, and make it more adolescent-friendly and acceptable to youngsters in the future.

The Reality of Fixed Behavior

The reality that not all teens are willing to change their behavior is something that you, as a parent, educator, social worker or other person concerned with them can face. Some of the participants who took these surveys felt none of this information was useful. They also felt the whole program was worthless to them. Some of them put the whole idea of positive ways to handle anger down. However, I truly believe that some of the ideas presented to them still registered in their minds. Whether they will do something different in the present or in the future remains unknown. Some need to save face or are just afraid that doing some of these things will open them up to further pain and vulnerability, things they've experienced all too often in their lives. Some, like many adults, are just afraid of change.

The way they have acted has protected them. Change may take away that protection. All we can do is try to expose them to some alternatives to destructive behavior, and hope to influence their actions, in some of their relationships, at some point in their lives. Maturity, peers, experiences—who knows what and when—lead to changes in these "hardened" youngsters' lives. I put this piece of reality in, because it is something we all have to contend with. My hope is that you and I can influence young people enough to help them create a better, more peaceful life. It is a goal that I feel we must strive for, no matter how many pieces of reality, challenges, obstacles or whatever you choose to call them, try to block us from reaching it.

For parents trying to help their children, youngsters' reactions can be gauged by their ability to stay focused on particular elements, for example, causes, effects or situations, different looks they have, whether they are wide-eyed enthusiasm or glazed, sleepy expressions. For areas that get the best kind response explore them well. Your children are continuously evaluating your efforts. Knowing what is working means staying with it and exploring it fully with your teens. It also means bringing up points in small doses and not over talking subjects, that is not, going on and on about them, a behavior that is often met by looks of disgust. Let what is going to be discussed come from the teens. In other words, to help them deal with their anger, see what are the concerns they bring up. We have explored this idea throughout this book in the chapters on unexpressed causes, different feelings that accompany anger, and experiences relating to adolescents.

Background Information on the A.M.P. Follow-Up Survey

The A.M.P. Follow-Up Survey was administered about one month after youngsters completed the entire Anger Management Power Program. Its intent was to discover what parts of this learning process were actually used by teens. Some were able to use at least part of the experience, some didn't have the chance to try or think about it, and some, who were part of that "reality" group mentioned before, totally ignored what they heard and saw during the course of the program. The importance of peer thinking and actions in stimulating changes in behavior should not be underestimated. Our purpose in using this information, as we look at an adolescent, thinking, hoping and praying that they see the light, can be expressed by the remark, "Hey, kid, look at some of the ways that people your age thought were ways to handle anger, (and for that matter better deal with stress and anxiety) without causing further hassles for themselves. Then adding, "Wouldn't it be great to have some of these things working for you?" The acknowledgment of this possibility comes not only by nodding their heads (certainly a start) but in knowing how strong an influence their peers' thoughts have on them. For most teens, what their friends think and do is really important. Their need to belong, fit in, and be recognized as one of the group, is very strong.

For others what peers do has little meaning. These are the adolescents who are often ostracized for being different, feel as if they are not liked or are sometimes the victims of bullying or other kinds of abuse. These youngsters are also those who suddenly react strongly to their treatment. They are the teens that often fall between the cracks until they either lash out at others (Columbine as an example) or themselves (instances of suicide). The ideas found in the Follow-Up Survey can be categorized as things for this group of adolescents to think about. They can serve as the source of discussion with them at some time after the initial training is given.

How to Use These Facts

The kinds of situations that were described in this survey are common to teen experience. The way survey respondents handled these incidents can encourage other adolescents to manage them using the same methods. The remark, "Here's how some other kids used this idea" may start a teen's thinking in this direction. Once this statement is made, wait for some reaction, whether it is verbal or non-verbal, to help decide whether or not to continue following this thought process. For the other, more independent group, having them choose from a list of Anger Management ideas to use with recent incidents is an effective path to take.

Look at the specific elements of the training emphasized in this document and some of the reactions of adolescent participants. From this knowledge you can get a better idea of the kinds of things that are effective and those that aren't. In essence, you don't have to reinvent the wheel if you use some of the information gained from this evaluation.

The first question focuses on the causes of anger. Most teens responded that knowing the reason for their anger was helpful because it helped them either to understand how situations that already took place could have been prevented, or to stop those that can occur from getting out of hand. The idea of knowing what really gets adolescents mad can help them avoid the circumstances entirely, or allow them to enter them more calmly. One situation that was described when adolescents disagree with their parents about spending time with a particular person, someone their mom or dad doesn't like. Instead of talking about it or trying to convince their parents that this person is okay, youngsters will totally avoid the situation, and the hassle it brings.

A situation that is impossible to steer clear of is one in which teens are aware that when they come home late their mom is going to be on their case. To prepare themselves for this showdown, adolescents can come into the house, taking many deep breaths before entering, and realize that the best way to deal with this situation is not to answer their parent back and apologize before their mom or dad reaches the out of control point. This is a way for young people to avoid major hassles. Describing these kinds of situations and the benefits of certain kinds of behavior is useful. These advantages can be provided in a list for teens to choose from.

Incorporating "The Top Ten Causes of Anger in Teens" or having teens describe their own top (any number) reasons for experiencing this emotion, in an individual's or group's training plan makes sense since it also offers the opportunity to then discuss ways to diminish the intensity of this feeling when it occurs.

The second question in this survey deals with the effects of anger. Adolescents responded by describing two kinds of reaction. The first involved knowing about the physical results of anger. An awareness of their own body's reactions, as well as those in others, pointed out the need to do something to calm themselves or the other people. Once youngsters had this knowledge they were able to chill out by using some of the methods taken from their training. Deep breathing, counting, and walking away were among the tools that were chosen most frequently. The second kind of reaction involved thinking about what kinds of things could result from letting their anger take control. Visualizing the result of losing it, or deciding if getting so angry over a particular incident was worth it, demonstrate Anger Managers that are helpful in limiting the effects of their anger. By providing a list of effects teens can choose from, bringing in peer reactions from this survey, or asking adolescents what happens to their bodies, what thoughts they have, or how else they feel when they get angry, they can decide how to handle the effects of anger. They may give some response, or none. Use the information in Chapter Six to help you get this information. I feel this is an integral part of any Anger Management program, since it provides an awareness of what can happen when this emotion is stirred up and how to limit its effect.

The final question related to the use of Anger Managers. It had three parts. The first indicated which Anger Managers were used. The most popular methods used by participants were noted. This information is helpful because it gives you ideas of which Anger Managers might appeal most to an adolescent. Once again, using peer appeal or a checklist is helpful. The next part asked the participant to describe the other person involved in the situation. Asking a young people to describe who they get the most hassles from points to particular situations that can be used with them. The last part of this question indicated the result of using particular Anger Management methods. Noting the replies in this portion of the survey is most effective with teens who value their peers' behavior in situations. In other words, how other people their age handled incidents gives an adolescent a reason to try to apply these methods in their own situations. The information furnished by this evaluation process provides you with the confidence of using ideas that passed this "Teen-Tested" training method.

Taking Anger Management Training in Other Directions

One way to take the idea of a follow-up to another point is to give teens the chance to express their interest in receiving more training. There are two ways this process can be accomplished.

The Objective of Developing Peer Workshops

This first kind of training has been used with several groups of adolescents. Its objective was to have young people develop and facilitate an Anger Management workshop for peers. These teens indicated their interest in this idea by providing contact information found at the bottom of the Follow-Up Survey. For an adolescent who has shown enthusiasm during their training with you, simply asking, "Would you like to get more training?" will accomplish this step. At this point, you can tell them about this method of expanding their knowledge or that of being a member of a focus group, a second method that will be described shortly.

Organizing and Qualifications for Peer Workshop Presenters

With the information provided at the end of the follow-up survey, student schedules were accessed and motivated students were contacted. The training periods were rotated as much as possible so no one subject class would be missed too often. This process took five to six class periods, or approximately three to four hours.

In addition to their teacher's consent to attend these sessions, the students who would facilitate the presentations (not just help plan them) were selected by their show of commitment to this task. There are several factors to judge teen dedication. One involves their belief in the ideas presented during original training. If they've used different Anger Managers and see the benefit of using these methods to handle conflict, then they have demonstrated their belief in this process. By taking this step they have shown that they can motivate peers to give these ideas a chance. Putting this concept another way, if someone believes in the value of the product they are selling, they have the best chance of selling it to others.

Youngsters' attendance and promptness in coming to the planning sessions is another indicator of their belief and commitment to becoming peer facilitators. If they forget that there is a meeting or the time it was to be held more than once, give some flimsy excuse, or they aren't there for a majority of the sessions, these students are ruled out as trainers. However, teens who missed training meetings because of exams or other school-related responsibilities are certainly not disqualified as peer trainers.

Another area of commitment is evident by an individual's effort and attitude toward the workshop planning and rehearsal sessions. Those who enthusiastically participate, share ideas and are supportive of their peers, display the kind of behavior that shows the necessary qualities that they need to become a peer facilitator. Those who sit back or misbehave, often treating the training as a way to miss their class or goof off, are eliminated as presenters.

The notification system found in an educational setting may be different in other agency or organizational environments. The qualifications for peer facilitators noted above can serve as a model for the kinds of behavior to look for in teens you feel can reach this goal. They can also be modified for use in different agencies and organizations.

How and Why to Create Peer Facilitated Workshops

1. Creating this type of training provides youngsters with ownership of the concepts involved in Anger Management. This means that they develop the workshop and it is theirs.

2. Developing the workshop can result in the increase in peer facilitator self-esteem, since it enables them to become leaders and "authorities" in this area.

3. Peers training peers is the most effective way to reach other adolescents. It's an example of peer power, something that can motivate other youngsters to take on this task.

Other Forms of Peer Training

Youngsters can also present their Anger Management ideas to peers in smaller groups, rather than in classes. Smaller group presentations may lend themselves to use in other than educational settings. They may take place in group homes, youth organizations, or as one of the services provided by religious institutions and other kinds of groups. This kind of peer "influencing" may also be accomplished with individual teens who are involved in peer mentoring programs or as a way for them to help family members and friends on a one-to-one basis.

The idea of being a leader, having control over peers in a positive way is an appealing thought to many young people. Earning this privilege must be tied foremost to their belief in the methods used in this kind of training, and their ability to follow whatever standards are set to earn this opportunity.

A Focus Group

This is another form additional training can take. The A.M.P. Program is a work in progress, changing as participants and colleagues suggest more ideas. This method was recently recommended and has become another opportunity for program participants to take a different road to extending their training. In this kind of group activity, participants speak about their experiences since receiving the initial training. One young lady came to speak to me about a situation she was having in her relationship. Although she wasn't part of a group, her time with me represented a variation of this kind of training. This format allows young people to have the opportunity to discuss what worked, what didn't, and share with each other alternative ways of handling different situations that occur. This group can meet at regular intervals, each month or couple of months, or at a time suggested during their initial learning experience. As with peer mediation, peer focus group facilitators can be taught how to establish group rules, maintain order and keep participants on track. This kind of leadership training is explained below. It uses the model of the preparation peer mediators receive to facilitate mediation sessions.

Teens who were being trained to carry out this method of third party intervention (See Information Booster section for an overview of this method) were given information on conflict and learned communication skills. They were taught the mediation process and were also given directions on how to make sure that order was maintained during this process. This knowledge enabled them to perform their duties effectively. Mock mediations were held to practice these skills and deal with challenges they might find during actual cases. To ensure a safe environment, an adult had to be present during all mediations. In addition to being a safety valve, this person provided feedback on the approaches peer mediators used, as well as what attitudes and actions were observed during this process. These kinds of comments were usually made as soon as the mediation ended or a short time after, possibly by the next day. This same process can be applied to teen facilitated focus groups.

One justification for offering a teen the opportunity to either lead, or become a member of a focus group, was made clear from the responses to the "Giving Ideas" and "Discussion" categories in the feedback survey, which expressed what participants in the A.M.P. Program liked most about their training. Having a focus group allows teens to discuss situations, a big preference for them, and also provides an excellent opportunity for an individual youngster to influence peers and increase self-esteem.

Chapter Summary

This chapter provided the results of the A.M.P. Program Feedback and Follow-Up Surveys. The conclusions that were reached by adolescent program participants provide ideas on what elements of this training may work with other young people. Methods of presenting these ideas to individuals, as well as groups of teens, were also offered.

The peer facilitated workshop and the focus group represent two ways to provide an adolescent with additional Anger Management training. The first described a way for them to present worthwhile information to peers. The second showed an adolescent a way to discover and share how the information received from the training was used.

Chapter Twelve

Some Parting Thoughts

We have almost reached the end of this journey together. You are about ready to "solo" with the information you have been given in this book. Before you do, I have some final thoughts. As a parent, educator, social worker or youth worker, this age group represents a great personal or professional challenge, or perhaps even both. For some people, dealing with an adolescent is characterized by the remark, "I wish Sam could have been frozen from the time he was thirteen until twenty-one." However, I would feel remiss if additional thoughts weren't presented to help you develop more confidence in handling this difficult, often scary, and ever-taxing age group. Some of these are general views, not specifically related to Anger Management. I am also including "Quick Tips for Keeping Peace with Teens" in the Information Booster Section of the book, as an additional resource for you to use to add to these ideas. Check them out. Enjoy using them and let me know what you think about them.

Thoughts for Parents

Being a parent of a child any age is a tough enough job, but with teens it is intensified many times. Fears for their safety outside of your home, in school or in your neighborhood, as well as other places they hang out in, the kinds of friends they have, their sexual activity, and their educational and life goals all characterize reasons to sprout gray hair or develop ulcers. You cannot be with them twenty-four hours a day, seven days a week. However, you have observed their behavior in many situations throughout their lifetime and have a running record in your mind of how different situations were handled. These experiences give you knowledge of some of the "How To's" of dealing with your teen. This information is a fear breaker, making some of your adolescent's behavior more manageable.

There are behaviors, attitudes and reactions that place adolescents in that hair-pulling, teeth-grinding, "out-of-control" category. These are the kinds of things that scare many parents and make them feel helpless. Physically acting-out toward you or other family members describes one such area. It is not something to be tolerated. First and foremost youngsters have to accept limits placed on them. For this type of behavior the "tough love" approach is essential. There are Tough Love groups that offer support and ideas for parents of adolescents who fit this profile. Look for local listings in phone directories, on the Internet, or get this information through school and/or mental health personnel. Locking a young person out of the house, calling the police or other authority and having the child removed from the home describe some of the more severe methods that fall into this category of behavior management. These may seem like extreme measures, but so are the possibilities of a young person causing injury, or even death, to those they physically act out against.

Other behaviors that fall into this group include:

> Cutting classes consistently or school entirely.
> Coming home at late hours.
> Involvement with peers who are engaged in criminal or
> destructive activities.

Obviously, such activities demand consequences. If remedies such as: grounding, loss of privileges (use of the Internet or television, having friends to the house, etc), spending extra time in school (attending night classes or summer school) don't work, then tough love decisions must be made. Seeing a child in jail, homeless, hurt or dead aren't alternatives any parent wants to face.

Other forms of difficult behavior can be met in different ways. These kinds of reactions are characterized as rebelliousness or stubbornness and can drive a parent crazy. Often a teen will throw a tantrum by yelling at the top of their lungs, throwing things or with non-stop cursing. Responding in unexpected ways to an adolescent's difficult behavior is useful. If for example, your child comes home demanding you get their dinner immediately after they have come home an hour after it was served, instead of running to prepare it, (often a real temptation just to shut the kid up) telling them to get something him/herself, or that the kitchen is closed are tactics to use. He/she still might demand his food. Ignore this command. If your child is hungry enough, he'll finally take his own dinner. At some time when he/she has eaten or calmed down, coolly explain that if they want you to give them dinner they must be home on time, or they'll just have to get something for themselves. A youngster often tests a parent by doing the same thing over again the next day and expects his/her mom's last reaction to his demand to have been due to her "temporary insanity." Consistency for children of any age is an effective way to be taken seriously. My message is, "Do the unexpected, and do it consistently."

An out of control teen doesn't mean *you* have to feel that way.

For many young people, when they yell they expect you to do the same, and that sooner or later you'll give in to their demands just to shut them up. If you don't, and speak softly, they need to listen more carefully and take their tone of voice down a few decibels. This kind of reaction allows them to see that making noise is not getting them what they want. This tactic takes time, effort and a lot of patience. However, isn't peace and quiet worth this price?

Another bone of contention between teens and parents revolves around carrying out responsibilities at home. These can include placing clothes in a hamper or taking care of their dirty dishes. In these cases doing the unexpected can also give a resistant adolescent something to think about. Leaving the clothes unwashed or serving your child on the same dirty dishes, illustrate this kind of behavior modification technique. Once again, doing these things consistently makes the message clear, and can produce hassle-free results. These changes take time and effort. The question to ask is, "will these changes mean less hassles in the long run?" If the answer is "Yes," give them a shot.

The following ideas summarize some ways to effectively handle an out-of-control teen.

1. Don't think a situation with an adolescent is impossible. Some measures involve more severe actions on your part, actions you must be willing to make and not reverse.
2. Changing your response to many of your adolescent's behaviors is another instrument of change. Think for a minute, of someone sneaking up on you and yelling. You jump! They say, "Gotcha!" Doing the unexpected and seeing your youngster's behavior change allows you to think to yourself that you got him or her to act correctly.
3. Asking for professional advice or speaking to other parents who have similar situations is another way to help you weather a youngster's emotional storms.

Other ways of approaching an adolescent's behavior are described below. These are some of the ideas that have been given to you throughout this book.

1. Understanding the reasons for a youngster's behavior and how to uncover them.

2. Different needs that a teen may have that may or may not be met.

3. Ways of dealing with an adolescent's anger without either party becoming more upset.

4. Some of the ideas suggested in this book can be helpful in handling the tension that can arise with other family members, or with the entire family.

5. Problems in relationships with peers, girlfriends, boyfriends, and those that arise in school or at a job describe situations that impact individual family members. There are those that can affect a whole family. These may include; economic hard times, changes occurring because of illness, death or divorce, or caring for elder members of your family.

6. Ways of modeling—or at least trying to show—positive ways of dealing with tough situations. Actions really do speak louder than words to your children. They provide methods for creating a more peaceful atmosphere in your family. Children do learn what they live, positive as well as negative.

Putting What You Found Helpful to Work

There are two ways to use the knowledge you've gained from this book. One way is to think of specific ideas that can be the most helpful to use with your child. Go back to the particular chapters that deal with the ideas that you think are useful. Once you have located them, jot down the pages or use some other method of noting important ideas for quick reference.

Perhaps you took notes as you read this book. There are different ways to arrange them. For example, different sections of a notebook can be arranged according to topic, with each area having different Anger Managers to use with it. Another possibility in dealing with the subject of Anger Managers involves categorizing them. Dividing these methods into those used to calm teens down and those used to help them express their anger can do this. Having easy access to this information will better prepare you to deal with the situations as they occur with your adolescent. For quick and easy reference, don't forget to put your notes in your cellphone, laptop, computer or any other device you carry.

Another approach is to anticipate a potential conflict that may arise and be prepared to handle it. Weekends or vacations are prime times for incidents to occur. They are occasions when young people want to go where they want to go, stay until they want to come home and be with whomever they care to be with—most often not family. These are the times when teens are free of school routines and don't want as many restrictions placed on them.

There are also other stressful times for adolescents and their parents alike. These often have to do with school. Upcoming exams, such as finals and standardized tests, report cards and parent conferences illustrate some of these sources of anxiety. Participating in or attending plays, dances, or athletic events are other predictable times for conflict to occur.

When these events do occur, it is necessary to be prepared for the reactions to expect from a youngster. This kind of "hassle-readiness" involves developing ways to keep these situations from getting out of hand before they happen. This means doing whatever helps you enter the situation calmly, or remain that way during a conflict. Here is where referring to the Anger Managers for parents in the Information Boosters section at the end of this book are helpful. Other categories of Anger Managers to have ready are those for keeping adolescents calm, or those that deal with coping with particular sources of stress that a young person has trouble handling.

Another thought occurred to me as a result of a conversation I had with my doctor who was talking about his fourteen-year old daughter. Often parents expect a teen to progress the same way and follow the same development as an older brother or sister. In this case this young lady's mom thought she had to concentrate and do better in math, just as her brother had done. Her dad saw that she was good in Science and felt that it was unnecessary for her to do as well in math as her brother. When one parent tries to push an adolescent in a particular direction, as this mom did, the result is yelling back and forth. The longer term consequences of these actions are that the mom's chances of influencing this young lady about school, or other areas in her life, becomes greatly diminished. In this case this teen was not being accepted for who she was and what she was capable of doing. Accepting what an adolescent thinks or does is very important. In this instance, seeing the daughter as being more interested in Science than in Math, without becoming stressed out about it, opens the door for having additional discussions and more influence with this young lady. A parent's attitude often means the difference between having an adolescent seek their advice or not.

The teenage years are often described as a time when an adolescent needs both freedom and security. The freedom to test their wings in different areas (school, career, relationships) conflicting with their need for support and assistance from their family illustrates this internal battle. This isn't often apparent, since you know how this age group can test adults to the ultimate limit of their patience. However, it is something an adolescent needs and wants. The idea is to keep the doors open. Let them experiment, as long as it isn't harmful to them or others. You don't have to like or agree with what they are doing, but accept it. Once this happens they will also feel the freedom to talk with you.

Thoughts for Educators

Teaching is without a doubt one of the most challenging professions there is. An educator is a combination of teacher, psychologist and parent all rolled into one person. To say the least, you are faced with many responsibilities, with many constraints. Among the most difficult of these duties involves classroom management. In other words, the question to be answered is, "How do I cover what I have to in the curriculum, with the time I have, and keep my students on track?" Limiting disruptions that take place is the key to resolving this problem. An unmotivated student or one with limited abilities often causes these distractions. Add to these factors increased hormones and attractions to members of the opposite sex, being "cool" and you know why being a teacher is so challenging.

As an educator for over thirty years in New York City, I know that the importance of classroom management cannot be emphasized enough. When I started as a teacher, this fact hit me square in the face, when all my efforts to teach a subject went down the drain, as disruptive students took charge of my time and efforts. Hindsight is a great teacher.

No doubt, many education courses emphasize the value and techniques involved in classroom management. The function of rules in a classroom cannot be underestimated. Having them established, written, and posted from the first day of class is stressed in many teacher education programs. Some "How to" develop these guidelines can be helpful. One idea involves having students suggest ways to help keep things going smoothly in the classroom. Since these are their thoughts, youngsters' willingness to follow these rules is strengthened. Rather than being called "rules" students can also come up with their own name for these guidelines. Accepting these thoughts demonstrates "ownership" and makes them part of "their" class-room. Using rules can also be a means of Objectification, something mentioned earlier. When an adolescent calls out, puts someone else down or curses, you can point to the rule and say something like, "We all agreed that no one in this class would do (whatever the offense was)." It takes direct blame off of this young person and points out a general standard. By taking this approach, a possible conflict can be avoided, and the time spent on this infraction can be minimized.

Handling a student who has come into the classroom upset is something else to explore. This is not uncommon. Arguments with parents, girl-friends or boyfriends, witnessing hostility between parents, fears of loss of a parent's job or knowledge of sudden illness or death of a family member, illustrate some situations that can occur prior to a student coming to class on a particular day. Other students may respond with "Oohs," or some other potential source of disruption when this young person may enter the classroom late, and is in this state of mind. (This particular scenario was used as part of the A.M.P. Program) When this happens there are several ways to handle this situation. Among the most effective are; ignoring the teen, provided they are not throwing things or doing something that can be harmful to you or the other students in the classroom, giving him a chance to calm down, and keeping the class focused on an assignment while quietly approaching this adolescent to try to find out why they were upset. One important thing to keep in mind is that if a teacher confronts a student in a classroom, this young person will react and do whatever it takes to save face in front of his/her peers. If a teen doesn't say anything, they face embarrassment and can be regarded as someone who is soft and takes [expletive] from another person, in this case, you the teacher. This is something that bears repeating. One of the strongest values for a teen is respect. One way to accomplish this is to speak with an adolescent privately, either softly in the classroom or arranging to speak with him/her after class. When this is done, the young person's emotions are kept from escalating. A valuable tool to use in this and many other situations that can occur in the classroom is to think in advance of situations that could occur and try to plan ways to calmly deal with them. Role-playing can be used with colleagues and students as an activity centered on different situations, or as part of professional development to better prepare teachers for different eventualities that occur within the school setting.

The "Hard Core" student offers another source of disruption in a classroom. This young person is often a bully, someone physically or verbally aggressive, or an individual who feels inadequate in school. This teen is possibly someone who has a limited understanding of English, an adolescent who is in foster care or a group home setting, or a long-term truant. Any of these possibilities can be the reason for this youngster's disruptive behavior. Often a colleague or other staff member has some knowledge of a particularly troublesome student and can suggest ways to keep the youngster's actions to a minimum. An immediate response to the disturbance a disruptive adolescent creates is to ask him/her if they like respect. This is something most young people find meaningful. It is something I have successfully tried with disruptive students during a workshop I recently gave with sixth graders. It is an attention getter, which can help prevent a situation from getting out of hand. For those of you who are fairly new to teaching, or working with teens, this preview of some of the areas that need to be addressed and how to deal with them, can take away some of your anxiety. This knowledge provides a way to control the classroom environment, and give yourself the best opportunity to teach your subject.

Time and the Teachable Moment

Time is a real challenge. Think of the ideas that have been presented throughout this book and couple them with the concept of the "teachable moment." This time may present itself when an incident takes place between students in your classroom or office, or one that you are informed about. It may also be something that is taken from the content of a particular subject area in which conflict takes place. This can occur during a particular period of history, in a Social Studies class, in a story or play in which two characters find they are having a problem with each other, in an English class, or as part of news stories being discussed in a Civics or Government class. Student perceptions of events and people, as well as incorporating Anger Management and other social skills activities, can take place within discussions that occur in these subject areas without requiring additional class time.

Advisories: Another Idea to Consider

The idea of "Advisories"—something found in many New York City high schools—is another path to take to institute Anger Management and other kinds of social skills development training with young people. Schools target groups that involve students who are considered "at risk," that is, those likely to become truants, or have a low academic success rate, are identified and placed in specific classes. Small groups of students (around ten) are assigned to specific staff members. These educators keep track of the identified students' grades, attendance and behavior, and provide them with more individualized attention. Once per week, they meet with their entire group and cover topics relating to academics, peer pressure, and social skills development. This concept is a holistic approach within the educational setting. It is something I believe is worthwhile. It can, in some form, be incorporated into other educational systems.

For Social and Youth Workers

Your services with young people take in a variety of clients and settings. They are provided to individuals, groups of adolescents, families or with school staff. Your career takes you into schools, agencies, and homes. Throughout this book, many approaches were described to help you understand anger in young people, and to empower them to handle this emotion in positive ways. In this chapter, additional ideas were given to parents and educators. They provide a menu of ideas for you to choose from as well.

In addition to that information, developing plans to work with youth in different areas of behavior management can be helpful to you. Even though ideas presented below are specific to providing teens with skills through an Anger Management program, they are adaptable to other areas of concern with adolescents.

Choices for Creating a Plan for Work with Teens

This method involves making several decisions. This first involves knowing what ideas you feel are most appealing to use with clients. The next step is to decide how you want to access ideas, that is, finding the tools and documents to use. With this part of the plan, using checklists offers a simple and efficient way to accomplish a task. It's also something that adolescents willingly do, since it requires a minimum of effort. These inventories include the different methods and thoughts that have been presented throughout this book. They provide ideas on what elements to consider in developing a plan to present the Anger Management Power Program training to teens. Use them as a guide. They can be applied to other areas you deal with as well. Try incorporating the concepts that you feel will work the best first. These tools are provided in the "Program Preparation Checklists" found in the Information Booster section at the back of the book.

Participants in the A.M.P. Program provided me with some great ideas. Many of these became part of this process and have benefited many people. It is here, that you and I can work together to discover the most effective methods to use with adolescents. Many thoughts, techniques and tools have been provided for you and the other people who have read, *Peace: The Other Side of Anger.* As you do more of this work with adolescents, different, interesting and effective ideas will come to mind. Don't hesitate to go with them. Working with youth requires flexibility. Feel free to share both the ideas that work and those that aren't as successful with your fellow readers and me in any aspect of your work with young people through my website, peacefforts.org.

The Importance of Following Up on the Training

The importance of following up is something that cannot be emphasized enough. It is all well and good to give teens ideas on how to handle their anger and opportunities to discuss issues, but without discovering if and how these ideas were used, the value of these opportunities becomes really limited.

In Chapter Eleven, the results of the surveys that were given to participants in the A.M.P. Program were evaluated. This process involved looking at what aspects of the program were used by participants. This was one means of gauging the effectiveness of some of the work done in this training modality. Besides knowing what ideas were used, an essential part of this method is also discovering what appealed to adolescents about the ideas they used, and what didn't have an impact on them. Obtaining this information can have great value in helping you decide to continue to use certain activities and ideas, expand on some, change others, or eliminate those that aren't valued at all. I have made many modifications, based on participant input, since I began to put the A.M.P. Program together. The responses to these changes have been mostly positive.

Dave Wolffe

Many suggestions have been made and ideas have been presented throughout this book. What happens with this information depends on you. How and in what forms you use this information are your choices to make. Once you have made these decisions and worked in this area with teens, having a dialogue with other readers and with me is important to consider.

The Importance of Your Feedback

I hope that reading this book has enabled you to identify ideas helpful in your work with youth. Feel free to join me at my website http://www.peacefforts.org to share experiences. Whether you indicate positive or negative results with the training, express doubts and concerns, or describe changes to the ideas that were presented in this book, this information is valuable. Our "conversations" will result in making this kind of Anger Management training more effective. I invite you to join me in this process.

Looking Ahead

Watch! Look! Listen! to the young people you want to help. That's the key to bringing more peace to their lives. How? When? Why? they decide to put the things you've provided for them into action will come when they want them to.

The ideas that have been presented have been based upon my experiences with many teens, as I developed, changed and tried to improve the Anger Management Power Program. It is a work in progress, as are our youth. Hang in there with it, and with them. Know that it's okay for you to make some choices and not make others. Don't be afraid to trust your gut. *Peace: The Other Side of Anger* was written for you. From it, hopefully, you've gotten some ideas to use in whatever way you feel can be most helpful. Whether you focus only on anger, or use this knowledge to help adolescents deal with a combination of feelings, is something to keep in mind.

235

My main goal was to give you more tools and ideas that will be helpful in understanding anger in young people, and help you empower them to handle this emotion in a positive way. I sincerely hope that it did.

I wish you good results!

Information Boosters

The Anger Scale
(Chapter One)

Rational*   *Irrational***

*Cool, Chilled-Out, Calm   ***O.D., Crazy, Psycho, Nuts*
(Use these terms or others that may be more adolescent-friendly)

You are in control of Anger   *Anger is in Control of You*

1	2	3	4	5	6	7	8	9	10

The Top Ten Causes of Anger in Teens
(Based on the responses of over 1,000 teen participants in this program)
(Chapter One)

1. Being lied to.
2. Being yelled at.
3. Being blamed for something I didn't do.
4. Being put down for something I did (grades, sports).
5. Being told to do something over and over again.
6. Someone's nasty attitude.
7. Boyfriend/Girlfriend cheating on me.
8. Telling a friend something personal and hearing about it from someone else.
9. Being ignored.
10. Someone making fun of me in front of my friends.

Adult Anger Managers
(Chapter Five)

Some of the methods found on the Anger Manager list are beneficial to adults. It is not always easy to deal with kids—they know your hot buttons! Try some of these tips, before the teen you deal with "gets your goat."

1. Physical outlets
    A. Deep breathing
    B. Exercise of any kind
        1. Running
        2. Walking
        3. Weights
        4. Dancing
    C. Counting
2. Avoidance: Cooling off period, tune out (emotionally remove yourself)
3. Chanting or saying a word or phrase
4. Visualizations (imagined or with actual pictures)
    A. Image of anger
    B. A calm scene (beach, forest)
    C. A special person
4. Throw yourself into your job or something you are interested in doing
5. Catch a breeze
    Go somewhere isolated, where there is no one else around. Sit down and let the wind blow against your face and feel the warmth of the sun.
6. Stress Putty
    Have something in your hand that you can squeeze or manipulate.

7. Take a bubble bath or shower
8. Anger Journal
   A. Indicate an anger-activator: What made me angry?
   B. Write: How do I resolve the situation?
   C. Note: How do I prevent it from happening again?
9. Talk it over with someone who is not involved
10. Listen To Music, Play An Instrument or sing
11. Quit trying to control others
12. Accept differences
13. De-personalize from the situation or person: It is not about you.
14. Focus on the angry person's issues not their actions (signs)
    Actions or signs of anger
    1. Sarcasm
    2. Personal attacks
    3. Using "always" or "never"
    4. Physically acting out
15. Make your muscles tense, then relax them.
16. Imagine the anger draining out of you.
17. Visualize a pleasant experience or doing something or going somewhere you would really enjoy (swimming, riding in a fast car on an open road, hugging someone special, shopping in Paris, getting a massage or some sort of pampering, etc.).
18. Ask someone who has done something to you, "How do you think that makes me feel?"
19. Sing a cheerful song in your head
20. Do something challenging like a puzzle, Soduku, or work on finding a solution to something that has been bothering you.
21. Question anger: What is its source? Is it something within you or something beyond your control?

The Anger Management Short List
(Chapter Eight)

This list represents what many A.M.P. Program participants felt were the Anger Managers most likely to be used by their peers. It was taken from a list of over sixty anger managers compiled as the A.M.P. Program was developed.

1. Anger Journal
   A) Indicate anger activator: What made me angry?
   B) Write: How do I resolve the situation?
   C) Note: How do I prevent it from happening again?
2. Talk it over with someone who is not involved
3. Accept differences
4. Treat others with respect
5. Tell others what bothers you. Be direct, specific and polite
6. Use the "I Statement"
7. Self-Talk and affirmations
8. Give the other person space, a time-out or leave him/her alone
9. Give the person a chance to express her/his anger without saying anything. In other words, *Just Listen!*
10. Listen to music, play an instrument or sing
11. Stay calm when another person is angry
    A) Take deep slow breaths
    B) Relax your jaw, neck muscles and body
    C) Maintain a healthy attitude
       1) Don't be defensive
       2) Be confident, not arrogant (acting smarter, cooler, etc.)

3) Don't take the other person's anger personally (his/her judgment is impaired)

12. Caucus (when you are a third party): One of the other two people involved is getting really angry. Take the person out of the room and speak with him/her to calm them down.

13. Catch a breeze: Go somewhere isolated, where there is no one else around. Sit down and let the wind blow against your face and feel the warmth of the sun.

14. Stress Putty: Have something in your hand that you manipulate.

15. Take a bubble bath or shower

16. Look at your angry face in the mirror

17. Think of someone you care about and how they would handle the situation

18. Physical outlets

   A) Deep breathing

   B) Exercise of any kind

      1. Running

      2. Walking

      3. Weights

      4. Dancing

   C) Counting

19. Is it worth it?: Look at the consequences of behavior before you react.

20. Chanting or saying a word or phrase

21. Visualizations (in your head or with actual pictures)

   A) Image of anger

   B) Calm scene (beach, forest)

   C) Special person

The Complete List of Anger Managers

*Please go to the website PeaceEfforts.org for a free
downloadable explanation of these Anger Managers.*

(Chapter Eight)

1. Anger Journal
   A. Indicate an anger-activator: What made me angry?
   B. Write: How do I resolve the situation?
   C. Note: How do I prevent it from happening again?
2. Talk it over with someone who is not involved
3. Accept differences
4. Treat others with respect
5. Tell others what bothers you. Be direct, specific and polite
6. Use the "I Statement"
7. Self-talk and affirmations
8. Give the other person space. (Give a time-out or leave him/her alone)
9. Give the person a chance to express their anger without saying anything. In other words: *Just listen!*
10. Listen to music, play an instrument or sing
11. Stay calm yourself when another person is angry.
    A. Take slow deep breaths
    B. Relax your jaw, neck muscles and body
    C. Maintain a healthy attitude
       1. Don't be defensive
       2. Be confident, not arrogant (act smarter, cooler, etc.)
       3. Don't take the person's anger personally (their judgment is impaired by anger)
11. Caucus (when you are a third party)

When one of two people involved is getting really angry, take the person out of the room and speak with him/her to calm them down.

12. Catch a breeze

    Go somewhere isolated, where there is no one else around. Sit down and let the wind blow against your face and feel the warmth of the sun.

13. Stress Putty

    Have something in your hand that you can squeeze or manipulate.

14. Take a bubble bath or shower.

15. Look at your angry face in the mirror.

16. Think of someone you care about and how they would handle the situation.

17. Physical outlets

    A. Deep breathing

    B. Exercise of any kind

        1. Running

        2. Walking

        3. Weights

        4. Dancing

    C. Counting

18. The "Is it worth it?" question combined with a light bulb going on or hearing a buzzer going off in your head. Look at the consequences of behavior before you react.

19. Chanting or saying a word or phrase.

20. Visualizations (imagined or with actual pictures)

    A. Image of anger

    B. A calm scene (beach, forest)

    C. A special person

21. Avoidance: Cooling-off period

    Tune out (emotionally remove yourself)

22. Wipe that frown off your face and relax

23. Quit trying to control others.

24 Ask, don't demand

    Learn to use wishing/wanting rather than telling someone what they should do or demanding

25. Reward, don't punish or threaten.

26. Be responsible for what you say.

27. Empathize with the other person (see things from their point of view), then deal with the situation.

28. Throw yourself into your job or something you are interested in doing.

29. Write to the other person (e-mail, letter). Then speak to them afterward.

30. Recognize that another person is angry by seeing the way they look (expression, body language, facial features (flushed face, veins showing, etc.)) or by the tone of their voice before trying to deal with them about a situation.

31. Listen to and respect another person's suggestions or opinions regardless of their position.

    Whether they are a student, teacher, supervisor, manager or staff member, professional or non-professional, in an institution, agency or other organization

32. Walk alongside the person.

33. Sabotage yourself: Put on a show for the other person of what your angry reaction is like.

34. Clarify the perception each of you has of the situation.

35. Leave the conversation or situation after saying something like, "We can talk when we are both calmer."

36. Use humor or a smile.

    Only use this with someone you've seen respond to it in some other situation or setting.

37. Hold the other person's shoulder or gently touch it
    Only use this with someone you know responds to
    this kind of physical contact.

38. Prayer.

39. Communicate your feeling to the other person as
    soon as possible.

40. Give out "Positive Karma".
    Your voice, body language and whole attitude tell the
    other person you are not out to hurt or fight with
    them, but want to help improve the situation.

41. Play video or computer games.

42. Offer to have something to drink or eat with the other
    person before discussing the situation that caused the
    anger.

43. The Two Minute Vent for the other person who is
    angry.
    For minor irritation, anger or annoyances
    1. Set boundaries for venting
    2. No physical or verbal abuse
    3. After the first minute you say or indicate the person
    should stop. Then ask, "Do you need more time?" If
    they do, then let them continue.
    4. Let go of the annoying thing
    5. Don't interrupt the person
    6. Don't tell the angry person to calm down

44. Use the power of silence with an angry person.
    Ask open-ended questions and just wait for a response.

45. Use the "Just Wait" method.
    A. Cut the person off when they become physically or
    verbally abusive, then just wait for them to talk.
    B. With a manipulative silent person (one who uses
    silence), say something like, "You're angry and not
    willing to talk." Then just wait.

C. If the person gives an "I Don't Know" response, ask, "If you did know, what would your answer be?" Then just wait.

46. Focus on the angry person's issues not their actions (signs).

    Actions or signs of anger:

    1. Sarcasm

    2. Personal attacks

    3. Using "always" or "never"

    4. Physically acting out

47. Admit mistakes to the angry person.

    A. Take responsibility for your part of the problem

    B. Indicate personal behavior change

    C. Avoid excuses (eliminate the word "but")

48. Map out an escape route.

    A. Move from a public to a private place (where no one else is around)

    B. Focus on the issues not the person

49. Transfer things the person has done right to an area they didn't do as well.

    A. Skill transfer is easier than character adjustment

        1. Example: "You did well in reading. Use the same skills to deal with math."

50. Allow an angry person to save face.

51. Guided problem solving with the angry person:

    A. Give limited options

        1. If you could have an ideal solution, what would it be?

        2. What are the pros and cons of this solution?

        3. What is the best case scenario for it?

        4. What is the worst case scenario?

    B. Zero in on key issues: What is important to the angry person?

C. Help the person choose from the options.

D. Get the angry person to commit to the plan

52. Pretend to blow up a balloon

53. Make your muscles tense, then relax them.

54. Imagine the anger draining out of you.

55. De-personalize from the situation or person: It is not about you.

56. Do something unexpected: Laugh at some behavior that was intended to be upsetting.

57. Question anger: What is its source? Is it something within you or something beyond your control?

58. Visualize a pleasant experience or doing something or going somewhere you would really enjoy. Swimming, riding in a fast car on an open road, hugging someone special, shopping in Paris, getting a massage or some sort of pampering, etc.

59. Go to a safe place where you feel you won't be questioned or hassled, and where you know it is calm and relaxed.

60. Ask someone who has done something to you, "How do you think that makes me feel?"

61. Sing a cheerful song to yourself

62. Take notes as a situation is occurring.

63. Do something challenging like a puzzle, Math, Physics or problem in a school subject, or work on finding a solution to something that has been bothering you.

64. Visualize the outcome of the negative behavior.

Dave Wolffe

The Situation Description Recorder(SDR)
(Chapter Nine)

Directions: Describe a real situation that occurred in which somebody got angry. It can be one that you observed or in which you were personally involved.

No names of the people involved are to be used

1. What was the situation?

2. Who were the people involved? (friends, parent/child, employer/employee, brother/sister, boyfriend/girlfriend, etc.)

3. Where did the situation take place (setting)?

The Anger Management Power Program Feedback Survey I

(Chapter Ten)

[The following is provided as a sample. Participants were asked to fill out a form.]

[Male/Female][Age][Setting]

1. Did you get any ideas from this workshop that you feel will help you? [Yes/No]
   If so, what was it or were they?

2. Which part(s) did you like the best? Can you tell us why?
   __a) Visualizing Anger
   __b) Human Anger Scale
   __c) Group Work
   __d) Role Plays
   __e) Giving Your Ideas
   __f) Telling About Your Experiences
   __g) Discussion
   __h) Other

3. Which part(s) did you like the least? Can you tell us why?
   __a) Visualizing Anger
   __b) Human Anger Scale
   __c) Group Work
   __d) Role Plays

__e) Giving Your Ideas

__f) Telling About Your Experiences

__g) Discussion

__h) Other

4   Which of the ways of handling anger do you feel you would try?

___ a) Is It Worth It?

___ b) Self-Talk

___ c) Chanting or Saying a Word or Phrase

___ d) Physical Coping (Deep Breathing, Counting, etc.)

___ e) Picturing Anger and Getting Rid of It

___ f) Other

5. How would you rate this experience?

(Put a circle around the number)

Want Less Time   *Want More Time*

1	2	3	4	5	6	7	8	9	10

The Anger Management Power Program Follow-Up Survey
(Chapter Ten)

[The following is provided as a sample. Participants were asked to fill out a form.]

[Male/Female] [Age] [Setting]

As a participant in the Anger Management Power Program given at [Place] on [Date(s)] you experienced various activities, were given different materials and discussed different aspects of anger and Anger Management. In order to see the impact of this training on those that took part in it, you are being asked to complete this survey. Please do so and return it as soon as you can. Thanks for your time and effort.

1. Has knowing the causes of anger helped you deal with the anger of others or your own anger? [Yes/No]

    If yes, how has it helped you? (Give situation, circumstance, outcome)

2. Has knowing the effects (physical, thoughts, feelings) of anger helped you deal with the anger of others or your own anger? [Yes/No]

    If yes, how has it helped you? (Give situation, circumstance, outcome)

3. Have you been able to utilize any anger managers? [Yes/No]

If yes,
a) Which one(s)
b) What was (were) the situation(s)
c) What was(were) the result(s)

If you are interested in additional training or to become a trainer please provide the following: (Circle One or Both)
[Name] [Telephone number] [E-Mail]

Statistical Overview of The A.M.P. Program Feedback Survey

(Chapter Ten)

As of this writing, the A.M.P. Program was presented to approximately 1000 teens, and 600 adult participants, a group that represents undergraduate and graduate college students, parents and professionals. My purpose in providing this information is to help encourage confidence in using the tools and ideas presented in this book.

The A.M.P. Program Feedback Survey
An Overview of the Information Gathered From Survey

1. The youngsters participating in this program were mostly older, (17-18 years old), more mature teens, who were upper classmen (Juniors and Seniors).
2. They may or may not represent the ages of the adolescents that you are dealing with.

Survey Results

The responses noted to the questions found in this survey, as well as those in the follow-up survey, are the ones that appeared most frequently, or those I have found to be the most effective to use with young people.

Question 1: Did you get any ideas from this workshop that you feel will be helpful?

Results: Three-quarters of the teens who responded indicated "Yes." These youngsters described many different reasons they felt their exposure to the A.M.P. Program was useful. Many of these ideas centered around the Anger Managers in general, with specific ones also being mentioned. Among the responses that fall into this category are:

1. Anger Managers give different ways to deal with anger.
2. Talking to myself
3. Is It Worth It?
4. Visualize anger
5. Visualize a calm scene
6. Deep breathing
7. Stay calm and relax
8. Walk away and calm down

More of these (thirty-seven) were given in response to this question. These Anger Managers, as well as others that were found to be the most prevalent for youngsters taking this survey, will be given.

Other ideas noted most often by adolescents from this program were,

1. Know how to control my anger better.
2. Different ways to control anger toward myself and others.
3. How to help and understand anger in others.
4. Channel or express your anger in positive ways.
6. How to express anger without hurting others.
7. Prevent anger or preventing it from getting worse.

Question 2: "What parts (of the A.M.P. Program) did you like best?"
Results: The top three choices and the reasons most often given were,

1. Role Plays
   A. They were funny/entertaining
   B. Better visual (see what is happening)
2. The basic conclusion that can be drawn from the teen participant ratings is that a majority of them felt the A.M.P. Program had value to them.
   A. Real life experiences

3. Group work
   A. Shared ideas
   B. Got to talk and listen to each other
   C. Got a chance to learn how others deal with situations
4. Giving your ideas (Discussions)
   A. Opened my mind to others' ideas
   B. Like to express myself
   C. People can hear me out

Conclusions About Responses To Questions One and Two

1. Young people like to be entertained and often learn from such experiences.
2. They respond to objective material (role play situations are objective, they don't focus on them directly).
3. Teens seek recognition for their opinions (they are valued by their peers).
4. They like to hear what their peers have to say and what they have done.
5. Many adolescents like to be helpful to others. It is makes them feel more valued, another form of recognition.

The conclusions reached from the information obtained from young people themselves may provide ways to reach their peers, in both a timely and efficient manner.

Now let's focus our attention on the flip side of this coin.

Question 3: "What did you like the least about this experience?"
Results: Here, again, we'll look at the top three choices and the reasons for them.

1. Survey
   A. Don't like writing
   B. Prefer talking
2. Anger Web
   A. Boring
   B. Not interactive
   C. Didn't like it
3. Group Work
   A. Boring
   B. Don't like it
   C. Some members of the group did nothing

As you have no doubt noted, the word, boring is a common expression among many youth. It can be found in this program's activities, as well as in other kinds of situations. This is not to say that teens have to be constantly entertained, stimulated, or otherwise part of the perpetual movement that are characteristic of this age group. However, in some instances, your desire to give an adolescent some experiences that will open their minds and eyes to the kind of Anger Management experience they will accept and perhaps incorporate into their lives can require some sort of stimulation. The overriding concern is to find whatever route can be taken to get these ideas across to a youngster. Keeping this goal in mind, after looking at these surveys, some modifications were made to the Anger Management Power Program. With all this said, let's move on to what I believe is the heart and soul of this program.

Question 4: "Which of the ways of handling anger do you feel you would try?" The survey itself listed five anger managers, along with the category of "Other." The following represent the most popular Anger Managers chosen by adolescent participants. (Keep in mind that many of these can be used with younger children as well.)

1. Physical Coping (Deep Breathing, Counting, Sports, Exercise)
2. Visualizing a Calm Scene (Beach, Forest), a Person You Love, or a Situation that Made You Feel Good and Helped You Relax.
3. "Is it Worth It?"
4. Picturing Anger and Getting Rid of It.
5. Learning to Use Wishing/Wanting Rather Than Should/Demand

The next six were listed in the category of "Other" and also range from the most popular down.

6. Self-Talk
7. Listen to Music
8. Ignoring the Other Person
9. Saying A Chant or Phrase
10. Talking to People
11. Anger Journal

Knowing what appeals to peers may be helpful to you in giving youngsters ideas on things that might work for them or that they may be willing to try. It certainly can narrow down the list for you and them.

The final question, relates to rating the Anger Management Power Program.

Question 5: "How would you rate this program?"

Results: Here is a scale ranging from 0–"Let me out of here, a waste of time," to 10–"I want more training," was used. The basic conclusion that can be drawn from the teen participant ratings is that a majority of them felt the A.M.P. Program had value to them.

6 - 10 Range = 55% of participants

5 Middle = 21% of participants
0 - 4 Range = 18% of participants
No Rating = .06% of participants

Statistical Overview of the A.M.P. Program Follow-Up Survey
(Chapter Ten)

Profile of High School Participants

Total number of participants = 421
 Ages: 17 year old =36% (most prevalent)
     16 year old =24%
     18 years old =15%
Grades: 12th graders = 31%
     11th graders = 18%
     10th graders = 9%

Information Gathered From Survey

Even though the number of teens involved in this assessment is less than those participating in the A.M.P. Feedback Survey, its results are helpful. This difference in the number of participants was caused by the lack of time to give this survey.

The youngsters participating in this program were mostly older, more mature teens who were upper classmen (Juniors and Seniors). They may or may not represent the ages of the teens that you are working with.
Survey Results

The responses noted to the questions found in this survey are the ones that appeared most frequently, or those that can be most effective with other young people. Some of these contain situations that participants described.

Question 1: Has knowing the causes of anger been helpful?

Results 53% of the respondents answered "Yes." Their responses focused on specific Anger Managers. Among this group of answers were:

1. I think about the situation before acting.
2. I know when I am faced with a situation, when it occurs I hold anger in, and let it pass.
3. When my mom and I disagree I would leave and take deep breaths and go on later and talk about it.
4. At home, my mom nagging, I ignore her.
5. It made me think about different situations and what the consequences would be if I did something.

The second category of responses related directly to general as well as specific reasons for anger. These included:

1. I realized what gets me angry and try to avoid it.
2. Whenever I wanted to get something or do something and heard the word "No," I would really get annoyed. Now I calm down and deal with it better.
3. I was very upset with situations (sisters, parents) in my family and instead of keeping my thoughts in I spoke to my family.
4. Knowing the causes, why you are angry, helps you to deal with anger in a positive way, rather than over-reacting.
5. By knowing how I react to certain things, I try to stay away from people that give me the wrong feeling and that get me angry.

There were over fifty responses to this question. If you feel more of these would be helpful, feel free to contact me by e-mail at peacefulyouth422@yahoo.com and I will happily send you all the survey results. This will hold true for the responses to both surveys.

Question 2: Was knowing the effects of anger useful?

Results: 43% of the participants answered "Yes."

Responses often included the use of Anger Managers. Some used in reply to this question were,

1. Think about the problem. Ask yourself, "Is it worth having a negative reaction?" The example given was, "A person pushes you. You're not having a good day. Think if it is worth fighting because you can hurt them or get hurt yourself,

2. I was mad at my best friend for something she had done. I thought of all the good times we had and just let it go.

3. I knew when I get mad I turn red. I try to remind myself to calm down and breathe.

4. Anger can lead you to make many mistakes as well as hurting others. When I'm angry I think of the effects anger comes with.

5. I understand why we get mad and why we have physical effects, thoughts and feelings, so I think before I do something.

The other group of responses to this part of the evaluation dealt with the general and specific effects of anger. These included:

1. I might not want that negative outcome so I avoid the situation.

2. When I see my friend is quiet I know he's upset about something.

3. It makes you try not to get angry.

4. When I get mad I get hot and irritated and don't like the feeling and try not to get upset. I start thinking mean thoughts, so I try to avoid anger.

5. When I am angry, I am stressed out and lose weight, so now I try to think positively to prevent it from happening.

6. Based on their physical appearance I can tell if something is bothering another person.

7. Made me realize all the danger people go through daily based on how they act.

Question 3: Have you been able to use any of the Anger Managers?

Results: About 30% of the participants answered "Yes." This question had three parts. The first indicated which Anger Managers were used. The next one described who the other person involved in the situation was. The last part indicated the result of using the particular tools. The Top Ten Anger Managers used by the participants (there were over fifty mentioned) are noted along with the use of multiple Anger Managers, that is, the use of more than one method in same situation Some of the young people indicated responses to all three parts, while others only noted the Anger Managers they used.

Top Ten Anger Managers

1. Is It Worth It? (also known as The Light Bulb/Buzzer Anger Manager)

2. Deep Breathing

3. Counting

4. Walk Away, while saying something like, "I need to calm down and then we can talk."

5. Think Before Acting or Speaking

6. Listening To Music

7. Writing(letter, poetry, Anger Journal)

8. Talking To Someone (close, who is not involved)

9. Exercising (sports, walking, etc.)
10. Staying Calm (Not yelling)

B. Multiple Anger Managers
1. Remain Calm/Is It Worth It/Walk Out/ Slow, Deep Breathing/Counting
2. Chant "Woo-Sah"/Take A Walk/ Breathe
3. Exercise (Walk)/Deep Breaths

These lists provide some of the most common Anger Managers adolescents used. Some of these tools will be listed again. This time they are shown in relationship to the responses that were given to the other two parts of this survey's question.

The Nature of The Situations Described

There are two kinds of incidents that will be described. The first category lists situations involving different relationships. The next grouping relates to more general types of events. All of these will appear under the headings of specific Anger Managers.

Anger Manager used: Deep Breathing
Situation: Argument with my mom.
Result: I calmed down.
Situation: Argument with siblings.
Result: I was able to calm down.
Situation: Brother gets me angry.
Result: I was able to talk to him.
Situation: I was going to fight someone.
Result: I cooled down and walked in circles.
Situation: Arguments with my girl.
Result: I got more angry. (Sometimes it doesn't work)

Situation: My brother got on my nerves.

Result: I didn't get angry like I normally would.

Anger Manager used: Is It Worth It? (Light bulb/buzzer)
Situation: Fight with brother.

Result: I got to calm down.

Thought: Now I bite my tongue more often and do my best not to do or say something harmful or something I don't mean.

Result: I didn't yell at anyone.

Result: Everything spoken about was done calmly and collectively.

Situation: Verbal fight with a friend.

Result: I realized after tensing that having a fight wasn't worth it.

Anger Manager used: Walking Away (Take a Walk)
Situation: I started an argument with my mom.

Result: I just got out and went back and spoke about the situation.

Situation: My friend and I had an argument.

Result: I walked away and let her calm down.

Situation: Argument with my boyfriend. I was mad and tried to explain, but it wasn't working.

Result: I calmed down and told him later that day. Everything was okay.

Situation: Argument with my mother.

Result: This helped me

Situation: Argument with a friend.

Result: I felt better and apologized

Situation: I was mad at my mom.

Result: Went to my aunt's house.

Situation: I was arguing with my sister.

Result: Walked away and ignored her.

Anger Manager used: Talk It Over With Someone Who
    Is Not Involved
Situation: Fight with mom. Went to aunt's house.
    Result: She calmed me down.
Situation: Boyfriend problems. Talked to my best friend.
    Result: She calmed my anger down.
Anger Manager used: Talking It Out
Situation: Argument with sister.
    Result: Resolved anger.
Situation: Fighting with parents/peers
    Result: No one was hurt.

The participant responses make these ideas credible to peers. The kinds of situations that were described in this survey are common to teen experience. The way survey respondents handled these incidents can encourage others to handle their situations using the same methods. The remark, "Here's how some other kids used this idea" may start the response ball rolling. Once made, let them decide. This is the point to wait for some reaction, verbal or non-verbal, to help decide whether or not to continue in this direction. For the other, more independent group, having these adolescents discuss what things were helpful or can be used in similar situations that arise, is a direction to take.

Program Modifications Based On Teen Responses

Elimination of the written survey. Better use of time, alleviating the "boredom factor" and eliminating the need for young people to write (something not among their favorite things to do) led to this decision. Why add another obstacle to our work? The questions found in this survey can be asked and answered as different activities are chosen to use from this program.

Elimination of the Anger Web, an early method in the program. Although having some value as a way for young people to see and accept differences in their perceptions of anger with their peers, time and boredom won over using this activity. In its place, we concentrated on having groups formed from an entire class focused on developing image of anger. (visualizing anger). Two-thirds of the participants felt this was what they liked best about the program. Their reasons were:

It was fun.
You can cope by visualizing [anger].
Good way to see anger.

The result of this activity turned out to be a popular Anger Manager.

With the elimination of these two activities in Spring 2008 came the use of an additional activity that was suggested by a teen participant. It was described as the Human Anger Scale. These changes also led to the modification of the questions used in the feedback survey.

Almost one-half of the participants found it was an activity they liked best. The reasons most given were:

You determine how angry you were.
Gave a visual of where our anger is.
It was fun.

Point of Information: Some youngsters were exposed to the full list of sixty-four Anger Managers. A short time ago, within the last few years (Fall, 2007), I felt this list was too overpowering. Based on a list developed for a peer facilitated workshop program, something to be discussed later in this chapter, the Anger Manager list used in Chapter Eight was created by teen presenters. There were seventeen anger managers on that list. Four more, based on common responses to this question were added to this original list. This is the list, as of Spring, 2008, used in all presentations of the program.

The following represent the most popular Anger Managers chosen by adolescent participants. Keep in mind that many of these can be used with younger children as well.

1. Physical Coping (Deep Breathing, Counting, Sports, Exercise
2. Visualizing a Calm Scene (Beach, Forest), a Person You Love, or a Situation that Made You Feel Good and Helped You Relax.
3. Is it Worth It? (Light Bulb/Buzzer)
4. Picturing Anger and Getting Rid of It
5. Learning to Use Wishing/Wanting Rather Than Should/Demand

The five listed above were on the survey and remained there. The next six were listed in the category of "Other" and also range from the most popular down.

6. Self-Talk
7. Listen to Music
8. Ignoring the Other Person
9. Saying a Chant or Phrase
10. Talking to People
11. Anger Journal

Here again, knowing what appeals to peers may be helpful to you in giving youngsters ideas on things that might work for them or that they may be willing to try. It certainly can narrow down the list for you and them.

Question 5: "How would you rate this program?"

Results: Here a scale ranging from 0 - "Let Me Out of Here, a Waste Of Time" to 10 - "Want More Training" was used. The basic conclusion that can be drawn from the teen participant ratings is that a majority of them felt the A.M.P. Program had value to them.

      6 - 10 Range = 55% of participants
      5 Middle = 21%
      0 - 4 Range = 18%
      No Rating = .06%

The Anger Management Power Program
Peer Training Workshop I
(Chapter Eleven)

This format was developed when the program was at its earliest stages. Substitutions of more recent activities will be added to some of those listed below. They will be noted with an asterisk.

If a group of teens has expressed an interest in putting together a peer workshop, what is most important to note are the activities that adolescents who put these initial experiences together chose. Along with the activities these young people were advised what and where certain elements of the program should be posted on a board or chart. These will be provided below.

(To be left up throughout the presentation)

Top
Anger Management Power Program
(Use the name facilitators give the program)

Left	Middle of the board	Right
Anger Managers (list to be developed)		Definition of Anger Management What do we want from this workshop?

1. What do you want to learn from the A.M.P. Program?

2. What does Anger Management mean? Here teens can list two or three responses, or they can give the program's definition: Expressing Anger without hurting yourself or others.

3. Anger Scale is place on the board. (Facilitators can choose terms to be used for describing both extremes) and briefly explained.

Calm, Chilled-Out   *Nuts, Crazy, Ballistic*

Person in control of Anger   *Anger is in Control*

1	2	3	4	5	6	7	8	9	10

4. What gets you angry?

The facilitators can use the, "Top Ten Causes of Anger in Teens" list and the Human Anger Scale exercise.

5. Responses to this question are taken and placed on the Anger Scale.

6. What was the effect?

A situation is described using any of the causes and the "Is It Worth It?" Anger Manager is described using the A-B-C format below.

A = Anger Activator: The cause of the behavior

B = Behavior: What a person did when they got angry

C = Consequence: What happened after the person acted on the anger.

7. From the causes put on the Anger Scale, choose another to describe a situation.

Adolescents can use the Situation Description Recorder(SDR) and distribute it to their peers.

8. Give out the list of Anger Managers.

9. Explain some of the Anger Managers which are often misunderstood. For example, the "I Statement," Self-Talk, Anger Journal, Look at Yourself in the Mirror.

10. Pick out three Anger Managers you would like to try to use.

11. Two or three situations, are chosen, either from Anger Scale or The SDR to either role play or discuss. What Anger Managers can you use?

12. What did you learn from this workshop?

The time available to do this workshop is something to consider with teens when they are choosing the activities and the method that they want to present them.

The Anger Management Power Program
Peer Workshop II
(Chapter Eleven)

The following description of the workshop was done and written by teens exactly as it appears below.

1. When you get into the room, one or more members of the team will put the following up.
A. "What do you want from this workshop?" (Right Side)
B. Write the words, "Anger Management" (underneath what they want from this workshop)
C. Write the words, "Anger Management Power Program, Center, at the top of the board.
D. Put the word, "Aim" ("Goal" can be substituted in a non-educational settings), center. E. Put the words, "Anger Managers" on the left side.
2. Introduce yourself and the peer trainer team members.
3. Say something like, "We are here to do a workshop with you on Anger Management as part of a program known as the Anger Management Power Program.
4. Ask: What do you want to learn from this workshop?
A. Take two or three responses and put them on the board.
5. Ask: What is Anger Management?
A. Take two or three responses. Use whatever words come close to "express anger without hurting others or yourself."

6. Ask: What do you think our goal is for today?
   A. Put it as the "Aim" on the center board.
7. Ask: What goes through your mind when you are angry?
   A. If no response, pause then ask, What thoughts or feelings do you have when something or someone gets you angry?
8. Ask:
   A. What happens to your body when you get angry?
      1. Put three or four responses on the center board.
   B. What can you do to relax yourself when your body starts to react this way?
9. Say: "These are some Anger Managers (put them on the left side of the board)
10. Put up the Anger Scale and explain it.
(These words can be added or others that teens suggest for these two ends of the scale.)

Calm, Chilled-Out　　　　　　　　　　　　*Nuts, Crazy, Ballistic*
You are in control of Anger　　　　　　　*Anger is in Control of You*

1	2	3	4	5	6	7	8	9	10

11. Ask:
    A. What makes you really angry?
       1. Get three or four responses.
    B. Where would you put them (the causes) on the scale?
12. Take one of the responses and show the A-B-C- Anger Manager
    A = Anger Activator
    B = Behavior
    C = Consequence

1. Ask: What A is in this situation? What is B? What is C?

  a) Write them in

2.. Ask: What is the most important part for this Anger Manager? (C)

3. Ask: What question might go with it? ("Is It Worth It?")

4. Add, A-B-C, "Is It Worth It?" to the Anger Manager List.

13. Give out Anger Manager list.

 A. Ask: Which ones would you liked explained?

  1. If no response, explain the "I Statement," Self-Talk and Affirmations, Anger Journal, Look at Yourself in the Mirror, are some that may be added to the others.

14. Say: "Choose three that you would like to try.

15. Role Play (If no volunteers, go to B)

 A. With volunteers

  1. Ask for a situation that shows people getting angry?

   a) You can also have them use the Situation Description Recorder and tell participants to write a situation

  2. Ask for volunteers to act it out.

  3. Direct actors to both get to a point where they are raising their voices (nothing physical) and stop.

  4. Ask: How could either one have managed their anger so it didn't get out of hand? Or what anger managers could have been used?

 B. If no volunteers.

  1. Ask for a situation.

2. Ask: What could be done so one or both people don't let their angry take control of them?

16. Summary.

   Ask: What did you learn from this A.M.P. Workshop?

The A.M.P. Program Mediation Process: An Overview
(Chapter Eleven)

1. Opening the Session: In this part of the process several tasks are accomplished. These are,

    a)   A warm, non-threatening atmosphere is created.

    b)   Information is given about the process and the role of the mediators.

    c)   Ground rules are established as a means of maintaining order during the mediation.

This is probably the most important part of the process. When it is done properly the tone for the rest of the mediation is set.

2. Gathering Information: At this stage the mediators and disputants hear both sides of the conflict described, and have the opportunity to clarify their perceptions of the incident.

3. Creating Options: During this step of the process what each disputant wants from the mediation is discovered, and ideas are generated on how to resolve the conflict.

4. Developing an Agreement and Closing the Session:

    a)   It is at this point that an agreement may have been reached and both parties feel that they have gotten what they wanted from the mediation. If this is the case, the terms of the agreement need to be described and modified to indicate the way each disputant wants things spelled out.

b) Whether or not an agreement has been reached, each disputant is thanked for their participation, and given the opportunity to return, or to refer others for this process.

c) If an agreement has been reached, a follow-up date is given to see if both parties are following its terms. If not, they are given an opportunity to return for additional work.

The Anger Management Program Preparation Checklist
(Chapter Twelve)

When planning to use the Anger Management solutions in the book, it's important to create a plan on what you think might work.

1. Write a list of chapters/pages to locate ideas, concepts and Anger Managers you want to use.
2. Make an outline of these key points.
3. Make further notes on how best to use this information.
4. Consider using Anger Manager combinations.

The remaining decisions have to do with the presentation format, approaches to be used and methods of gauging the effectiveness of the training given. The form these ideas are going to be presented in represents one of these choices. This can include one or as many of the ways you feel will facilitate the experience for the young person.

Will you deal with young people as a group?

1. Small (2-10)
2. Medium (11 or more)
3. Unsure at this point

If you plan to deal with individuals, how will you manage this?

1. One-on-One
2. Several one-on-ones through a period of time.

Will you elect to work with a larger group during a set period of time?

1. Lecture/Seminar
2. Discussion
3. Part of another program
   If so, decide which one(s)
4. Combination of these
   If so, which ones?

The next choices to make are what tools or documents would be used, and how and where they can be used.

1. Anger Scale
   A. As a chart (to be hung somewhere in your facility or office)
   B. Handout
   C. Other
2. Visualization of Anger (pictures, written descriptions)
   A. Displayed in a particular room in the facility
   B. Displayed in your office
   C. Other
3. Situation Description Recorder (like a suggestion box)
   A. Create situations to be discussed
   B. Record of personal situations
   C. Other
4. Anger Manager List
   A. Specific anger managers
      1). Hang in particular place(s) or office(s)
      2). Handout
   B. General List

      1). Hang in particular place(s) or office(s)

      2). Handout

  5. Other ideas you may have, not covered in this book.

The final decision is to figure out how effective this training was.

  1. Discussion

     A. Individual youngsters

      1). Result of personal experiences or those they witnessed.

      2). Something hinted at during a conversation

      3). Time designated during the Anger Management training experience

     B. Group

      1). Result of member experiences or a witnesses of a conflict

      2). Time designated during the Anger Management training experience

  2. Observation

     A. Visual: Situations that you saw youth involved in.

     B. Auditory: Situations you heard about from the individuals involved in them or others who witnessed these things.

  3. Creative Methods

     A. Situations: These provide the opportunity for the spontaneous follow-up.

  4. Combination

     If so, which ones?

  5. Other ideas you may have.

Dave Wolffe

Additional Resources for Parents, Educators, Social Workers and Youth Workers

(Chapter Twelve)

Each state has its own resources. Generally, look under the areas of, "Tough Love." "Domestic Violence," "Relationship Abuse" or "Child Abuse" on the Internet. You can also look under State agencies and mental health associations under these specific headings in a local phone book. In the case of someone in imminent or immediate danger, dial "911"!

The following telephone numbers are helpful to know and post.

Tough Love: http://toughlove.com/htm Telephone: 866-828-0178
Domestic Abuse Hotline: 800-799-SAFE (7233) TTY 800-787-3224
Child Abuse Hotline 800-342-3720 New York
Child Abuse Prevention Network http://child-abuse.com
Relationship Abuse: 800-621-HOPE (4673) New York

If in imminent or immediate danger, dial 911 in any state.

Quick Tips for Keeping the Peace With Teens

1. Speaking first makes things worse. Hearing a teen out before saying something prevents the, "You don't want to hear what I have to say, you only want to tell me what I did wrong" reaction.

2. Raised voices, means fewer choices. When an adult reacts to a teen's yelling in the same manner, it shuts down chances of finding out the source of problems and working with an adolescent to find ways to resolve these situations.

3. Embarrassment leads to harassment. When you embarrass a young person, you can bet on being verbally assaulted. If a criticism needs to be made do it in private, and without making a teen feel dumb.

4. Ask and you shall accomplish a task, demand and things can get out of hand. Putting things that you want from an adolescent as a request, rather than a demand or threat, has a better chance of getting a positive response.

5. Helping a teen fulfill a need draws them closer to you and the deed. When a young person has a need, for example, for recognition, and you accept or ask for their opinion, they will see you as somebody who's worth listening to and will be more likely to work with you.

6. A compliment works like relationship cement. Most teens are used to being told what they do wrong. Complimenting them takes their view and relationship with you to a different level. "What, someone actually sees when I do something right," makes this point.

7. Considering a teen's perception, can give you a better reception. "Wow, somebody really listens to what I have to say!" sums up this point. It clears the way for your opinion to be heard.

8. Asking a teen's desires, will help prevent emotional fires. When you enter a conversation with an adolescent ask what they want. Doing so pre-

vents incorrect assumptions from being made and avoids the comment, "How do you know what I want!" By not telling a young person how they think or feel provides them with the freedom to express what they want and gives them the knowledge that they can expect this kind of respect from you.

9. Listen and ask and accomplish a major task. Something that came from a teen that I worked with illustrates this idea. Asking an adolescent if they want you to just listen to what they have to say or want your opinion goes a long way toward working with them. Adults often jump into a discussion with their opinion, when all that is needed is a chance for a young person to get something off of their chest.

10. It's not a teen's personality or physical description that should be prominent, it's how they act that should be dominant. When you deal with an adolescent it's their behavior that needs to be focused on, not their looks or the kind of person they are. "You acted without thinking when you cut Mr. Brown's class," not, "You fat slob" or "You are stupid" illustrate this point.

11. Speak to, not at, a teen, and they'll be more attentive to you. No one likes to feel as if they are being put down. When having a conversation with an adolescent, speaking about their behavior rather than telling how bad or wrong they are will encourage them to listen to you, rather than shut you out.

12. Give a teen a chance to explain, chances are your words won't be in vain. Hear what a teen has to say and then he/she will be more open to listening to your thoughts.

13. When a teen is misbehavin' provide them with an emotional safe haven. When a teen is upset he/she sometimes needs to go somewhere, where they feel they won't be scolded or judged. This is often a counselor's, or social worker's office.

Dave Wolffe

About the Author

Dave Wolffe earned his Bachelor of Arts Degree and Masters Degree in Education from Queens College. He has been an educator for over thirty-five years. He taught grades 1-9 for most of his over thirty years with the New York City Board of Education, and was a high school guidance counselor for the last thirteen years of his career. For the past six years he has been an Adjunct Lecturer at John Jay College of Criminal Justice in New York City, where he teaches Sociology of Conflict, a course in the Dispute Resolution Program.

Mr. Wolffe was certified as a Peer Mediation Specialist from the International Center for Conflict Resolution of Columbia University Teachers College. While working as a high school counselor this training enabled him to teach high school students to facilitate peer mediation sessions with other students. During this experience he and many of these young people helped to establish, facilitate and participate in school wide and borough wide violence prevention programs. In addition, he is a certified mediator. Westchester Mediation of Cluster, located in Yonkers, N.Y. granted this credential to him.

He developed an Anger Management program known as the Anger Management Power (A.M.P.) Program on which this book is based. He has facilitated this training experience with over 1,000 high school students and well over 600 parents, educators and other individuals who are concerned with youth in this area. He also developed and presents violence prevention workshops based on this program for New York City area Teacher Education college programs, has worked with mediators in this area, and has created a facilitator training method for presenting these Anger Management skills.

Subject Index

A

B

Breinigsville, PA USA
21 November 2010
249771BV00004B/1/P